"Fast-paced yet beautifully evocative, *Devil's Moon* is a thriller that will keep you guessing until the very end."

~ J Carson Black, Author of *The Shop* and the Laura Cardinal crime fiction series

"Matt Marine has crafted a page-turning suspense in *Devil's Moon* that immediately envelops the reader and sucks them into the seedier side of the touristy/upscale environs of Sedona. Strong but flawed characters battle more than the crime scene and keep you involved to the very last page."

~ Jude Johnson, Author of *Dragon & Hawk*

"What appears to be an open and shut case dissolves into an emotionally charged investigation by an FBI Agent trying to conquer his own demons. Complex characters in a compelling story hold you captive from the first page to its stunning conclusion."

~ Carol Costa, Author of *The Dana Sloan Mysteries*

MATTHEW MARINE

DEVIL'S MOON

Open Books
PRESS

Published by Open Books Press, USA
www.openbookspress.com

An imprint of Pen & Publish, Inc.
Bloomington, Indiana
(812) 837-9226
info@PenandPublish.com
www.PenandPublish.com

ISBN: 978-0-9852737-5-0

This book is printed on acid free paper.

Printed in the USA

Dedication

For my wife and children.
This book would not have been possible without your support
and love.

Acknowledgements

I'd like to thank a great many people for their help in making *Devil's Moon* a reality. To all my writing friends (especially the Gecko Gals), thank you for your encouragement and friendship. It meant a great deal to me to have you by my side.

To Paul Burt and everyone from Open Books Press, thank you for working with me and giving me this wonderful opportunity. Your professionalism and sincerity are refreshing.

Special thanks to Arlene W. Robinson, freelance editor extraordinaire, for your knowledge, patience and wit as you helped me shape my words into meaningful prose. You're the best!

Finally, I'd like to thank my wife, Katherine, and daughters, Jennifer and Sydney. You never complained when I was squirreled away in my office for hours on end during one of my writing frenzies. You were always happy to read and reread my story until I got it just right. Thank you, thank you, thank you. I love you!

Chapter 1

Amanda Pearce scrambled up the dark earthen embankment, the shine of fresh blood following in her wake. Cresting the rise, the surface beneath her feet was level, less rocky.

A road. *Thank God.*

She looked down at her bare feet. Blood oozed from a dozen wounds and she doubted she could continue much farther across the harsh desert floor.

Pushing back a tangled strand of hair, she looked to her right. The moon's pewter glow fused with the shadows of juniper trees, making them appear as demonic skeletons. Above them, iron-black peaks blotted out the stars. Her eyes followed the winding dirt road until it disappeared into an abyss of empty desert.

Not good. She swiveled her head in the opposite direction. A few lights twinkled in the distance. Sedona. Just a few miles away. The road aimed straight for them. She was close this time.

So close.

She shivered in the cool night air, then began limping toward the lights. He wouldn't find her. Not again.

She remembered his words when he caught her the last time. "I trusted you," he'd said, his face red and sweaty in the lantern's glow.

Trust? He doesn't know a damn thing about trust.

Then his eyes became dark pinpoints and the pipe crashed down. She'd bitten down on the filthy rag he'd stuffed in her mouth, her scream smothered in her throat.

"Don't ever try to leave me again," he'd said, the pipe's onslaught continuing until her mind darkened into unconsciousness.

That was a week ago. Maybe two. Locked in a cinder-block basement, she only marked time by his frequent visits. When he brought her food, or came to … *came to …*

Tears threatened. She bit down on her lip, forcing them back. She wouldn't let him do that to her again. Subconsciously, her hand went to her neck, searching for the angel that had hung there for eight years. She needed its comfort. Now more than ever. But it was gone. It had disappeared the day he abducted her.

Keep moving. That's what was important. She willed her legs to move her farther into the quiet night.

A coyote's howl broke the silence. Her head spun toward the sound. Another answered the call. Then another, and another, until a chorus of voices echoed off the ethereal mountains behind her. Rather than terrifying her, she welcomed the coyotes' presence. It meant she was no longer alone.

She'd been alone for so long.

And the coyotes' calls seemed to be beckoning her. Summoning her forward. Showing her the way ... or ... *or ...*

Warning her.

A faint musty odor drifted on the breeze.

She froze. Sniffed the air. *She knew that smell.*

Then the coyotes' cries went silent.

A shiver raced through her. He was out there. Looking for her.

She stood in the middle of the road, knowing if he caught her again, he would kill her. That assurance had been in his eyes the last time he'd swung the pipe. Eyes that could be full of caring one second, enraged the next. Amanda shook off the memory, took a deep breath. She wasn't going back. Ever.

Her eyes searched the desert behind her. A gust of wind stirred a copse of trees, their shadows dancing to some silent chant. She watched in horror as one seemed to break away from the others. A dark apparition flowing onto the road.

She held her breath. Nothing. Maybe it was just her tired eyes. Seeing things. Then she spotted the glint of metal in the moonlight.

The pipe.

Her chest tightened as terror flooded her mind.

"I told you not to run away," the shadow said.

She stumbled, tendrils of panic making her legs weak.

"What do you want from me?" she said, but knew his answer before she finished the question.

"Lauren, please, all I want—"

"Go fuck yourself!"

She wasn't going to beg. She'd done two weeks of that. It hadn't helped. And she wasn't going back to that awful room.

The shadow edged forward.

"You're a freak! A monster!"

He paused his advance, as if her words had a physical impact.

"And fuck your precious Lauren too," she continued, knowing what her insolence would bring. She hoped he'd make it quick. Use the gun, not the pipe. Hearing the heavy thud of steel striking the palm of his hand, she knew she wasn't going to be that lucky.

"You aren't any different," he said, his voice now hard with rage.

She took a few steps backward.

"No different. Just like the others."

She stopped. *Others*—?

Then the pipe came up and she didn't have time to think about it.

She turned to run, but he was already on her.

She opened her eyes. Blackness. All around her. And the smell. Musty. Foul. Sickening.

Oh, God. She was back in the basement.

She lay in the suffocating tomb as currents of pain surged through her broken body. Her forehead seemed to be on fire and she felt something warm trickle down her face. She tried to push herself into a sitting position, but her fingers kept slipping on the slick surface. It took her a long time to realize what it was: plastic. Thick with her blood.

Exhausted, she collapsed back on her side.

And waited.

Waited for him.

Her fading heartbeat her only company.

The sound of the lock opening came first. Then a sliver of light pierced the darkness. She watched him enter, a lantern in one hand, the pipe in the other. She tried to scream, but he'd stuffed the rag in her mouth again and nothing more than a soft gurgle escaped her lips. Her mind was beyond fear. Beyond terror.

All she could do was watch.

And listen.

"This is for you, my love," he said, holding up a plastic container about the size of a shoebox.

She drew a few shallow breaths through her nose. One final attempt at sympathy. Understanding. "I'm ... I'm not Lauren," she said through the rag, her voice so weak she didn't think he'd heard her.

To her surprise, he nodded. "I know."

Then he turned the box so she could see what he'd written on its end: *Amanda Pierce.*

No ...

He bent down and picked up something off the floor. "One last beautiful smile for me?"

Please ...

When the flash lit up the basement, she knew he was planning something even darker than just her murder.

Chapter 2

The house wasn't what he expected. The ones that harbored monsters never were. Set back on a couple of acres of high desert, the one story ranch was a few miles west of Sedona, Arizona. The front yard was neat and well kept; flowers bloomed in large clay pots under an open porch. The late afternoon sun, showing through a line of thin clouds, cast the house in a soft orange glow and gave it a homey feel.

Any American family could have lived there. He could have lived there. Nothing about it hinted at the atrocities found inside. So much for judging a book by its cover.

Shaking his head, FBI Agent Stuart Ransom steered his government-issue Crown Victoria onto the gravel driveway. Two black-and-white Sedona police cruisers, looking as out of place as a panhandler in Tiffany's, were parked in front of the house.

No officers were visible, but he expected that. Local police never laid out the welcome mat for the feds. Not even when they were knee-deep in their own shit. Small-town cops took care of their own.

Ransom braked to a stop. Killed the Vic's engine. But he didn't exit the vehicle. Not yet. The ninety-minute drive up from Phoenix hadn't gone well. He reached into his pocket, pulled out a flat, smooth crystal the color of black obsidian. It was a little over an inch long, with a depression in its center the size of his thumb. A worry stone. His daughter had bought for him, thinking it would help. He closed his eyes, rubbed his thumb in its hollow. Felt the smoothness. Tried to let everything go.

When the stone began to get hot, he opened his eyes again. Looked down. After two years of use, he'd almost worn it through. Although he'd never admit it to his daughter, sometimes he *did* feel a little better after using it.

Not today. Not with what was waiting for him. He put it back into his pocket. Time to get to work.

Snatching a thick folder from the passenger's seat, he angled his six-foot-one-inch frame out of the car, then attempted to smooth the wrinkles out of his standard FBI attire: dark suit, white dress shirt and midnight-blue tie. The wrinkles held fast. The four-year-old suit was two years beyond its life expectancy. He combed his fingers through his unkempt sandy-brown hair. Next week, he told himself, a new suit and a trip to the barber, before the FBI's fashion police came knocking on his door.

Finished with his futile attempts at tidying up, he turned full circle. The nearest neighbor was a good quarter mile down the road. Too far away to hear what had taken place in the basement.

The two-car garage door was open and a thin man in a dark blue uniform leaned out of the entryway. "You the FBI?" he called out with about as much friendliness as a junkyard dog.

Ransom smiled anyway. "Stuart Ransom, from the Phoenix office."

Wasted effort. The officer's scowl held fast. "Chief Parker's waiting for you inside."

"Hope he hasn't been waiting long," Ransom replied, knowing he was almost an hour late. "Traffic was a bitch." Which was true, but not the only reason he was late.

The officer grunted and adjusted small oval glasses on a nose as sharp and angled as a hawk's beak.

Ransom noted the lack of crime scene tape on the doors. Two days since the bodies were found and these guys had already solved the case. Or at least that's what they thought.

He made his way to the door, not bothering with further niceties. He wasn't here to make friends either. As he passed the officer, he noted the nametag. *J. Mosner.* Strange name.

He crossed the threshold and the atmosphere shifted. Gone was the cheerful feeling he'd experienced outside. In its place was a sense of emptiness. The feeling of loss and the foul smell of death only murder can emit.

"He's in the dining room," Mosner called out behind him.

Ransom passed through a small kitchen. A pizza box, two paper plates and two bottles of Bud Light sat on the Formica counter. He sidestepped to the counter and studied the bottles. Both were about half full.

He shifted his attention to the pizza box. Printed on its top was a logo depicting a howling coyote wearing sunglasses and the name "Blue Moon Café."

"Take out or delivery?" he asked.

"Take out," Mosner replied.

He took a pen from his pocket and pried up the lid. Pepperoni. Two slices gone. The rest was shriveled and looked plastic. He'd seen pizza in a similar state. In his own house after his son's death.

"The dining room," Mosner reminded him.

Ransom let the lid fall, stuck his pen back into his pocket and stepped through the doorway into the dining room, Mosner following close behind.

The first thing he noticed was a man about the size of a side-by-side refrigerator leaning against the far wall. His uniform seemed two sizes too small, but it wasn't due to bulging muscles. More like too many trips to the donut shop. Ransom's assessment was confirmed by a dark food stain below the officer's right pocket. This, combined with a lopsided grin and a crown of pink skin on top of his head, reminded Ransom of an overstuffed teddy bear. The officer gave Ransom a sociable nod. Maybe not *everyone* in Sedona hated him. At least not yet.

Another man, this one in striking contrast to the first, sat on a wooden chair next to a square farmer's table. He was fit looking, probably mid-fifties, with gray hair in a military cut and handsome Nordic features. This one's uniform was pressed and spotless. With the look of a war veteran who'd seen most of life's hardships, his eyes scanned Ransom for a few long moments. And Ransom knew which one was Chief Parker. He held Parker's gaze, stuck out his hand and introduced himself. Again, wasted effort.

Parker pressed his lips together. "Why are you here?"

"To assist in the investigation." The official line sounded too well used, even for Ransom.

Parker refused to bite. "There is no *investigation*. The man responsible put a hole the size of New Jersey in the back of his head. He's already started his eternal sentence in hell. Case closed."

"Craig Adams?"

Parker nodded.

"He committed suicide?"

Parker looked at him as though he were the most dim-witted agent on the planet. "Putting a gun against your forehead and pulling the trigger pretty much defines suicide in my book. Or didn't they teach you that at the FBI Academy?"

Ransom nodded. "If you don't have someone helping you."

Parker's face went red. "I don't know what you've heard to bring you all the way up here from your cushy office in Phoenix, but it's all BS. It was suicide."

"No question about it?"

"Not in my mind. So my first question still stands. What's the FBI's interest in this?"

Ransom took out his pen again and tapped it against the wooden table. "I received a call yesterday, asking for our assistance."

Parker's eyes widened, then flicked to the hefty officer slouched against the wall. "Someone from my department?"

"I can provide access to the FBI's resources."

"We don't need any of your help."

"What about the girl? She was from here too, right?"

Parker said nothing.

"Have you found … uh … the rest of her?"

Parker sprang from the chair. "Christ! Don't you know when to stop? I know her family. I held her when she was two days old. And now she's dead!" His face was now the color of an overripe plum. "And luckily for us, the bastard who killed her is too. If he didn't do it himself, I would have."

Ransom raised his eyebrows at Parker's declaration.

Then all the hot air rushed out and Parker let out a heavy sigh. "This is a local issue. I don't need anyone … any outsider … coming in here and stirring things up. We survive on tourism here, Agent Ransom. And this business is bad for tourism." His lips curved into a cross between a grin and a snarl. "We'll give you a call if we need any assistance." Parker began to turn away, dismissing him.

Ransom pulled a neatly folded piece of paper from his folder and held it out. Parker eyed the paper, but didn't reach for it.

"A letter from my boss, Special Agent in Charge Roger Phillips, authorizing my involvement, access to any evidence collected, and asking for your support."

Parker's eyes narrowed, locked onto the paper in Ransom's hand.

Five seconds.

Ten.

Ransom had been through this before. He could wait until it snowed in Phoenix.

Fifteen seconds.

Parker shrugged. "Go ahead. If you want to waste your time, that's up to you."

Ransom put the email confirmation for his hotel room back into his pocket, let out an imperceptible sigh. He had asked Phillips to let him come to Sedona, but was turned down. "Looks like his guilt got the best of him," his boss had said. "Let the locals handle it." And that was that. The SAC didn't often change his mind once he made a decision. Neither did Ransom. So Ransom was on his own.

Parker pointed to the heavyset officer. "I'll let you tag along with Officer Hilderman. But if you start getting in the way, I don't care what paper your boss signed, I'll kick your ass out of here so fast you'll be wishing you never left Phoenix."

Ransom offered his best *we're on the same team* smile. "I'll be a fly on the wall."

Parker snorted, then continued speaking to Officer Hilderman, "Show Agent Ransom around. Give him the five-cent tour and access to whatever he wants."

Ransom smiled. "Thank—"

Parker's upraised finger stopped him. "You've got twenty-four hours. Then my patience runs out." Parker nodded to Officer Mosner, and they both strode out the door.

Hilderman watched the cruiser drive away, then looked to Ransom. "I don't think he likes you much."

"You catch that too?"

Hilderman's lips curved into a hint of a smile. "He's usually not so … angry. But this business has him … has everyone in town … on edge. Just don't get on his bad side."

"You mean I'm on his good side?"

A full-blown smile on the meaty face. "Not even close. But if you *were* on his bad side, your ass would've been hittin' pavement by now."

Ransom's eyebrows arched in surprise.

"Or maybe not. But don't underestimate him, he can be downright nasty when he wants to be."

"I'll keep that under advisement," Ransom said. He clicked his pen. "Okay, tell me about Craig Adams."

Hilderman shook himself as if something had just burrowed under his skin. "Jesus, I can't believe it." A deep breath. "He was a cop. He was one of us."

Chapter 3

There it was, the crux of the problem. The man who appeared to have brutally murdered a young girl, then killed himself, was a Sedona cop.

But he already knew that. He'd done a background check on Craig Adams before leaving Phoenix. He also knew that the data garnered from database searches didn't mean much. Better to get a more personal view.

"So tell me about Craig Adams," Ransom said. "What's his history?"

Hilderman slouched a little more, thought a moment. "Moved here from California when he was about fifteen."

"Did you know him then?"

A nod. "Everybody knows everybody in a small town. And Sedona was small back then." He scowled. "Not the big city it is today."

Big city? Ransom wondered what Hilderman thought of Phoenix.

"He was two years younger than me, but my family had moved here the year before, so I sorta showed him the ropes."

Two years younger ... Craig Adams had turned forty-four a few months ago, which would make Hilderman only forty-six and five years older than Ransom. He would have guessed early fifties.

Hilderman caught the surprise in his face and grinned. "I know, I know." He patted his sizable belly. "I've gotta weak spot for good food … or bad food … or any kind of food." His eyes turned upward. "And my big bald dome doesn't help me with the ladies either."

"Bald's making a big comeback," Ransom said.

Hilderman chuckled. "If you say so, boss, but I ain't been on a date since my divorce."

Ransom scribbled a few notes in his notebook.

"Anyway, like I said, I showed him around, but we weren't close or anything...." His eyes went distant. "My baby brother did date his sister for a while in high school."

He'd smiled when he'd said it, but Ransom thought he detected a trace of jealousy. "Do you remember anything unusual about him when he was growing up?"

"My brother?"

Ransom hoped this guy wasn't Sedona's finest. "No, Craig Adams."

A shrug. "Right. He seemed like a good kid. Never got into any serious trouble. Maybe a little shy. Didn't seem to go out much. After high school, he went to college in Phoenix and I joined the force." He grinned. "Something I always wanted to do. Loved playing cops and robbers since I was knee-high to a grasshopper. Then I—"

Ransom held up his pen. "Can we get back to Adams?"

A rueful shrug. "Right. Craig came back to Sedona when he was about twenty-five, said he wanted to be a cop. Help people."

"Was he a good one?"

Hilderman stiffened, and the question hung in the air for a long moment. Ransom knew Adams had been given the Medal of Service award twice during his time on the Sedona police force. No black marks in his personal or professional records, until about a month ago, when Chief Parker wrote him up for failure to notify a supervisor that he was arresting a juvenile. That was it. A good record. Nothing to indicate he was capable of the brutality discovered in his basement.

Hilderman swallowed hard. "Was he a good cop? Yeah, I thought so ... at least ... until ... shit ... I've got a sixteen-year-old daughter. She made a 'mistake in judgment'—her words—about a year ago. Craig picked her up for shoplifting some lipstick from a drugstore. He cuffed her, put her in the back of his car and played it up real good. Scared the crap out of her. I thanked him for that." His eyes went to the floor. "When I saw what he'd done ... Jesus, my daughter was with him. Alone. *She* could've been down there instead of..."

Hilderman let the words trail off, as if saying them might actually change history. Ransom nodded in sympathy. It wasn't an act. He also had a daughter. Morgan was eighteen, and since the accident that claimed his son, she was his only child. The thought that she could also be so easily taken away made his stomach constrict into a tight ball.

Hilderman continued. "It's ... it's just so hard to believe he could do that."

"Can you think of anything that might've given you a clue to what happened? Or why?"

"Nothing," Hilderman said, but it was clear there was more.

Ransom tapped his pen on the table, making each tap deliberate. *Tap. Tap. Tap.*

Hilderman's shoulders sagged. "I don't know … I've been thinking about Craig since we discovered what he did. You know, thinking if I could've done something, noticed something … I liked the guy … but …"

"But?"

"Shit, I really didn't know much about him. He didn't have kids or an ex-wife, so we didn't have much in common."

"Girlfriends?"

"I don't think he was dating any local girls. Always said he preferred them from Flagstaff or Phoenix."

"Anyone in particular?"

Hilderman's brow furrowed. "Can't say. He was a private person. Spent a lot of time working on his house."

Ransom jotted notes. "How did he get along with everyone on the force?"

"Fine, I guess."

"What about Parker?"

"They weren't best buddies, but as you saw, the chief don't show much love to anyone." He pursed his lips. "But something happened … maybe a month ago … the chief seemed to have it out for him since then."

About the time Adams received the one black mark on his record. "Any reason in particular?"

Hilderman's eyes jerked left, then right, verifying they were alone, then he whispered in a conspiratorial tone that seemed familiar ground. "The chief wrote him up for failure to notify. A bullshit wrap."

"Why did Parker do it?"

A shrug.

"And Adams. What did he think about it?"

Another shrug. "Like I said, Craig was a private person." Then his voice lowered again. "But, he was pissed. Anyone could see that."

"Any good friends on the force?"

He thought for a moment. "He was always sociable, but he was—"

"A private person," Ransom finished.

A grin. "You got it, boss."

"What about enemies?"

Hilderman shook his head. "Not until we found out what he did. Now his only friend seems to be his sister."

"No other family?"

"Just his father … Jesus, he's the one who found the body. He's taking this real hard."

"And the girl?" Ransom looked at his notes, then back up. "Amanda Pearce?"

"Popular, but no boyfriend. Hometown girl. Pretty … well, she used to be. Her eighteenth birthday would have been next week, so she was a couple years older than my daughter. A party girl. Her dad had to bail her out of trouble a couple of times. Underage drinking, smoking weed. Not too unusual. 'There ain't nothin' to do around here,' should be the Sedona teenager's official motto."

"When did she go missing?"

"Almost a month ago. A Saturday night. She left her best friend's house sometime around 11:00 p.m. Her friend admitted they'd been drinking and smoking pot."

"She drive home?"

Hilderman shook his head. "Walked. She still lived at home, and her dad had taken away her car privileges after her most recent drinking incident. Less than a mile to her house, but she never made it. No evidence of foul play. At first we thought she'd run away. No one was surprised. She made it known she wanted to leave town, but no one ever thought she'd throw away her allowance."

"Allowance?"

"Robert Pearce. Her father. He owns Bell Rock Jeep Tours. And about half of everything else in town." He made counting-cash motions with his hands.

Ransom nodded. "Then what?"

"After a week and still no word from her, we started getting worried she hadn't just run away…." He looked down at his feet and balled up his fists. "And she was right here all this time."

Ransom put his pen away and tucked the folder under his arm, but Hilderman didn't move, just stared at the floor and muttered, "It was real bad down there. Real bad."

Ransom thought of the folder in his hand. Thought about the pictures inside. A shiver ran down his spine. Hilderman was right, it was real bad down there.

Chapter 4

"Howard Adams—Craig's dad—said when he didn't show up for dinner, he came here looking for him. Jesus, finding your own son's body … and Amanda … her head was set on his workbench, like some kind of trophy. And the pictures … the dispatcher said he was freakin' hysterical."

Ransom chewed on his bottom lip. "You ever been in the basement before?"

"Not until two days ago."

"Show me."

The officer's face paled, but he nodded and pointed toward a door on the other side of the kitchen, an open-shelf pantry next to it. "Down there."

Hilderman led him back through the kitchen. The pantry shelves held canned soups, vegetables and fruits, boxes of cereal and microwave popcorn. The door was cracked open, the space beyond dark and silent. Basements weren't common in Arizona, but some of the older ranch homes were built to eastern construction standards, to help make recent transplants feel more at home.

Ransom stepped forward, grabbed the handle and pulled the door open. Steep, angled steps disappeared into the gloom. Damp air wafted upward. His nose picked up the unmistakable stench of decaying flesh and dried blood. This was where the monster had his fun.

"The basement," Hilderman—the master of understatement—breathed from somewhere behind him.

Ransom sensed movement over his shoulder. Hilderman had backed up a good five feet. "You don't need me down there, do you?" Hilderman said. "Once was enough for me."

Ransom shook his head.

"Light switch is on your left," Hilderman said, then disappeared from view.

Ransom turned back to the door, found the light switch and flicked it on. The darkness below brightened a few lumens. He placed a foot on the topmost wood stair, waiting for a creak. Silence. The hairs on the back of his neck tingled, thinking some sound would have been better than nothing. He sniffed the air, thought about turning around, thanking Hilderman for his time and driving back to Phoenix. He didn't need to be here. Wasn't *supposed* to be here. But, he'd made a promise.

Ten steps and he was down. The basement wasn't much of a basement. Maybe twenty feet square, cinderblock walls, concrete floor and a lone light bulb hanging from the ceiling. Empty except for two metal shelves and a workbench. The shelves were filled with old paint cans, roof coating, paint thinner, oil, a five-gallon gas can—things the typical homeowner needed to keep the house in shape.

He stepped over to the workbench and ran his fingers along the edge. Oak. The surface was clean, but marred from years of heavy use. A piece of pegboard was anchored to the wall behind the bench. The basement's light reflected chrome-handled tools. He looked, but couldn't find any evidence of the grotesque trophy Hilderman said had once graced the room. Nor any sign that the monster had killed the girl here.

His eyes shifted to the opposite side of the cellar. A message, written in black permanent marker, was scrawled on the far wall:

Help me
Will God ever forgive me?
I am a monster
Please forgive me
I love you, Lauren

He had to squint to read the last two lines of Craig Adams' epitaph. They were almost illegible, as if the words themselves had driven him crazy.

Dark bloodstains splattered the wall, and a large pool of dried blood colored the concrete floor below the writing.

That's where he killed himself, he could almost hear Hilderman say.

Ransom opened a copy of Chief Parker's preliminary report. It contained little more than what had been found at the scene, but he wondered what Parker would do if he knew Ransom had it. Probably turn *downright nasty* as Hilderman put it.

He scanned the first few pages again. Nothing new came to him. No surprise there. The file was only a day old. Not enough time for anyone to do a thorough investigation. But Parker had already made up his mind.

When his fingers touched a thick divider near the end of the report, he lingered, unsure. He knew what the file did contain—copies of digital photographs.

It was bad down there, Hilderman had said.

The pictures.

He took a deep breath and turned the page.

The first photograph, taken by the medical examiner's office, was of Craig Adams, his body collapsed in the corner of the basement. Ransom looked up from the picture and matched it to the scene in front of him, flipped through the next few pictures showing the body from different angles. Parker was right about one thing; there *was* a large hole in the back of his head.

The close-up of Adams' face stared back at him. A ragged hole ringed with black powder marks was centered in his pasty white forehead. A thin line of dried blood ran between his eyes, around his nose and over his blue-black lips. His eyes were still open. The irises were a dull black, the whites a spider web of broken blood vessels. Ransom knew the zombie look was caused by the .40 caliber breaking every blood vessel in his eye, not from a horror-movie makeup artist. But it still looked as if Adams might rise up, take to the streets with an insatiable desire for human flesh.

The last picture was Adams' official police photograph. He'd been a handsome man, and hadn't yet taken on the hard look many veteran cops acquire. Delicate features, with short dark hair, a wide smile and bright green eyes—nothing like the ones in the previous photo. Ransom stared at the picture, dissecting the man's eyes. They didn't seem the eyes of a brutal killer. But he knew that humans could be extremely adept at deception.

He turned to the final section of the report. This one separated the pictures taken by the police from those *found* in the basement. Although he'd looked at them once before, he had to prepare himself. He took a deep breath and flipped the divider over. The first picture depicted a naked body so mutilated, if it weren't for the subsequent close-ups, it would have been impossible to tell it had once been a seventeen-year-old girl. He skimmed over the next series of pictures: a pulp of torn flesh that used to be an arm; amputated fingers; broken toes; a torso struck so many times that a portion of her ribs were exposed.

It had been a rage induced beating. Every inch of her touched. Except for her head. At least when it had still been attached to the body.

He paused. As bad as those pictures were, he knew the others were worse. He swallowed hard. Why in the hell didn't he just take over Dad's plumbing business? He wouldn't be here, looking at these damn pictures. *Because you wanted to be the big, tough FBI agent, helping ladies in distress. And you didn't want to deal in other people's shit. Literally.*

Although he knew he would never take over the family business, sometimes he felt better fantasizing about it.

Back to this shit. He turned the page. The photo was probably the last one taken while the woman had been alive. It was a headshot of her face, skin stark white from fear and the camera's bright flash. A rag had been stuffed in her mouth, and her eyes were spread wide with a terror he recognized. In the same style print as on the basement wall, the words *forgive me* had been cut into her forehead.

Amanda Pearce had known she was going to die. Horribly.

"Shit," he muttered, then flipped to the last page. A beautiful dark-haired girl with vivid eyes and an infectious smile looked up at him. Amanda Pearce's senior picture. She could have been one of Morgan's friends. *Hell, she could have been Morgan.*

The air in the cellar suddenly felt ten degrees colder. He glanced up at the door, half expecting it to somehow have shut and locked itself, sealing him in this tomb forever.

A shadow drifted over the threshold. His hand went for his Glock.

"You okay down there?" Hilderman's voiced echoed off the barren walls.

He breathed out. "Be right up." He closed the folder and climbed the stairs in three leaps, almost bowling Hilderman over as he barged through the door.

Hilderman led him back into the kitchen. "Creepy, huh?"

Ransom nodded. He didn't blame Hilderman for not wanting to go down there again. *He* didn't have any desire for a return trip to Craig Adams' hell.

Hilderman grinned. "Nice to see that tough FBI agents get a little spooked too."

"You'd have to be inhuman not to be."

"Inhuman …" Hilderman looked back toward the basement. "Let's get outta here."

"Good idea." It felt as if he'd been breathing polluted air, his lungs blackened from the stench of death, and he wanted out of the damn house as fast as possible. Once outside, his chest felt lighter.

Hilderman leaned against his cruiser. "Where to now, boss?"

Ransom didn't answer right away. He was still thinking about what he'd seen in the basement. "Who's Lauren?" he asked.

Hilderman shrugged. "Dunno."

When he didn't say anything further, Ransom said, "Parker is trying to find out, right?"

"I'm not following you," Hilderman said. "Who's Lauren?"

Christ. The big lug couldn't be *that* dense. "Lauren," he said. "The writing on the basement wall. *I love you, Lauren.* That Lauren."

"Ohhh," Hilderman said catching on. "The last few lines are hard to read. It's not Lauren. It's Laura. That's his sister. Her name's Laura."

"Are you certain?" Ransom asked.

Another confused look. "Sure. I know her. And her name's Laura, not Lauren."

Ransom gave up. Hilderman was probably right. The writing had been almost unreadable. He looked back at the house. "Where's the … evidence?"

"The station. At city hall."

"I want to see it."

Hilderman's face blanched. "Jesus, I think I'd rather go back in the basement."

Chapter 5

Hilderman pulled his cruiser into the small parking garage, while Ransom parked the Crown Vic in a visitor's space out front of Sedona's city hall, impressed by what he saw. Just off the city's main drag, highway 89A, the graceful arches, red clay mission tiles and tasteful artwork made it more closely resemble a Mexican hacienda than the blocky utilitarian design normally selected for government structures.

He stepped out and threw on a light jacket. A cold breeze had whipped up and the sun was setting behind a thick layer of violet, indigo and pink clouds. Set against Sedona's famous red rock, it was one of the most beautiful sunsets he'd ever seen. He stared at the darkening sky, wondering how a world full of such splendor could produce such horrors.

"Storms coming in."

He swiveled to his right. A woman stepped around his car to stand next to him. She pointed westward. "Those types of clouds always bring rain."

He nodded, but didn't look back at sky. He was more interested in her. She looked to be in her late thirties, wore faded blue jeans, a denim jacket and hiking boots. Straight jet-black hair danced in the gathering breeze. But it was her green eyes that kept his own eyes on her. He could envision them smiling, but today they seemed heavy with sadness.

And familiar. The last time he'd seen them was on a monster who'd just murdered a teenage girl.

She opened her mouth to speak again, but labored breathing behind them stopped her. Hilderman, his face ruddy from the walk to Ransom's car, drew up his great bulk next to them. Ransom looked him over and shook his head. If Hilderman ever had to chase a suspect farther than the length of his cruiser, he'd probably die of a saturated fat-induced heart attack.

Hilderman grinned. "Too many of those damned Big Macs," he said between gulps of air. "But don't worry, heart's strong as a bull."

"Hey, Hildy," the woman said.

Hildy?

"Laura," Hilderman replied, eyes going to the ground.

Ransom tried to hide his surprise. These two knew each other. Maybe even had some history together. But that shouldn't be too surprising. Sedona was a small town.

The woman said, "Want to introduce me to your friend?"

"Uhhh …" Hilderman shifted from foot to foot as if standing on a hot stove.

Unwilling to wait for Hilderman, Ransom stuck out his hand. "Stuart Ransom."

"Laura Adams." She took his hand and her handshake was firm, yet feminine, fingers soft and smooth. She held his grip for a long moment before letting go.

Hilderman finally recovered. "Laura is Craig Adams' sister. The one I told you about."

Laura began to say something, but Ransom gave her a look that told her to keep quiet.

"Agent Ransom's with the FBI, Laura," Hilderman continued. "He's looking into Amanda's … uhhh … and your brother's …"

"Murder?" she answered.

Hilderman shrugged.

Laura's eyes darkened. "He didn't kill anyone, Hildy. You know that. He couldn't have done those things. He didn't have a bad bone in his body. He was a cop … just like you."

"Laura," Hilderman's eyes cut to Ransom, "I can't talk about the case, not until the investigation's over, you know that."

Right. Ransom noted that if he wanted information leaked into the local gossip circuit, Hilderman was his man. It was the reason Ransom didn't want Laura to say she'd been the one who called him.

"This *investigation* is a joke," Laura said. "Parker's in maximum CYA mode, and as far as he's concerned, the investigation is over. He'd rather blame Craig than find the truth." She turned to Ransom. "Have you talked to Parker yet?"

He nodded.

"Been to Craig's house?"

He nodded again, but she didn't reply, obviously wanting some sort of report.

"I can't say anything yet." He angled his thumb toward the city building. "I've got to look at the evidence, then—"

"The evidence is bullshit!" She moved close to Hilderman. "Tell him, Hildy. Tell him my brother was no killer."

Hilderman's eyes flashed between her and Ransom. Ransom could tell he wanted to say something, but couldn't bring himself to.

Laura shook her head, disappointment replacing the anger in her eyes. "It's wrong. Everything is wrong," she said, stepped off the sidewalk and walked away without looking back.

Ransom watched her climb into an old Honda Civic, one of the tiny ones from the seventies. Then he looked back at Hilderman. He'd also been watching Laura. But with big, sad eyes.

And something else. He caught Ransom's stare and shook himself out of it. "She hasn't accepted her brother's ... involvement in this yet."

The king of the obvious strikes again. Ransom wondered if Hilderman was really that thick, or if it was just his dry sense of humor. Ransom's lips curved into a hint of a smile. Either way, he was beginning to like the big buffoon.

Hilderman cleared his throat. "She's a stubborn lady."

Ransom nodded. He learned that when he talked to her on the phone yesterday. As she angled the car onto the street, her green eyes caught his for a heartbeat. Stubborn *and* beautiful. Even more so than her picture had promised.

Hilderman escorted him past the bored-looking officer at the reception desk, and they worked their way to the police department offices. It was quiet inside; the afternoon shift was still out, and the evening shift was yet to arrive.

"How many officers work here?" Ransom asked.

"Thirty-two," Hilderman said. "We cover nineteen square miles in and around Sedona."

A Native American officer peeked out of an office door, pressed her lips together when her eyes found Ransom. He felt his skin tingle under her intense stare. Nice to know word had gotten around so fast and he was making friends.

After skewering Ransom, her eyes went to Hilderman. "Enjoying your babysitting, Hilderman?"

Hilderman grunted in response, reached out and pushed through a swinging door. "Evidence room's in the basement."

Ransom followed him down a flight of stairs "What about your medical examiner?"

Hilderman shook his head. "Not much violent crime in Sedona. All we've got is a temporary facility and we borrow the ME from Yavapai County when we need one. But you're lucky, the Yavapai ME's been busy, so he isn't coming to pick up the bodies until tomorrow." Near the bottom of the steps, he groaned. "Bad knee," he said over his shoulder. "High school football."

Ransom wanted to add that his weight didn't help. Instead he asked, "What's your opinion on all this?"

Hilderman stopped on the bottom landing, then, without turning around, said, "Not sure."

"Come on. You knew both Craig Adams and Amanda Pearce. You know this town, these people."

"Chief Parker—"

"I already know what Parker thinks. I want to know what *you* think."

At this, Hilderman turned around and looked up at him, a shadowed sadness in his face. "Look, boss, I'm not the smartest guy around—"

"A large portion of a man's intelligence can be measured by the company he keeps," Ransom said.

Hilderman's eyes were thick with suspicion.

"Look, it doesn't seem like I'm making friends too fast around here, so you're going to have to do for now."

Hilderman gave him a wary smile. "Neither of us are gonna win any popularity contests right now, that's for sure."

"So, what do you think? Was Officer Craig Adams capable of what you saw in his basement?"

The dark stairway went silent for a moment. "My gut tells me no," Hilderman said. "Not the Craig Adams I knew. But … I've been wrong before. Jesus, you spend a few hours a day at work with each other, but you don't know what they do when they're alone, right? Like all of those Catholic priests, abusing children. It's a crazy world out there."

"Remind me to never ask you to be a character witness," Ransom said with a grin.

With a "*Hrmph*," Hilderman opened the door to a narrow corridor. Nondescript doors drew off on either side. He ambled up to the second door, a polished brass nameplate at eye level reading *Evidence / Storage Room*. He reached for the outsized combination lock securing the door, but his hand froze. "Damn," he muttered under his breath.

The lock's clasp hung open.

Chapter 6

"Not again," Hilderman said with a shake of his head.

Ransom gave him a curious look. "This sort of thing happen often?"

"The damn lock's a little touchy. If you don't close it right, it can pop back open."

"Time to buy a new lock."

"We did. Second one this year. Heavy-duty, with four number combinations. Cost about $350 a piece."

"Not worth a penny if they don't stay closed."

"The chief thinks a batch had a defect and the company won't admit it. They say we aren't closing them properly." A small grin. "You'll find the chief a stubborn man. He won't buy another lock. Wants the lock company to reimburse him for this one and the previous one."

"Sounds like Parker's stubbornness might have just cost us the chain of evidence."

Hilderman took down a clipboard hanging next to the door. Ransom glanced over to see that it was an access sheet with dates, times and names of people who opened and locked the door when leaving. Hilderman reached into his breast pocket, took out a pair of reading glasses. "Getting older sucks," he said as he put them on. "I usually wear contacts, but my new ones don't come in until next week, the ladies—"

"Don't like guys with glasses," Ransom finished. He moved closer, scanning the list as Hilderman did. His eyes jumped to the last name on the sheet: *Parker*.

"Goddammit," Hilderman mumbled. He put his glasses back into his pocket, unclipped the radio from his belt. Once the dispatcher answered, he said, "I need the chief," he said. "Down in the evidence room."

"He's not available," the dispatcher's voice echoed back.

"It's important."

The officer sighed over the radio. "I'll check with him."

Hilderman hooked the radio back to his belt and gave Ransom a sheepish look. "Uhhh … the chief don't think too highly of me."

"Maybe he's afraid you'll be taking over his job soon," Ransom said in a light tone, but Hilderman's face remained humorless.

Ransom pointed to the lock. "What are you going to do about that?"

"The chief might be stubborn and cheap, but he ain't stupid."

Hilderman signed the access sheet, noted the lock's open state and that Ransom was a visitor, and pushed open the door. He flicked the light switch and they were instantly bathed in bright light. The room measured about fifteen feet square, with a small metal desk shoved into one corner and tall steel cabinets lining two of the walls. At the far end of the room, four square silver doors were embedded into the masonry wall.

Temporary storage coolers.

Hilderman motioned Ransom to follow him. Two of the four doors had yellow tags hanging from their handles. Printed in black marker against the yellow background were the names *Amanda Casey Pearce* and *Craig James Adams.*

Hilderman tugged on each handle; neither budged. He pulled a massive set of keys from his pocket, spent a few minutes finding the right one and unlocked both doors. Looking up at Ransom he said, "The chain of evidence is still intact."

"Hooray," Ransom replied. He pointed to a cooler labeled with the victim's name. "Care to do the honors?"

Hilderman recoiled as if it contained a viper. "Be my guest."

Ransom pulled on the handle, and suppressed a gag as the stench escaped on a cold rush of air. The dark interior appeared empty. He grabbed the icy gurney and slid it out. The first few feet showed only a bare white sheet and he thought maybe someone had done something with the evidence. But near the end of the gurney, the sheet curved upward into a bump about the size of a soccer ball.

Shit. He didn't want to do this. He gathered himself, took a corner of the heavy sheet between two fingers and lifted. But even the pictures hadn't prepared him for what lay on the rack. Amanda Pearce's head, severed at the neck, faced him. Her eyes were open and they appeared to be staring into his soul. Asking him *why?*

It was a question he didn't have an answer for. Not yet.

He sucked air between clenched teeth. Cleaning crap from a clogged toilet for his father's plumbing business was looking damn good right now. He bit his lip and pressed forward.

Unlike the rest of her body, Amanda's head hadn't been bludgeoned to a pulp. It was as if two different people had murdered her.

One had taken his rage out on her body, the other had sought absolution by preserving her face and head. With utmost care, the killer had washed all the blood from her face. Even the wounds left when he'd taken a knife and carved *forgive me* into her forehead looked as if they'd been cleaned. The only other trauma to her head was a thicket of her black hair had been sheared off. Something the killer had kept for himself.

Ransom tore his eyes from hers and looked at the other items the monster had left for display. Four amputated fingers. The tips raw, the fingernails broken and torn. Impossible to tell if they were clipped off while Amanda screamed or after her heart had stopped.

The final item Parker had found in the basement was a gold necklace. The killer had draped it across her severed head, as if it had significant meaning. Now, it lay on the cold laboratory sheet in front of her unblinking eyes. Ransom took his pen from his pocket and lifted it up. A tiny golden angel, wings outstretched as if ready to take flight, swung lazily from the delicate chain and for an instant, it seemed as though the angel *was* actually flying. He laid the necklace back down, replaced the sheet and slid the gurney back into the dark cavern.

Next came Adams, whose tall frame took up most of the gurney. Ransom inspected the bullet's entry and exit wounds, then the rest of his body, noting that his arms, face and torso were free of defensive wounds. Either Amanda didn't fight back, or he'd come on her so quickly, she never had a chance to.

Ransom closed the door to the cooler, leaned heavily against the wall. Hilderman had been right, it was worse here. He turned to Hilderman, who was sitting atop the desk. "What else did you find down in the basement? Find any tools he might've used to do this?"

Hilderman shook his head. "They were clean. Couldn't find blood on any of them."

"And the pictures?"

"On the workbench. Arranged in a circle around Amanda's head."

"Any blood or fingerprints on them?"

"No blood, but Craig's fingerprints were all over them."

"Ideas on where he cut her up or what he did with the rest of her?"

Hilderman shook his head again. "We've been all over his property, no sign of a fresh grave."

"What about the necklace? Parker have any ideas on why that was left for us to find?"

"Uhhhh … I don't think so."

"How about Adams? Anything interesting on him?"

"Nope—" Hilderman's eyes cut to the tall cabinets. "Just his weapon."

"Can I see it?"

Hilderman grunted, went over one of the tall cabinets, unlocked the door and handed Ransom a plastic evidence bag containing Adams' service pistol, a .40-cal Glock Model 23. He inspected the weapon inside the bag, noted the white residue left over from fingerprinting.

"Fingerprints?" he asked.

Hilderman nodded but looked away.

Oh, no.

"You *did* find fingerprints on the gun, right?"

"Yes," Hilderman said shuffling his feet.

Ransom would've liked to be playing across the poker table from this guy, the man just wasn't good at deceit. Or maybe he was and he was hiding something?

Ransom fixed him with a level stare. "How many?"

"Two clean ones and—"

"Two? That's it? How in the hell did Adams accomplish that?"

"He couldn't have, but—"

"And Parker's explanation?"

"A mistake," came a voice from behind them. Ransom twisted around. Parker filled the doorway, arms crossed over his chest. "We believe the first officer entering the residence inadvertently contaminated the crime scene as he secured the weapon." He raked Hilderman with his eyes.

Ransom turned to Hilderman. "You were the first cop to arrive on the scene?"

He nodded.

"Lucky you."

"Yeah, lucky me."

Parker moved into the room. "We're not *CSI* … or the *FBI*, Agent Ransom. And this isn't LA. The last homicide here was in 2004. Most of my officers will never encounter a murder scene during their entire career here. It was an unfortunate mistake," he glanced at Hilderman again, "but I've dealt with it."

Ransom bet he had. And Hilderman had been paying a steep price ever since. He felt a pang of sadness for the big, bumbling cop.

Keeping his eyes on Hilderman, Parker said, "Now that we've cleared that up, was there something else needing my attention, Officer Hilderman?"

"The door lock. It was—"

"Not again. What about the cabinets?"

"All secure."

"Who was it this time?"

Hilderman passed him the clipboard. Ransom watched Parker's face turn red. It seemed that Hilderman was a one-man wrecking crew, with a specialty of undermining Parker's image in front of Ransom.

Parker passed the clipboard back to Hilderman, who said, "You said you wanted to know—"

"Note it in the log—"

"Already done."

Parker's face was now so red that Ransom wouldn't have been surprised to see steam rising from it.

With, "Then make sure the damn thing's secure when you leave," Parker gave each of them a hard stare, did an about-face and was gone.

Uncomfortable silence filled the room for a few long seconds. Hilderman's eyes were on the floor. He cleared his throat. "Like I said, it was real bad down there. Craig was … Jesus … he was in the corner, half his head gone. Then there was Amanda … or what was left of her … the pictures … the writing on the wall …" He took a deep breath. "And his old man. He was down there. Going crazy. Crying, screaming … Jesus … if it had been my son who'd done that …"

He finally looked up at Ransom. "He was talking about killing himself. He wouldn't leave Craig's side. I saw Craig's weapon laying next to him and thought I'd better get it away from his old man.…"

Then Hilderman was looking at his feet again.

"Shit happens," Ransom said. "Maybe you saved the guy's life."

"Maybe."

Ransom turned back to the weapon. "But what I don't understand is if you picked up the gun, why aren't your prints on it?"

"I used a rag from the workbench. I guess it took off some of Craig's prints."

"Leaving your prints on the weapon might've given people the wrong idea."

A knowing smile. "Sometimes I ain't as dumb as people think."

Ransom wasn't so sure.

Hilderman's smile turned into a frown. "Parker didn't tell you everything."

Ransom blinked in surprise.

"It's true we only found two clean prints, and both were Craig's. But there was a partial print on the barrel." He took a deep breath. "And it wasn't his."

Chapter 7

"Another person's fingerprint was on the weapon?"

Hilderman nodded. "Badly smudged, but we don't think it came from Craig."

"Yours?"

A shrug. "I don't remember touching it without the rag … but, the print's still under investigation. Be at least a couple days before they can make a match … if ever."

Ransom thought a moment. "What about the father? Did he touch Craig's weapon?"

"Not while I was there."

"Did Parker fingerprint him?"

A nod. "Match not probable."

"Then whose?"

Another shrug.

"What does Parker think?"

"He thinks I screwed up big time."

Ransom closed his eyes. Parker was right. Hilderman *had* screwed up. Hilderman should have secured the father, not the gun. Parker also seemed right about another thing. From what Ransom had seen so far, everything pointed toward a murder-suicide, and he shouldn't be here.

Still …

Images flashed before him: Amanda's severed head on the workbench, Craig Adams' crumpled body, the writing on the wall, the pictures, the fingerprints. Something wasn't gelling, and he couldn't squelch the anxiousness in his stomach. The same feeling he'd gotten when he first talked with Laura Adams.

She had suggested her brother was being framed and Parker was covering it up. Although he'd heard similar stories hundreds of times, for some reason he wanted to believe her. He didn't understand why and he tried to drive the feeling away, but it was like pushing a balloon under water. It always bobbed back to the surface.

He spent another thirty minutes going through all of the evidence collected by Parker, but didn't find anything that led him to believe Adams was a brutal killer. But he didn't find anything that told him Craig wasn't the killer either.

Hilderman locked the door, tested it three times to make sure it was secure, then escorted him back to the parking lot. The sky had turned dark and the cold breeze had become a biting wind. He felt the low clouds overhead, their heaviness bearing down on him. Laura Adams had been right. A storm was coming.

"Looks like rain," Hilderman said.

"That'd be my guess," Ransom replied while he pulled his keys from his pocket. "Recommend a good place to eat?" After more than an hour in the ME's room, his appetite wasn't strong, but breakfast had been a long time ago.

"George's Mexican Restaurant," Hilderman said without hesitation.

Ransom gave him a skeptical look.

"Trust me. It's good." He patted his large belly. "I oughta know. Besides, it's my little brother's restaurant. I taught him everything he knows about cooking."

Ransom grinned. "Can't turn down that kind of endorsement."

Hilderman gave him directions, and Ransom said, "Meet you back here at seven tomorrow?"

"Seven a.m.?" Hilderman said, making it clear he wasn't a morning person.

"I've got a serious case of insomnia."

Hilderman shrugged. "Okay, boss. You get the coffee, I'll bring the donuts."

It was a quick walk to the car, but Ransom was shivering by the time he was behind the wheel. He looked at his watch: 7:40. Shouldn't be much of a crowd at George's.

The rain, fat, cold drops blown by a strong wind, began just as he pulled into George's. It was a seat-yourself restaurant and he took a booth in the far corner, his back to the wall. He shed his wet jacket, placed it on the red vinyl bench, then sat the folder on the table in front of him.

The waitress, a gray-haired plump woman in her fifties, gave him a stained paper menu. "The chimis are our specialty." Her smile was warm and friendly and made him forget the cold rain outside. At least not everyone hated him on sight. Then again, she had no reason to know who he was. To her, he was just another tourist or businessman.

"Sounds good," he said. "I'll take the chicken chimichanga and a bottle of Bud."

She wrote down his order, shoved his menu under her arm and headed toward the kitchen. He drew in a deep breath. Stared at the folder. Pushed it away. Enough for tonight.

He looked up and took a few minutes to get to know the place. The restaurant was small, maybe fifteen tables and no bar. Worn, but clean. Four tables contained customers. Two older couples, a lone man talking on his cell phone and a family of four with two elementary-age children, a boy and a girl.

The boy, who looked about ten, took two French fries and stuck them between his upper front teeth and his lips. He turned to his older sister, put his hands up in the air and tried to make a scary face. She burst out laughing and Ransom couldn't blame her. The boy had tried for Dracula, but looked more like a walrus than the Prince of Darkness. Another man would probably have smiled at the scene, but Ransom found his chest tight with grief. He looked down at the marred butcher-block table. Trevor would have been almost eleven now, about the same age as the mischievous boy at the other table.

Christ. A day didn't go by that he didn't miss him. It had been exactly seven hundred and eight days since his death. Seven hundred and eight days since he held Trevor's lifeless hand. Seven hundred and eight days since he told his son that he loved him. Seven hundred and eight days since his life went to hell.

The waitress set the beer on the table with a soft thump. Without looking up, he grasped the cool bottle.

Seven hundred and eight days of anger. He put the bottle to his lips. Seven hundred and eight days of guilt. In three gulps, the bottle was half-empty.

He looked at the brown bottle and the fury inside him almost consumed him. He felt like tossing it across the room, smashing it against the table. Something. Anything. The bottle was both heaven and hell—all in one package. Like drinking the blood of the enemy.

It had taken his son from him.

He was still staring at the bottle when the waitress brought a plate overflowing with chicken in a fried flour tortilla, cheese, lettuce, rice and beans. "Need another one, sweetie?" she said, motioning toward the beer.

"This one's fine."

She nodded and ambled off.

The smell coming from his plate was fantastic. He threw all thoughts of his son, Amanda Pearce and Craig Adams away and picked up his fork. A flurry of fork revolutions later, his plate was empty and his belly was full. He pushed the plate and still half-empty beer away. He'd have to thank Hilderman. He was right. His little brother *could* cook.

He looked around the restaurant. Thankfully, the family had left. He didn't want to think about Trevor right now. Ransom's waitress and a coworker were talking quietly near the cash register. The man who'd been talking on his cell phone was still sitting there. On his phone. Staring at him. Mid-thirties, curly brown hair and a two-day beard, dressed in a colorful western shirt and dark leather jacket. The face pinched with anger.

Shit, Ransom thought. *Might as well have a big neon sign over his head that reads FBI.*

He shifted his eyes back to his waitress, still chatting with her coworker, and was about to wave her over for his check when she went stiff, lips frozen in mid-sentence. His eyes followed hers to the restaurant's entrance and he saw who had just pushed her way through the door.

Laura Adams.

Laura stopped just inside the door, and her eyes zeroed in on Ransom. He nodded in recognition. She fixed him with a level stare and strode his way, the two waitresses whispering as she passed. She edged up to the booth, her body rigid, eyes ready for a fight. "Shouldn't you be looking into who really killed Amanda Pearce instead of filling your face?"

He held up his hands, palms out. "A man's got to eat sometime."

"And the beer? Isn't it against FBI regulations to drink on duty?"

Ransom felt a rush of guilt surge through him, but willed it away. He looked at his watch. "I went off duty two hours and fifty-seven minutes ago … about the time I was looking at Amanda's remains and wishing I were home sitting in front of the TV instead."

The fury evaporated out of her. She sighed. "Right. Sorry. I haven't slept much since Craig died … I just keep thinking I'm going to wake up from this nightmare … but I don't." She slumped into the seat across from him, her hair and jacket damp from the rain.

He wished he could reach for her hand and tell her that everything was going to be all right, but he couldn't lie. Not about that. He still hadn't recovered from his own nightmare seven hundred and eight days ago.

"Want anything?" His waitress was back, standing at least two arm-lengths away from the table, her friendly demeanor gone.

Laura turned to her and attempted a smile. "No. Thanks, Beth. I'm just staying a minute."

Beth flinched at the mention of her name and whirled away so fast, Ransom felt the vacuum left behind.

Laura shook her head. "They all believe Craig was some sort of monster. And they're glad he killed himself." She grabbed a paper napkin and began twirling it tight with her hands. "They seem to have forgotten all the good he did. Hell, he helped Beth and her family move into their new house two years ago. They stick their collective heads in the sand and don't really want to know the truth."

"It's human nature to want quick closure when something terrible happens. We want to forget about it and put it behind us." Ransom listened to his voice as he said it and wished he could take his own advice.

The napkin was now about the thickness of a pencil and she continued to twist it into ever-tighter knots. "Screw human nature. People I've known for years turn their backs on me, like I'm also to blame. They think that *I* can't accept the fact that he … he …"

Ransom looked from the napkin into her eyes. "Can you?"

Her hands froze and she met his gaze. After a long moment, she nodded. "Yes. It would be terrible, but I think I could."

He raised his eyebrows slightly.

A thin smile cut across her face. "Okay, so maybe I lied. Maybe I could never accept it. But that's only because it's not true. He just couldn't have done that—"

"Even if the evidence is irrefutable?"

"The evidence is far from irrefutable. He didn't do it."

"That's what you said on the phone yesterday." He tapped the folder in front of him with his finger. "But nothing in what you sent me tells me otherwise."

"Someone framed Craig for Amanda's murder and made it look like he committed suicide." Her eyes locked onto his as she untwisted the napkin and tore it to shreds. "There hasn't been a murder in Sedona for almost five years. The police aren't exactly experienced when it comes these things. Either they missed something big." She took a deep breath. "Or they're covering it up."

"That's why I'm here," he said.

He could lie too. Though he felt a pang of regret doing it. He couldn't help looking down at his hands. Damn. Maybe he wouldn't take *all* of Hilderman's money at a poker game after all. He let out a long breath. At least he wasn't entirely insincere. That bad feeling in his gut *had* formed when Laura told him her suspicions over the phone. And her suspicions were one of the reasons he was here.

He looked up.

The other was sitting across the table from him.

Chapter 8

"Parker's dragging his feet," Laura said. "He's taking Craig's … involvement and suicide as fact, unwilling to listen to alternate explanations."

Ransom considered this. "Parker's no Sherlock Holmes. And his office has made some mistakes. But from what I've seen so far, he's not intentionally covering anything up. He's in a delicate situation. On the surface, all the evidence points to one of his officers brutally killing the daughter of a leading town citizen." He nodded toward the waitress. "And they believe your brother got his just rewards. Parker's got to be careful. If he openly gave credence to your suspicions, this town could implode in on itself."

"I don't—"

"Think about it. If your brother didn't kill Amanda, it means the murderer's still out there. Combine that with your accusations of a police cover-up. If I were him, I'd be keeping this as quiet as possible too."

"Yes, but—"

"Give it some time. The truth usually comes out."

She leaned forward, her face inches from his. "The truth? No one wants to hear the truth."

"And what is the truth?"

"My brother didn't kill anyone. He just couldn't have."

He shook his head. "I've seen cases where a mother smothered her three children in their beds, then set the house on fire. A father sexually abuses his own daughter and threatens to slice open her throat if she tells anyone. Humans have the capacity for unimaginable evil."

She slumped back in her seat. "Not Craig."

"Listen, you said on the phone you had proof that your brother didn't commit murder. That Parker wasn't conducting a thorough investigation, possibly even covering something up. But there's absolutely no evidence to support your claims. Your brother's fingerprints are on the pictures of the murdered girl—""

"Put there by the real killer."

He sighed. "Look, I'm not even supposed to be here. My boss thinks I'm working another case. You've got to give me something."

She grabbed a handful of sugar packets and began placing one atop the other in the center of the table. When the pile was about two inches high, she said, "Do you think Amanda's murder was sexually motivated?"

His brow furrowed. "The pictures showed no evidence of rape, only anger and rage. But that doesn't mean she wasn't sexually assaulted."

She placed a few more sugar packets on top of the pile.

"Most extremely violent crimes against women are sexually motivated—even if the victim wasn't raped," he continued. "So, yes, my guess is that her murder had sexual overtones."

The pile wobbled, then tumbled over, spilling packets across the table. She stared at the fallen contents. When she didn't say anything, he said, "I don't know why—"

"Craig was gay," she blurted in a hushed whisper.

"What?"

"He told me about a month ago." She took a deep breath. "I didn't know what to say. He'd gone out with a few girls in high school, then he seemed to be interested in women from bigger towns. But now that I think about it, that was all a big cover-up. I don't think he ever had any other women in those cities … I think he went up there to see men."

Ransom struggled to take this in. "Does anyone else know?"

She shrugged. "I don't think so. He made me promise not to tell anyone."

"You haven't told Parker?"

A shake of her head. "The only reason I told you is that you aren't from here. Once Parker knows, it'll be all over town. Craig wasn't ready for this to come out. He was a very private person. And my father …" She sucked in a deep breath. "Our father … he would … I just don't know what he'd do. If it came out that Craig was gay on top of everything else … and what if nothing came of it?"

Ransom hardened his heart. "In the town's eyes, your brother has already been condemned for killing a young woman. Any information you have to help clear his name—no matter how painful—needs to be given to the chief."

She started picking up the sugar packets and placing them back in the wire container. "I'll think about it."

"Fair enough," he said, trying to soften his tone. "Why did he tell you after all this time?"

"Maybe he finally just had to tell someone. And … he told me he thought he'd finally found someone special."

"Your brother … did he give you a name?"

She tossed in the last of sugar packets. "Please, don't keep saying 'your brother.'" It feels so cold. Like he wasn't a person. Call him Craig, that's what he liked to be called."

"Okay, did Craig give you a name?"

She shook her head. "He said he needed more time … and he was afraid that his *friend's* family might not understand."

"You think it was someone local?"

"No. He was always going to Flagstaff and Phoenix. I think he found someone there."

Ransom stared at the sugar packets for a long time, thinking about what he was going to say. Finally, he looked up. "Statistically, gay men don't commit violent crimes against women … and if Craig was gay—"

"He didn't kill Amanda Pearce."

A cold wind bit into Kristen Tovar's exposed flesh. A few drops of frozen rain pelted the dark pavement. Her skin tingled with icy prickles and she pulled the hood of her black sweatshirt farther down over her pale face. She peeked around the corner of the old train depot.

The streets of Flagstaff's historical district were almost empty, the tourists unwilling to brave the cold and rain. Not more than a handful of students like her dared to be out in this weather. She wrapped her arms tighter around her and edged closer to the building's massive stone walls, out of the rain. The train depot, built in 1889, was across historic Route 66 and the majority of the tourist traps here. Now, it was a visitor's center. But at this late hour, all windows were dark.

Kristen glanced across the tracks behind her. Two large warehouses, slowly deteriorating. Both deserted and hard to distinguish against the black night sky. Shit. She didn't want to be out here. Not at night. Not in the rain. *Why can't David do business in the middle of the day at one of the coffee shops?*

Because David's business was selling drugs.

She rubbed her hands together. And she wouldn't be here either if she didn't really need some weed. Where in the hell was he? The asshole was always late. She thought about leaving, going back to her warm apartment. Make the son-of-a-bitch wait for her for a change.

Who was she kidding? He wouldn't wait for her. He'd drive by, see she wasn't here and take off. Then she'd have to call him to set up another *appointment*. He'd put her off a week, maybe more. And she needed the shit. Finals were coming up.

She shivered. Another fifteen minutes. That was all she'd give him.

Headlights flashed into the parking area. About time. She peered around the building and was momentarily blinded by the bright lights. She shielded her eyes with her hand and started out from her hiding place.

She froze. It wasn't David. It was a cop car.

Shit. Had the cops busted him and he was ratting her out? Her hands went to her pockets. Was she carrying anything incriminating? What was she going to tell her parents?

She thought of making a run for it across the empty parking lots and dilapidated buildings across the tracks. But when her pockets came up empty, she decided not to. She wasn't doing anything wrong. At least not yet. The car hadn't moved since it caught her in its headlights. No red and blue flashing lights. She looked closer. In fact, there weren't any emergency lights on top of the car at all.

Maybe it wasn't a cop car. Maybe it was just a lost tourist who happened to own a similar make. She tried to peer through the rain-splattered windshield, but couldn't see anything beyond the dark glass and windshield wipers swiping from side to side.

For over a minute, they stared at each other. She was about to flip the driver off when the car slowly backed away, turned around and drove out of the parking lot. Maybe they hadn't seen her? Maybe they had been lost tourists?

But there had been an eerie presence about the driver's behavior. They hadn't turned on an interior light, so they weren't checking a map. She'd been caught dead to rights in their headlights, so she was sure she'd been seen. And whoever was in the car had looked her over for a full minute. Why? The thought made her shiver more than the cold.

She crept back into the building's protective shadows and started breathing again. Screw fifteen minutes. Five minutes. That's all she was going to give that asshole. Then she was out of here.

"Okay, now that it's settled that my brother isn't a killer—"

"Whoa." Ransom held up his hands. "I never said that. Statistics are only one part of the equation. And I've been bitten too many times to put all my money on them."

Laura's eyes softened. "You'll find they aren't lying this time."

"That right?"

She held his gaze. "I've got a good feeling about you, Agent Ransom."

"I'm Stuart to my friends," he said, though he couldn't recall the name of a single friend at that moment.

A smile. "Okay, Stuart. Then I'm Laura. Anyway, I think you'll find out the truth, even if Parker can't see it."

"And what makes you say that?"

"You're FBI. One of Hoover's Henchmen … a G-man and all that. They always get their man, right?"

"Fidelity, Bravery, Integrity, that's me," he deadpanned.

For an instant the sadness, fear and anger was gone from her face. Her green eyes sparkled and a wide smile played on her lips. Then, as if she caught herself doing something she shouldn't, her expression became serious again. "So, uhhh … as you so eloquently pointed out, if Craig didn't kill Amanda, who did?"

He turned toward the rain-splattered window, wishing he could be here for different reasons. That he could be having dinner with this woman instead of discussing who killed her brother. Or that he could be planning a fishing trip with his son instead of continuing to mourn his death. *Why did he have to die?* he asked God for the millionth time. *Life isn't fair, Stuart,* his father's words came back to him. No shit. That much, he'd learned seven hundred and eight days ago.

His eyes searched the parking lot's darkness for a good answer: to both questions. "I don't—"

The flash of brake lights. A barely discernable figure in the rain.

A man—

"Get down!" he shouted as the window exploded into a thousand sharp fragments. Something heavy crashed onto the table then tumbled to the floor. Screams erupted from across the room.

He grabbed Laura's hand and pulled her toward the exit. "Go! Go! Go!"

Broken glass crunched under their feet as they raced for the door. The waitresses and the other customers were two steps ahead of them. They burst out the doors and the freezing rain hit Ransom like an icy blanket.

"What the hell was that?" his waitress shouted.

Ransom's eyes darted around the parking lot. Nothing. Damn, he was on the wrong side of the building. An engine roared in the distance. He pulled his gun from its holster. "Stay here," he told Laura. "Make sure everyone got out all right."

As he raced around the corner of the building, two faint taillights disappeared in the night.

He turned and trotted back to the restaurant's entrance. Laura, the two waitresses, and a young man who looked like he'd been washing dishes were huddled together in the rain. Four people. Someone was missing. He racked his brain for the mental image of the customers he'd seen when he entered the restaurant. The family—no, he'd seen them leave. The older couples? Gone. He thumped his head with his fist. There was someone else…. Then he had it. The guy in the leather jacket. Mr. Cellphone. He'd been talking on it when Laura came in, but he wasn't here now. Was he still in the restaurant?

He started toward his waitress, but she'd already crossed the few feet between them.

"George is still in there," she screamed.

George?

A huge man wearing a white apron shoved open the door. "It's okay," he said holding up something in his hand. "It was only a brick."

It took Ransom a second to see the resemblance to Hilderman. To realize this was George, Hilderman's younger brother.

A few choice words emanated from the staff as they rushed back inside to get out of the rain. George stopped Laura when she walked by. "I think this was meant for you," he said handing her the brick, his face drawn with sadness.

Laura's face went white. She looked at the brick for a moment then passed it to Ransom. It was cold and slick with rain. He turned it over. Written in black permanent marker were the words: *Leave it alone.*

Kristen covered her mouth with her hands and blew warm air between her fingers, temporarily postponing the numbness creeping in. She shoved them back into her jacket pockets. Fucking David. Fucking wind. Fucking rain. It was really coming down now. Fat drops mixed with icy sleet. She could barely see the buildings across the highway.

Where the hell was he? She hadn't seen anyone since that creepy car had left ten minutes ago, but she hadn't totally given up yet. Partially because she really wanted her weed, partly because David would give her a ride home. She really didn't want to walk the six blocks back to her apartment in the rain.

The cold wind crept under her wet clothes and chilled her inner core. Fuck it. She was going to freeze to death out here. She edged away from the wall.

Lights flashed behind her. She whirled around. Through the driving rain, she could just make out twin headlights coming from the abandoned warehouse's parking lot.

A horn beeped twice. David. He'd probably been there the whole time, just screwing with her. Anger flared and the rush of heat momentarily drove away the cold. She strode off toward the car. She was going to place her cold, numb hands around his neck until he gave her the shit for free.

The sound of a car door opening and closing came as she crossed the tracks. She put her hand over her eyes, screening them from the rain. All she could see were the lights. What the hell was he doing? He must be high on his own weed to come out of his warm car into the rain. She smiled. David always said he was his own best customer.

She tripped over a black railroad tie bordering the parking lot and went down to one knee. Red-hot pain shot through her leg. *He better have some good fucking weed this time.* She rose to her feet, brushed away the volcanic cinders clinging to her jeans and … froze.

She'd gotten close enough to recognize the car's headlights. They weren't David's. It was the car that had come into the visitor's center.

She started backing away, realized she wasn't moving fast enough, whirled around to run and bumped into a man dressed in a dark rain slicker and wide-brimmed hat. The car's headlights gleamed off his wet glasses.

"Hello beautiful," the man said, sliding a sharp knife against her throat.

Chapter 9

Two officers arrived ten minutes later. By that time, George and the cook had taped large black trash bags over the broken window. Ransom sat with Laura at a table away from the broken window, and was turning the brick over in his hand. Nothing special about it. Except for the writing on one side.

He looked up at Laura. Some of the color had come back to her face. "You said that people here were getting tired of you proclaiming your brother's innocence."

She nodded.

He set the brick on the table with a solid *thunk*. "Can you think of anyone who would resort to this?"

She pressed her lips together. "If you'd have asked me a week ago, my answer would have been an emphatic no, but now," she looked at Beth, who was sweeping up the glass shards, "I don't know. Anybody I guess."

"Who knew you were here?"

"Only Hilderman," she said. "I called him to ask where you were."

Ransom thought a moment. If he took Hilderman out of the equation, only two other possibilities came to him. Someone who saw Laura enter the restaurant, or someone inside the restaurant. The first theory didn't seem likely in the dark rain. That left the people at the restaurant.

Mr. Cellphone.

"What about the guy who was at the table over there?" He pointed to the now vacant table where Mr. Cellphone had been sitting.

She shook her head. "Don't know. I was looking for you. Didn't notice who else was here."

The waitress finished sweeping a pile of glass into a dustpan, and he waved her over to the table.

"Yes," she said through gritted teeth, her eyes hot pokers aimed at Laura.

Ransom thumbed toward the empty table. "Who was that man sitting by himself when I walked in?"

She thought for a moment. "Not sure if I remember—"

"He was wearing a leather jacket and talking on his cell phone," he reminded her.

"What color hair did he have?" This from Laura.

"Dark brown. Curly."

Beth's eyes shifted between Laura and Ransom. "With all the excitement, I can't remember."

Ransom decided she wasn't a good liar.

"Could it have been Evan?" Laura said. "Doesn't he come in here after work a few times a week?"

"Christ, I don't know. Maybe. What in the hell does it matter anyway? He wasn't here when that brick came through the window." She let out an exasperated sigh and huffed off toward the kitchen.

"Evan?" Ransom asked.

Laura nodded. "Yeah, Evan Parker."

Ransom felt his eyes go wide.

"You got it, G-man. Chief Parker's son."

Ransom closed the door and tossed his luggage and laptop on the tan-and-emerald bedspread. He set the still-damp brick down on the desk. The room had forest-green carpet, cream-colored walls and a small desk in the corner. Not a five-star resort, but the Kokopelli Inn seemed clean and comfortable.

He shrugged out of his wet coat and hung it on the back of the desk chair. It had saved his sport jacket from most of the rain, but his pants hadn't fared so well. They were soaked from the knees down. He removed his Glock and holster, gently placed them on the chair's seat, then tossed his car keys, the worry stone and his wallet on the desk. His wallet tumbled twice and a picture fell out. His breath caught in his throat.

Trevor looked back at him from his third grade picture. His *last* school picture. He was smiling, one front tooth missing.

Three days before the picture was taken, the tooth fairy had traded him cash for the incisor.

Trevor shot out of his bedroom early that morning. "Five dollars!" He jumped up and down. "I can't believe it. Five dollars!"

Ransom bent down and gave him a hug. 'I told you, Trev, the Molanator always pays more for front teeth."

"*Tooth fairy*, Dad." Trevor gave him a playful jab in the ribs. He always loved it when Ransom called the tooth fairy the Molanator.

"Hey, now that you're rich can I borrow some money?" Ransom said as he made a playful grab for the bill.

"No way!" Trevor replied, skipping back to his room. "I'm savin' up for the new Guitar Hero game."

An icy chill raced under his skin as he came back to the here-and-now. Ransom shoved the photo back into the back of his wallet, behind a stack of credit cards. Tested it. It felt secure, but he wasn't convinced. No matter where he placed the photo in his wallet, it always seemed to find a way out.

And every time, the old feelings of sadness, guilt and anger flared up, but he refused to get rid of the picture. Somehow he felt closer to Trevor knowing his picture was with him.

He pushed the memory away, determined not to dwell on it anymore … at least not tonight. Better to concentrate on work. He thought about the warning scrawled on the brick.

George had said it was meant for Laura, but Ransom wasn't so sure. Although his presence here wasn't supposed to be publicized, it could hardly be called a secret. He could count at least five cops who knew he was investigating the Craig Adams suicide. One of those cops was Hilderman. Ransom wouldn't be surprised if half the town knew who he was. Maybe the brick was meant to warn him, not Laura, to stay out of it.

Laura. What was her part in this? He thought for a moment. She was Craig's sister proclaiming his innocence. But there was more to it than that. He had the feeling she wasn't telling him everything. That she was leaving something important out. What that could be, he had no idea.

He remembered those green eyes as she'd driven away. They were hiding something. But they were also beautiful. Damn, *she* was beautiful.

He stripped off his wet clothes, took a long shower and slid beneath the sheets. Waited for sleep. Realized it wasn't going to be easy tonight. He took a deep breath. Like it ever was.

The room was quiet, the soft patter of rain against the window mixing with the sound of his own breathing, his heart beating. As he stared at the dark ceiling, he couldn't stop thinking about Laura. She was convinced that her brother wasn't the monster the evidence conveyed. But that wasn't anything unusual; family members generally didn't accept the truth for a long time. Still, for some reason, there was something different about this case.

Although he was trying to be objective, the nagging feeling in his gut just kept getting worse. He couldn't ignore it. Not from the first moment he'd talked with Laura. For some reason, he knew he had to be here. Why? No clue. But he'd been in law enforcement long enough to know one didn't ignore gut instinct. It usually pointed the agent in the right direction.

Usually.

He studied the clock's red LED numbers: 4:47. Two minutes had passed since the last time he looked at it. Ransom groaned and threw the covers back. It wasn't any use, he'd been awake for almost an hour, and he wasn't going back to sleep anytime soon. Not that he hadn't expected this.

He rarely slept through the night—not anymore. Anxiety, stress, panic attacks, all stemming from his son's tragic death: that's what his doctor had said. No shit. He hadn't needed to spend $100 an hour for a shrink to tell him that.

He retrieved the black case off the floor and walked over to the desk. Five minutes later, he was accessing the FBI's network through the in-room high-speed Internet and his secure modem. He scanned his email. Twenty-three new messages.

"Christ," he whispered. "I've been gone for less than a day."

About ten of the messages were from other agents, inviting him to meetings and asking general questions. He took care of them. Another six were spam. These asked if he wanted great deals on Viagra, low-cost stocks or 7-day Caribbean cruises. He clicked on each one and reported them as spam, though he didn't know why he went through this every day. Even with the FBI's resources, spammers somehow managed to sneak through the anti-spamming filters on a regular basis. Sometimes he wondered if the good guys were winning the war.

Five emails were forwarded jokes from his sister in Portland. He deleted them without reading them. He stopped on her last email. In large bold letters she asked—again—if he'd thought about coming up there to spend Christmas with her family. He stopped short of deleting it, but didn't answer it either. Later, he told himself. Again.

The final two emails weren't so easily deleted … or ignored. He mentally flipped a coin: work or personal? The coin landed on heads and he clicked on the email titled *Status on Longely case*. It read:

Stuart,
What's the status on the Longely case? Have you heard anything from the Vegas office? Will you be ready for a case review on Monday?
Roger Phillips, SAC

The Longely case was what Ransom should be working on. What Phillips *thought* he was working on. Longely had ties to the mob, and his mistress had found him dead one morning in their Scottsdale getaway. OD'd on prescription sleeping pills. Might've been an accident, but rumor was he'd been skimming more than his share off the take. The FBI thought it was the latter, and Ransom was assigned the case. Two months and he'd made no headway, much to the SAC's dismay.

He hit the reply button and typed:

Roger,
I haven't heard any more from Vegas, but I'll keep bugging them. Monday's not looking good, how about Wednesday?
Stuart

He clicked the send button and let out a sigh. Most of it was true, but he doubted he'd have anything before Wednesday—even if he was working on the case as he was supposed to.

The mouse pointer hovered over the last email. It was from Miatagirl292@hotmail.com. The subject line read: *Weekend*. Not descriptive, but it didn't matter, he knew. He thought about not opening it. But he'd learned that ignoring it never helped. Of the two of them, she was the more persistent.

He double-clicked the email.

Dad,
What are we doing this weekend?
Love,
Morgan

A simple question, but one he fought with ever since the divorce agreement. Despite himself, he had to grin. She sent the same point-blank question once a month—she had never been one to beat around the bush. No, she preferred the most direct path to his heart. Which is just where he didn't want her to go.

Not yet. He wasn't ready.

His grin faded. After the loss of Trevor, he'd gone inside himself, unable and unwilling to express his anger and guilt. The sadness that swept over him was so intense, he pushed his daughter away instead of embracing her. Somehow, he believed his own distorted logic that he couldn't be hurt so terribly again if he closed his heart.

At least that's what his therapist had told him. And for the most part, it was true. Over the last two years, he'd pulled away from his daughter, while she tried her best to reel him in. But he couldn't help it. He couldn't endure the seemingly bottomless sadness he went through—was still going through—after Trevor died.

No. It was too hard.

He clicked on the reply button and typed:

Working in Sedona for the weekend.
Sorry.
I promise we'll get together next month.

The mouse floated over the send button for a few seconds. Then he deleted the words *I promise*. He'd already missed about half of this year's weekends. The guilt eating through his soul didn't need to be magnified by breaking a promise. At least that's how his screwed-up mind thought about it.

He would hide in Sedona for the weekend. Bury himself into his work … again. He knew that was another reason he'd come here. To get away. Have an excuse not to get close to his daughter … no matter how hard she tried.

He slammed a fist on the desk. The accident had not only cost him his son, but his wife and daughter too.

Why did Trevor have to die?

Ransom tried to remember a happier time. His mind went back to a family vacation to Disneyland about four years ago. The kids had loved it. He had loved it. If he could go back in time, back to Disneyland, stay there forever ...

Enough! He couldn't think about it anymore. The past was the past. There was no changing it. He clicked the send button and told himself to focus. *Concentrate on the present.* That's what his overpriced shrink always told him. With a great effort, he pushed all the memories away and centered his mind on Craig Adams, on what had bothered him since last night. His subconscious had worked it out during his few hours of sleep.

The murder of Amanda Pearce had all the signs of a serial killer. Of someone who'd done this before. If that were true, where were the others?

Chapter 10

The thick scent of pine blended with the damp earth woke her with a start. She opened her eyes, but the world swirled in a confusing array of light and shadow. Her head throbbed. She shook it an attempt to clear the fog and the pain began to subside.

A spear of light cut through the inky darkness. Long, thin, spaghetti-like shapes came into focus in front of her, looking like a tangled mass of pickup sticks. Her brain fought for understanding. After a few moments, she matched the sight with the aroma of pine: She was lying in a bed of pine needles.

That mystery solved, she willed herself to concentrate on what was happening more than a few inches away from her face. The world was dark and gloomy, a lone light came from somewhere out of sight. Tall shafts thrust upward. Trees. She was in a forest.

What was she doing there? She didn't like the woods, especially at night. She'd told her dad she didn't want to go camping anymore. Why had he taken her here?

And she was cold. No. Beyond cold. Numb.

Slowly, she turned toward the light.

A car.

Headlights.

The shape.

Everything came back to her. All of it. The car, the man in the rain, the knife … what he did to her … his fists smashing down on her … the pain, then the darkness.

A shadow cut across the car's headlights. It stopped near the edge of light, turned in her direction. Kristen dared not breathe. Although she couldn't see his face silhouetted against the light, she could feel his dark eyes upon her.

Finally, as if satisfied she was either unconscious or dead, he reached for something on the ground, picked it up, and continued his trek into the darkness until he stopped in the shadows between two enormous trees.

Shwuck.

Shwuck.

Her eyes strained through gloom, but the shadows refused to reveal their secret.

Shwuck.

Shwuck.

What was that sound? Its cadence was a regular as a heartbeat.

As her mind worked to decipher the sound, her eyes saw a glint of metal. Then she knew. A stifled cry escaped her lips, the terror ripping through her.

The sound was a shovel digging in the soft mud.

He was digging her grave.

The abduction, the mutilated body, the trophies, the pictures, the confession on the basement wall—everything about the murder screamed serial killer. And the apparent ease in which it was accomplished made Ransom believe the killer had done it before.

He signed into the FBI's secure search program using his fourteen-digit password and code from his keyfob. A list of his most recent searches were displayed in a table, in case he wanted to review them. He didn't. He clicked on the button for a new search. A multipage form appeared, with over one hundred text and dropdown boxes to conduct anything from a general to a detailed search. This one was going to be general. At least for now.

He searched the FBI and regional law enforcement databases for murdered girls between the ages of thirteen and twenty-one, within the last five years, in the states of Arizona, New Mexico, Nevada, California and Colorado. It took the computer system a few moments to display the results of his search.

"Whoa," he whispered. Two hundred and twelve. Way too many. He asked the computer to display only those that hadn't been solved. Better. Nineteen, including Amanda Pearce, since her case was still officially open.

He scanned the records for any similarities to her murder. Twelve died of gunshot wounds, three by knife, three beaten to death.

One mutilation. Edith Harshaw. A blonde twenty-year-old from Silver City, New Mexico. She'd been found in a shallow grave just outside the city, her hands and feet missing, vagina and breasts mauled beyond recognition. Not exactly the same as a beheading, but the amputations made it close. No suspect named.

He saved the case under his current search title. Next, he told the computer to include women who were believed to be abducted, but their bodies were never found. That bumped up the number to fifty-four, nine in Arizona alone. Mostly teenage girls. There didn't seem to be any similarities in nationality or location. He looked at the pictures of each one. Six had dark, straight hair similar to what the killer had taken from Amanda Pearce. But there were just as many blondes and brunettes.

The Arizona disappearances showed that five were from Phoenix, one from Flagstaff, one from the Navajo reservation, two from Tucson and one from Camp Verde. Nothing definitive.

He thought back to the basement. To the writing on the wall and the last line: *I love you, Laura.* True, the letters hadn't been much more than scribbles, but they'd looked like *Lauren* to him.

On a hunch, he scanned through the names of the fifty-four women. Damn. None were named Lauren. He expanded the search to include those committed up to ten years ago. Nothing. Twenty years. One hit. Lauren Castle. A thirty-four-year-old woman from LA. Someone had broken into her apartment, raped her, then cut her throat with such force she'd almost been decapitated. Paul Lacross, a neighbor three doors down, was the prime suspect, but police couldn't find sufficient evidence to officially charged him with the crime. Five years later, he moved to Vegas and has been a person of interest in two more rape-murders, but has yet to be convicted of any crime. One slippery son-of-a-bitch.

He saved the results, then expanded the search one last time. Forty years. Two more hits. The first was Lauren Martin. She'd been beaten to death by her husband, John. Right in front of sixteen-year-old James Martin. Fearing for his own life, James had killed his father. Due to James' age, most of the information regarding the case was sealed in juvenile records.

The final hit was the murder of Lauren Castle from Phoenix. Her husband, Robert Castle, had found her with another man, then killed her in a jealous rage with a hunting knife. Robert Castle was convicted of second-degree murder, but was released on parole two years ago for good behavior. He now lived in Flagstaff.

That was it. Nothing popped out at him. Most likely, he was just wasting his time. He didn't even know if any of the missing women were actually dead. It was possible that some, maybe even most, were runaways, now living in LA or Vegas, hooking or dealing drugs.

He stared at the computer for a few long minutes. What if a few of them had been Craig Adams' previous kills? And if so, what had he done with them? Amanda Pearce's head had been made a trophy. What had he done with the others? And the pictures. Where were the pictures of the ones before Amanda Pearce?

Ransom pushed back from the table. The chair's wheels squealed in protest. If this wasn't Adams' first time, he might've kept trophies from his earlier victims.

He needed another look at Craig Adams' basement.

Kristen couldn't move. Her terror paralyzing. He was going to bury her somewhere out in the damp forest. But why? She didn't even know the man. After he'd raped and beaten her, he'd said, "You're not the one," whatever that meant.

But she was still alive. She'd pleaded with him to let her go, though deep down she knew he never would. She began to quietly weep. "Please, please, God. Don't let me die." She tried to remember the words of the Lord's Prayer. She hadn't uttered it once since she'd stopped going to church at twelve. "Our Father who art in Heaven …"

Shwuck.

The shovel hit soft mud.

Shwuck.

He would finish digging her grave, come back and use the shovel to finish what his fists failed to do. Dump her body into the muddy hole. Cover her with fresh soil and let the worms do their work.

Shwuck.

Shwuck.

The man was relentless in his digging.

Please, God. Don't let him kill me.

Then another thought, even more unsettling, forced its way into her head. *Why hasn't he killed me already?* But she already knew the answer. He wasn't going to kill her at all. No, this man wouldn't show her that much compassion. He was going to bury her alive.

The thought sent such a river of terror through her, that it finally released her from her paralyzing fear. She wasn't going to let him bury her alive. No, not alive. This much she vowed.

Cautious, she tried to move her legs. If she could get away and find some place to hide in the forest. Wait until it was light. Then make it back to the city.

She pushed again. Her legs failed to respond. At first she thought it was just the numbing cold, but she could wiggle her toes. She looked down. It wasn't the cold. The asshole had bound her ankles together.

Even knowing what she would discover, she tried her arms. They were bound too. Straining, she tried to push herself upright. Maybe she could crawl far enough away … But after two minutes, she collapsed in exhaustion, having not made more than a few feet headway.

She watched in despair as the barely discernable figure dug her grave ever deeper. How dare he? He had no right to do this to her. She didn't deserve to die like this.

Like a small inferno, the anger warmed her. She began to work at the ropes binding her wrists together, immune to the pain as they cut into her skin. She felt her own blood, sticky and warm, flowing from her wrists.

After what seemed an eternity, the bindings began to loosen. Renewed hope surged through her. A few more minutes …

Shwuck.

Shwuck.

She listened. The sounds of the man scooping soil from the forest floor had slowed. Now they were coming farther and farther apart. He was tiring.

Or … he had almost finished.

She fought the ropes with a ferocity she'd didn't know she possessed. The cord tore at her skin, chewing at the sinewy muscle beneath. Her arms were on fire, but the more she worked the bindings, the more they began to unravel. With a final tug and searing pain, her right hand ripped loose.

She didn't congratulate herself. No time. She immediately went to work on her ankles. In less than a minute, she was free.

Breathing hard, she took a moment to rest. Figure out which direction to run. As she swiveled her head around, she sensed something missing. She held her breath, but all she could hear was her own heart thumping inside her chest.

No drum of the shovel.

Oh, God.

And now that she thought of it, it had been a long time since she heard the digging sounds.

A shadow moved across the car's headlights.

No, no, no.

He was done.

And he was coming for her.

Chapter 11

The shrill ring of the bedside phone made Ransom jump. He glanced at the clock as he reached for the phone. 6:17. His wakeup call was almost fifteen minutes early.

He picked up the phone. "Yeah."

"Good, you're awake," the female voice said.

What kind of wakeup call was this?

"Gabe said you would be, and with the light in your window—"

His eyes shot toward the thin curtains covering the window. *Who ...?* Then he recognized the voice. "Laura?"

"We need to talk. I'll meet you in the lobby."

"I'm not even—"

"Fifteen minutes." And she clicked off.

"Crap," Ransom mumbled. He put his computer away, then quickly shaved, combed his hair, brushed his teeth and dressed. He was down in the lobby in twelve minutes. Laura was waiting for him, dressed in black jeans, a plain teal t-shirt and her denim jacket. Her hair looked freshly washed and still damp. Her green eyes held his gaze for a few heartbeats.

He pointed to the small room where the hotel provided a complimentary breakfast. "How about some coffee?"

Her eyes shifted to an older couple sitting at one of the small tables. After a quick review, she seemed satisfied they weren't going to bother her, and nodded.

They each filled their cup, Ransom taking his black, Laura with cream and one packet of sugar substitute. They slid into empty seats in the corner of the room. Laura stirred her coffee in slow motion, apparently not willing to rush into whatever brought her here at such an early hour.

He took a sip from his cup and grimaced. It was scalding hot and black, but that's about all the resemblance it had to real coffee. He grinned. "Just like Starbuck's."

"I'm sure," she said continuing to stir her coffee. She was in no hurry to confirm his opinion of the coffee.

Not knowing what else to say, he said, "Tell me about your brother."

Her stir stick froze for a heartbeat, then continued its slow rotation. "He was a good brother." She looked into her cup as if she could see him in the swirling brown liquid. "I remember when he told me he wanted to be a cop. He'd been out of college for a year or two. Had a job as an accountant for some big bank in Phoenix. And hated it. He wanted to do something worthwhile with his life."

Ransom dared another sip.

"Dad wasn't thrilled at his announcement. Went a little ballistic, in fact. I guess he didn't want to chance losing someone else."

"Someone else?"

"My mother," she said, but didn't offer anything else.

Under other circumstances, he would have pressed her. He didn't. "And you? What did you think of his choice?"

"I thought it was a great idea. He was such a giving person. Just like Mom." She looked up and a ghost of a smile crossed her face. "A true momma's boy." She shook her head. "Craig hated when I teased him about that, but they'd always been close." Her eyes turned serious. "And he was a good cop."

Ransom nodded. "That's what Hilderman said. Until about a month ago, about the time he told you he was gay."

"Yeah. When he said he'd found someone special. But I could tell something was bothering him. He wasn't himself. Preoccupied. Detached."

Ransom did some mental calculations. "I'm sorry, Laura, but I have to ask … did he start acting strange before Amanda went missing … or after?"

She physically flinched and stopped her relentless stirring. "I'm not sure," she said at last.

"I have to look at every angle," he said. "You want me to find the truth, right? Whatever that might be."

She gave an almost imperceptible nod, clearly shaken. "I believe it was after Amanda went missing. But it doesn't mean he killed her."

"True."

A silence fell between them. Ransom took a few sips from his coffee. Finally, he said, "You said you wanted to tell me something?"

She took a deep breath, her previous determination returning. "I think I found out who Craig's lover was."

Ransom's eyebrows rose. "You know who your brother was seeing before he died?"

Her eyes caught his. "And you do too."

Kristen raced through the trees in the predawn light, the wet underbrush clawing at her clothes. Briars and tiny tree branches grabbed at her as though they were the Devil's own minions. But she couldn't let them slow her down. She was being hunted. He was somewhere behind her. She could feel it.

Although she'd managed to escape before he returned from digging her grave, she *knew* he was coming for her, that he wouldn't give up until he caught her and returned her to the grave. When she stopped to catch her breath, she could hear sounds among the trees. Footsteps. Branches breaking under his feet.

So she ran. Ran in pure, unbridled terror. Ran amid the dark trees. She had no idea what direction she was heading, only that it was away from him.

She was so tired. Had no idea how long she'd been running. Ten minutes? Fifteen? Thirty? Her breaths came in gasps, her legs were on fire, and she had puked twice from the stabbing pain in her side.

Her foot caught on a root, spilling her onto the damp ground. She used a nearby tree to help her to her feet and brushed the dirt from her hands.

So tired.

A large pine tree, its trunk about two feet in diameter, stood to her left. She hobbled behind it. A rest. Catch her breath. Give her legs a chance to recover.

She put her head between her legs. Dizziness rippled through her, but it passed without her vomiting again. She looked at her wrists. They were caked in black dirt and dried blood, but the cold helped numb the pain.

When she was able to breathe without gasping, she took a moment to look around. She seemed to be in an endless forest of ponderosa pines and young seedlings. The local terrain was hilly, but not mountainous. A large rock outcropping, maybe twenty feet tall, was a hundred yards in front of her.

And dawn was coming. She didn't know if she should be relieved or frightened. The encroaching light was making it easier for her to work her way through the dense brush. But it also made hiding more difficult … and finding her easier.

But *where* was she?

He couldn't have taken her too far since last night. With miles of forest surrounding Flagstaff, she could even be just a few miles outside the city.

But in what direction? North, south, east or west?

She felt despair filling her chest, her hope surrendering to exhaustion. She couldn't last much longer. If she was lucky, she might outlast the sun. But if she had to spend the night, wet and cold, in the forest, she would die of exposure.

That was assuming he didn't find her before then.

She was still leaning against the tree when her eyes caught the first trace of sunlight glinting off the treetops.

Glorious sunlight. Warm sunlight. She envisioned its rays warming her body and trembled in anticipation. A glint of hope raced through her. She had no idea if east was the direction of her salvation, but somehow it felt right.

She pushed away from the solid trunk and began running toward the rising sun.

"Me?" Ransom said. "How do I know—?"

"You saw him last night … at George's." She leaned in close, lowered her voice. "Evan Parker."

Ransom almost spilled his coffee. "Chief Parker's son? How did you know that?"

Laura hesitated, then sighed in resignation. "Gabe told me."

"Gabe?" It was the second time he'd heard that name this morning. "Who's Gabe?"

"A … friend."

He felt his chest tighten, wondered if it was jealousy. Jesus. He hadn't felt that inner demon for a long time. His voice turned harder than he expected. "And how did he come by this information?"

"He knows."

"How—"

"Does it really matter?"

"Do you have any evidence? Pictures? Notes or emails to confirm what your ... friend told you?"

She shook her head. "You've got to trust me. Please. Talk with Evan. Ask him."

Ransom looked down at his coffee. "Okay," he said. "I'll talk with Evan." It wasn't much of a concession, since he wanted to talk with him about the brick incident anyway.

"Good." She pushed away from the table and stood. "You'll keep in touch, right?"

He nodded. She reached down and touched his hand. "Thank you," she said, then turned and walked away, leaving her coffee on the table, untouched.

He watched her go, feeling the lingering touch on his hand. Her stroke hadn't been overtly sexual, but it had been warm and left him thinking there could have been more than friendliness behind it.

He shook his head. Who was he kidding? This wasn't some singles bar. And he wasn't Brad Pitt trolling for coeds. It had been so long since he'd been with a woman, he was seeing things. Impossible things. Even if she *was* interested in him, it was a bad idea. He was putting his neck out far enough just being here without authorization. Better stick to business.

He was still staring at the hotel's entrance when a man with shoulders as wide as a meat locker stormed in. Had to be six-four and weigh at least two-fifty.

And he was clearly pissed. His eyes seethed with anger as they searched the room like twin gun sights hunting for a target.

They found Ransom.

And he knew the man had come for him.

Chapter 12

A branch snapped behind her and she whirled around, eyes searching the endless sea of green and brown.

No movement.

Was he toying with her, or was she going crazy?

Although Kristen had given up running for walking a while ago, her legs were still wobbly. Worse, her throat was parched and she felt drained to her bones, physically and emotionally spent. Dehydration had set in. And she was cold. Her previous anger and terror-produced warmth had given way to the cold morning air.

She realized she'd been wrong earlier. She wasn't even going to make it to dinnertime.

The man pushed between the empty tables like a linebacker through a weak offensive line, his eyes never leaving Ransom's. He wore crisply pressed khaki Dockers and a dark maroon polo shirt with a bright yellow logo on the right chest.'

Ransom didn't rise to meet the oncoming bull—that might have been considered aggressive, something he didn't think was in his best interest right now. Instead, he offered a friendly expression while grasping his coffee in one hand. It had cooled a bit, but a two-hundred-degree java face-wash would probably slow down even the most rabid bull.

The man stopped at Ransom's table. Put both meaty hands on the surface, almost causing it to flip over. He had numerous scratches on his hands and arms, as if he'd been working all day in a field of thorny roses.

"You Ransom?" he growled.

"Not if you're here to kill me," Ransom said.

The bull puffed out his cheeks. "Thinking about it."

"Not sure that would be a good idea," Ransom said, "for either of us." He nodded at the cup in his hand. "Looks like you need a cup. It's hot."

"I'm not here for coffee."

"Good choice."

The man's fist slammed the table, startling the older couple. "Enough. I know why you're here."

Ransom refused to bite. He stared at the logo. It showed a Jeep crawling over Sedona's trademark Bell Rock. The words below read: *Bell Rock Jeep Tours*.

"You're gonna try to prove that monster didn't do it."

Ransom met the man's eyes. "Monster?"

"Craig Adams. The bastard who killed my daughter."

"Mr. Pearce, I'm terribly sorry about your daughter, but that's not why I'm here."

"Not what I heard."

Ransom took a sip of coffee. "Then you heard wrong."

"Then why the hell are you sitting in my hotel, asking questions about my daughter's murder?"

"Listen. If Craig Adams murdered your daughter, fine. I'll drive that to ground— "

"He did."

"But … what if you're wrong?"

"I'm not."

"A million-to-one shot. What if someone else did those horrible things to your daughter? Wouldn't you want the guilty person found?"

"He's dead. Leave it alone."

Those words again. He was getting tired of hearing them. "Are you sure the murderer's dead?"

"Yes." Pearce's eyes were hard, mouth set tight.

"Don't—"

Pearce leaned closer, inches from Ransom's face. "I don't care what line of crap you've been fed, but I'm not going to sit by and let you muddy the waters. Craig Adams killed my daughter, then himself. That's it. No amount of meditating, crystal reading or speaking with angels will change that."

Crystal readings? Angels? Ransom had thought Pearce's fury had been fueled by the sadness and anger of losing a child, but maybe there was a bit of old-fashioned insanity mixed in. "I'm sorry?"

"Go back to Phoenix, Agent Ransom. Today. You're not welcome here."

Ransom wondered if he should remind the man that he was threatening a federal agent. Probably wouldn't do any good. Pearce already knew he was FBI … and didn't care. "I'll take that under advisement."

Pearce's eyes, pinpricks of rage, stared at him for a long moment, his ragged breath hot on Ransom's face. As though making a decision, he grunted and walked away. But not out the door. Instead he went to the front desk.

Ransom watched as he spoke to the clerk in hushed tones. Then, without looking back, he stomped out the door, climbed inside a Cadillac that matched the color of his shirt and sped away.

Ransom looked at his watch. Almost time to meet Hilderman. He rose from the table and filled another cup with coffee, stuffed a few creamers and sugar into his pocket and made his way to the reception desk.

The clerk, a petite woman with stringy brown hair and a silver stud through her nose, looked up from her computer. "Checking out?" she asked tentatively.

"I'd like to stay another day," he said.

She looked back down to her computer. "I'm sorry, Mr. Ransom. You only reserved last night, we're full tonight."

"Full?"

"Yes, sir."

Ransom chewed his lower lip. "A convention just book the place?"

"Something like that," she said, unable to meet his eyes.

He shrugged, knowing he wasn't going to win this fight. "Let me get my things. I'll be down in five minutes." He paused, then nodded to the door Pearce had just left through. "Think I'll be able to find another hotel for tonight?"

With an apology in her voice, the clerk said, "I wouldn't bet on it."

Neither would he, Ransom thought as he started for his room.

Twenty minutes later, Ransom angled into the spot he'd parked in last night. Overnight, the rain had stopped and the air was crisp, the morning sky a dazzling robin's egg blue.

Hilderman, a bag of donuts clutched in his hand, ambled up to the car, held up the white bag like a prized catch. "Donut?"

Ransom rolled down the window. "Get in."

The officer made his way around the car; the suspension gave ground as he slid into the passenger's seat. "You sure? It's the last one."

Ransom noticed the white frosting on Hilderman's lips, and wondered how many donuts had started out in the bag. "I'm good."

Eyes gleaming as though he'd just struck gold, Hilderman thrust his hand into the bag and hauled out the final frosted donut. "I heard about your bit o' fun at my little brother's last night."

"Yeah, you've got a real friendly town here."

Hilderman shrugged. "It is … usually." He held the donut in front of him for a moment, contemplating it. "Just finished talking with Chief Parker."

"And?"

"He wanted to make sure I kept your ass out of trouble this morning." He took a mammoth bite from the donut and mumbled around it, "And that I wouldn't forget to wave goodbye when you left town this afternoon."

"Awful nice of him."

Hilderman wiped his mouth, leaving a white line of frosting on his uniform's sleeve. "Yeah, Mr. Considerate."

Ransom put the car in reverse, pulled out of the parking spot.

"Where we goin' boss?"

"Back to Craig Adams' basement."

Hilderman stopped chewing, replaced the half-eaten donut into the bag. "I think I just lost my appetite."

Ransom's mouth twitched in a grin. *Bet that doesn't happen often.*

They drove in silence for a few minutes until Ransom's cell phone chirped. Keeping one hand on the wheel, he used the other to unclip it from his belt and glanced at the screen. Not a number he recognized. He put the phone to his ear and said, "Stuart Ransom."

Deep silence for a few breaths, then, "Chief Parker gave me your number."

Ransom didn't remember giving it to Parker, and wondered how he'd gotten it.

"I'm Howard Adams. Craig's father."

Ransom noticed the present tense and he felt a sudden pang of sympathy for the man. When Trevor died, it had taken him over a month to have the courage to use the past tense when talking about him.

"I'm sorry for your loss, Mr. Adams."

"Thank you," he said, his voice heavy with sadness. "I need to talk to you … before you leave tonight."

Parker was sure making it clear Ransom wasn't invited for an extended stay.

"I've got a few things to do this morning, how about after lunch?"

"Good. Come by my house."

Ransom made note of the address. The line went dead and he snapped the phone shut.

"I can't even image what he's going through," Hilderman said.

Ransom nodded. He could.

Hilderman's eyes suddenly went wide. "Oh, shit."

Ransom followed his gaze out the front window. A black plume rose like a phantom against the blue sky. Ransom felt his gut wrench. They were headed directly for it.

Chapter 13

The forest opened up into an immense sea of ankle-deep grass. Yellow goldeneyes and zinnias were sprinkled throughout the meadow. Butterflies, warming in the morning sun, drifted lazily from flower to flower. Under different circumstances, Kristen would have thought the scenery beautiful, but survival was all that mattered now.

She eased out from the tree line, swallowed hard and pushed down the apprehension about leaving her cover. She would be visible to anyone—him—if he were close by.

Two thoughts drove her to expose herself. The need to feel the sun's heat on her face, and finally having an unobstructed view of the surrounding area. Out of the cover of trees, she might be able to see Humphrey's Peak, part of the San Francisco peaks northwest of Flagstaff. Rising to almost 12,000 feet, they were the tallest mountains in Arizona. If she could see the mountains, she could tell where Flagstaff was.

Her eyes constantly moving, she walked into the meadow. Goose bumps formed on her arms as the autumn sunlight blazed against her skin. After a cold, wet, terrifying night in the claustrophobic forest, the meadow's open warmth felt as though God himself was now watching over her.

Squinting, she looked toward the azure sky ... and saw it. Humphrey's Peak. Closer than she ever could have hoped. Joyous tears ran down her cheeks.

The decision to head toward the sun had been right. If she continued walking toward the mountain, she would hit the busy road heading up to the Grand Canyon.

She went to her knees, closed her eyes and clasped her hands together in front of her. "Thank you," she whispered. After rising to her feet, her eyes shifted back to the meadow. What she saw brought a gasp. Her focus on the mountain was so intense, she hadn't seen the muddy scar cutting through the grass just twenty feet in front of her.

A road. Well, sort of, she thought after a longer look. Maybe an old logging road. From her previous trips to the Grand Canyon, she knew that dirt logging roads angled off the main road like the branches of a tree. Regardless, it was a road, and roads always led somewhere.

She limped up to it, looked in both directions and could see signs of use; tire tracks showed in the less muddy spots. Though it didn't look like anyone had come through since last night's rain.

To her right, the road wove through the meadow before plunging back into the trees and heading straight for Humphrey Peak. Just where she was headed, and she'd make better time on the road. With renewed energy, she set off down it.

She was halfway through the meadow when she heard a car's engine.

Behind her.

Oh, God. No!

Ransom's foot goosed the accelerator just as Hilderman's radio came to life with the dispatcher calling fire crews to a house fire. A house at 12105 West Kachina Drive. Craig Adams' house.

Dark smoke blossomed ahead. The Crown Vic's engine roared. Mailboxes flashed by. Ransom glanced at Hilderman. He'd gone pale, becoming one of his frosted donuts, and a hand clenched the armrest. He gave Ransom a nervous smile. "We're gonna beat the firefighters."

Probably. And for a moment, he thought about Hilderman's unspoken question: what would getting there ahead of the firefighters accomplish? They had no firefighting equipment. They would be spectators, watching the home turn to ash while they waited for the fire crew to arrive. But, he urged the car faster. Something was telling him to hurry.

Less than a minute later, he swept into Craig Adams' driveway, fishtailed in the gravel and almost clipped a car blocking the entrance. Flames blackened the garage door, licking at the fascia along the roof. Smoke billowed out the broken living room window.

What in the hell is going on? The house was empty. How could it catch fire?

But *was* it really empty? He looked back at the car he'd almost crashed into. He'd seen it somewhere before. A tiny—

"Jesus," Hilderman said. "It's really cooking."

A scream pierced the fire's roar.

Who—?

Then he remembered. He'd seen the car at the police station. Green eyes. Black hair.

Laura.

Another scream.

She was inside the inferno.

Kristen ran as fast as her exhausted legs could carry her. Had he been playing with her this entire time? Watching her? Waiting for her to feel a sense of hope before pouncing on her? Was it all some kind of game to him?

She raced along the road. If she could make it to the trees, she might get lost in the forest again. She felt as though she was dreaming, her legs leaden weights, moving in slow motion.

The trees seemed miles away. The engine noise grew closer. She dared not turn around. The sight of his car speeding toward her might push her over the edge.

Her feet splashed through a muddy puddle. Panic consumed her, as she raced along the road's uneven surface. Her breaths came in sharp gasps. She heard the car splash through the water behind her.

Run.

Fire burned in her legs. She ignored it.

Run.

Her eyes locked onto the trees in front of her. The stoic sentinels, unwavering. Waiting for her. Offering their shelter.

Thirty feet. Twenty. Then her foot caught an exposed rock. She threw her arms out in front of her, but couldn't stop her fall. As she crashed to the ground, she heard the crack of bone breaking. Searing pain shot through her arm and fireworks exploded in her brain.

Run! her mind screamed. But her legs wouldn't respond. She couldn't move. She was beyond exhaustion, her body and her spirit spent.

Her eyes were open and she looked up at the flawless blue sky. And in that instant, the terror that had consumed her for the last twelve hours was gone. Even the pain in her arm seemed to detach itself from her soul. All this was replaced by sadness.

A car door opened and slammed shut. Footsteps rushing toward her.

She blinked back tears. All she could think of was that she didn't want to die on such a beautiful day.

"Are you okay?" came a voice barely audible below the thunder of blood in her ears.

With tremendous effort, she turned her head.

The man's face came into view, silhouetted against the bright sky.

No … not *the* man's face.

Another's.

Blue eyes. Young eyes. Eyes showing concern. Genuine concern.

Movement in her peripheral vision. Another figure, emerging from a yellow Jeep.

"Is she all right?" another voice called out.

Her relief was too great. She couldn't speak.

"I don't think so," said the man, his voice low and anxious. "She looks beat up pretty bad. We need to get her to a hospital."

Chapter 14

Ransom threw open the door and shot out of the car. Even from twenty feet away, the fire was hot enough to sear meat.

Laura was in there.

Despite the heat, the thought sent chills through him. Shielding his face from the flames, he raced for the door. His hand went for the door handle. But at the last second, he drew back at seeing the door's paint peeling from the fire boiling behind it. He stuck his hand into his jacket pocket and tried the doorknob. It felt as though he were grabbing a hot iron. He held on, twisted the handle and pushed.

Flames and black smoke surged outward. He recoiled from the heat.

More shouts. Panic-stricken screams.

"Jesus," Hilderman said as he edged next to Ransom.

"Use the hose." Ransom pointed to a neatly coiled garden house a few feet away. "Maybe you can beat the flames back enough to get inside from here. I'll see if I can get through the back door."

Then he was sprinting off toward the back of the house. Along the rear, a bedroom window had blown out and smoke billowed from the opening, but the heat didn't seem as intense.

The sliding glass door leading into the dining room was intact; the curtains were drawn and he couldn't see inside. At least they weren't on fire.

He tried the door. Locked.

More screams. Closer this time.

He drew his pistol and fired. The bullet smashed through the door, and glass cascaded like a million water droplets in a silver waterfall. Smoke rushed out, though it wasn't followed by a burst of flames. He waited for the smoke to subside somewhat, then threw the curtain aside.

Acrid fumes burned his eyes and the overwhelming heat made him gasp. To his left, the living room was ablaze. Furniture, carpet, walls and ceiling, fully engulfed. The kitchen fared better: the counter and appliances weren't as combustible as the furniture. In front of him was the dining room. The table and one of the chairs smoldered, but somehow weren't enflamed.

A sickly sweet smell permeated the smoke.

Bang. Bang. Bang.

His head swiveled toward the sound. Through the kitchen. Where—?

Jesus, no. The basement.

"Laura!" he yelled above the fire's angry roar.

For a heartbeat nothing happened, then the pounding started again, at such a furious rate it sounded like the chatter of a machine gun.

Keeping his head below the smoke-filled air, he raced to the basement door. It was closed, but shaking from the violent beating on the other side.

He grabbed the knob and twisted. It didn't budge. He swiped at his burning eyes, tears from the heat and smoke rolling down his cheeks. He tried it again. Harder this time.

Nothing.

A loud cracking. The sound of beams giving way. Then *whoosh*—a rush of superheated air. Smoke laced with glowing embers spilled around him. Flames swallowed up the kitchen.

"Shit!" he half coughed, half spat, now having to kneel just to breathe.

He returned his attention to the door and immediately saw the problem. It took his breath away, almost as much as the smoke. The door was locked.

Someone had locked Laura in the basement!

He released the catch and the door sprang open, slamming into his head. Reeling backward, he crashed into the shelves beside the door, cans of soup and boxes of cereal raining down on him.

Laura was like a caged animal suddenly set free. Her eyes went wild with terror as she saw the raging inferno. Then they met Ransom's. A split second of surprise.

He struggled to untangle himself from the pantry's contents. She offered her hand. He pulled himself into a crouching position, gasped, "Come on, time to get out of here."

And then they were through the dining room's door and into fresh air.

Ransom pushed the oxygen mask away and coughed up a black glob of phlegm. It hit the pavement, joining the ten or so already there.

"I'm good," he said, his voice sounding like he'd just eaten a bowl of volcanic gravel.

The fireman looked at Hilderman, who nodded his approval. The fireman shrugged, took the oxygen mask from Ransom and turned his attention to his other patient. Laura, sitting next to Ransom on the ambulance's rear bumper, gave a thumbs-up. The guy took off her mask too. She'd been coughing, but nothing like Ransom. In the end, she'd been lucky; the locked basement door had saved her from most of the smoke.

Ransom turned his attention to the smoldering ruins in front of him. Despite the torrents of water the firefighters sprayed into the burned-out shell, a few pillars of smoke resisted their efforts. Most of Craig Adams' ranch house had collapsed into itself, gutting the interior.

He shook his head. Everything was lost. He'd heard the basement's ceiling give way, felt the rush of heat as the chemicals and paints inside erupted in a ball of flame. Whatever was hidden there was going to stay hidden.

He coughed again, but couldn't conjure up any more black spit, and was wondering if that was good or bad when he heard a small commotion in front of him.

"Damn," Hilderman said in a whisper.

Ransom shifted his eyes in time to see Parker striding through a couple of fireman.

The police chief's face was the color of the fire trucks, eyes blazing hotter than coals. They found Hilderman, then Laura, then Ransom. "What the hell's going on?" he said.

"We're roasting weenies," Ransom shot back, not in the mood for Parker's crap.

Parker ignored Ransom's jab and turned to Hilderman. "Well?"

"Craig Adams' house burned down, Chief," Hilderman said.

"No shit. I'm not fucking blind." Parker's face was so red it seemed ready to burst. "Care to tell me how that happened?"

"Gas," Ransom said.

Parker looked at him as though he might just be the dumbest FBI agent in the world. "These homes don't have gas."

He met Parker's stare. "Gasoline, not propane."

"What?"

"Someone soaked the place in gas. Smelled it in the dining room."

"Arson?" Parker said, sucking in his breath.

Ransom shook his head. "No. Attempted murder."

"Attempted murder?" Parker's voice was heavy with sarcasm. "And just what makes you say that?"

Hilderman cleared his throat. "We found—"

Parker gave him a venomous stare. "I want to hear it from *him*."

"I'll go talk to the fire chief," Hilderman said and slunk away.

Parker watched him leave, then turned back to Ransom. "Start at the beginning. What the hell were you doing here in the first place?"

"I wanted to go through his basement again. Thought I might have missed something the first time."

Parker's eyes narrowed. "Like what?"

"You went through his entire basement?"

"This isn't Mayberry, Agent Ransom. We had to look for … for the rest of Amanda."

"Which … you didn't find." This came from Laura as another dig at her brother's innocence.

"We found enough," Parker shot back.

"But," Ransom injected, "did you find evidence of any *other* murders?"

Laura blasted Ransom with a reproachful look that said, *I thought you were supposed to be helping me!*

"One was plenty for me." Parker looked at Laura. "But that's all moot now, right? I'm guessing the fire didn't leave much behind."

"I didn't start the fire," Laura said, disbelief in her eyes.

"Then what were you doing here—?"

She looked at Ransom. "After we talked this morning, I wanted to look for … something."

Parker asked, "And what was that?"

"For a … friend."

"What the hell does that mean?"

She shook her head. "It doesn't matter. He was my brother, I can—"

"No, you can't," Parker said. "This house is off-limits to anyone not officially on the investigation—including family."

"I'd hardly call what you're doing an investigation!" Laura spat.

Parker didn't flinch. "You didn't answer my question."

"I …" she looked at Ransom, then back at Parker. "I don't have to answer to you."

Parker pointed a finger at her. "I could arrest you for interfering with an investigation."

"Then do it. At least you'd be doing *something*!"

Parker stepped forward, eyes glowering, but Ransom forced his way between them. "Okay. We're losing sight of what's important here."

Parker hesitated, then took a few steps backward. "And what's that?"

"Someone locked Laura in the basement, threw gas all over the place, then lit it."

Hilderman, who had slowly eased next to Parker, said, "I just talked with the fire chief. He thinks the fire was intentionally set, starting from multiple locations within the house and some type of accelerant was used."

"Gas," Ransom said.

Parker put his hands on his hips and his brow knitted in thought. He seemed to be fighting some inner demons, not wanting to accept the news that someone in his elite town was capable of murder. Again. After a long minute, he looked at Ransom. "Why?"

"That depends," Ransom said, "on whether his original target was Laura … or the house."

"Maybe I was just in the way," Laura said with wary relief. "They were after the house, not me. I didn't even know I was coming here until after I saw you this morning."

Parker gave them a look like they were conspirators in some crime.

Laura shrugged. "I just happened to be in the wrong place at the wrong time."

Ransom wasn't so sure, but he kept his thoughts to himself. "Either way," he said, "I think this proves that you've got more going on here than a murder-suicide."

Again Parker fell silent, then shook his head. "No. What we have is someone who wanted to rid our town of this ... place of death. Clean house. Rid the town of evil." He took a deep breath. "We've got a good town here, Agent Ransom. A town that depends on tourism. This isn't LA or Phoenix. We don't breed thieves and murders. We've got decent people here."

"Other than someone who decapitates young women and an arsonist who's into human barbeque."

Parker gave him an unwavering stare. "Your presence here is causing exactly what I didn't want to happen. First the brick, now this. Go back to Phoenix, Agent Ransom. Tonight. Before things get out of control."

"Out of control?"

"If you're right about this. About this being more than arson," Parker said, his eyes shifting to Laura, "it doesn't look like I can guarantee her safety." Then he whirled away and stalked off toward the smoldering house.

Chapter 15

Ransom weaved the Crown Vic through the Sedona's red rock sentinels as though he were training on the FBI's evasive driving course. Parker had taken his sweet time getting their official statement on the fire, and he was late for his meeting with Craig Adams' father. Talking with Evan Parker would have to wait until later this afternoon.

"Easy," his passenger said. "Parker would find great pleasure giving you a speeding ticket."

"I'm FBI, remember?" he replied with a mischievous grin. "We're allowed to speed. It's in the FBI handbook."

Laura chuckled. A nice soft laugh. Then said, "I didn't think G-men had a sense of humor."

"They usually perform a humor lobotomy the first week of the Academy, but I happened to be sick that day and missed my appointment."

Another chuckle. "Good for you." She studied him. "You're definitely not what I expected."

Was she flirting with him? Suddenly, he was tongue-tied. It hadn't been the FBI who had eliminated his ability to flirt. Sixteen years of marriage had done that just fine.

Looking for a distraction, he put his hand out the window. Let the rush of air wash over his arm and face. Thankfully, the October sun had warmed the air. "Maybe we'll get the smoke smell out by the time we get to your father's."

"Sure," she said, then turned to watch the scenery race by.

He felt a guilty pleasure for agreeing to let her accompany him. How could he have said no? He was driving to see her father. But he knew it was more than that. He wanted her along. He'd felt inexplicably drawn to her since he'd pulled up her DMV picture during his initial background search. Even the notoriously bad DMV photographer couldn't hide her beauty. But it was more than that. He was surprised how much he wanted Laura to be single and available, and just how much his jealousy flared when she'd mentioned Gabe.

A friend, she'd said. But he could tell it was something more. Her husband? She wasn't wearing a ring, so that meant boyfriend. But that didn't feel right either.

Damn, it was going to drive him crazy. Maybe if he asked her like it was part of the investigation. Which it could be.

He took a deep breath, blurted out, "Who is this Gabe who told you about Evan and Craig?"

Laura jerked in surprise at the question, but didn't face him. "Uhhmmm. Like I said, a friend."

What was she hiding? He put on his most official-sounding voice. "I might need to talk to him. You know, about Evan and Craig."

She didn't respond. Just kept looking out the window.

He decided to change tactics. Ask her something nonthreatening. Small talk. "So … what do you do here in Sedona?"

This made her look at him. "What is this? Twenty questions?"

He shrugged.

She stared at him for a long time. Appraising him. Then, she seemed to relax. "I'm sorry. You really are a G-man to the core. I guess it's something I'll have to get used to."

What did she mean by that?

She grinned. "I'm surprised Hildy hasn't brought you up-to-date on everyone in town yet. He'll never admit it, but he's a huge gossip."

"I got that far," he said. He wanted to ask her what was going on with Hilderman and the way he looked at her, but decided now wasn't a good time for that either. Better to let her continue talking.

"How long did it take you to make that discovery?" she said.

"About five minutes. But, you … you, I haven't figured out yet."

She took a deep breath. "Okay. Here's me in one minute or less. I'm thirty-seven years old. Lived in Sedona since I was ten, and when I graduated high school, I thought I wanted more out of life, so I moved to LA. Got married." A long pause. "It lasted more than ten years, but I should've left after two."

He gave her a questioning look.

"Found out I didn't like LA, or my husband." A thin smile. "Maybe that was part of the problem. He loved LA. Still does as far as I know." She sighed. "Anyway, after the divorce, I moved back to Sedona."

"And you like it here now?"

She thought for a moment. "I did, but after this business, I'm not so sure anymore."

"And … you live here all by yourself?"

She shook her head.

There it was.

Then she grinned, patted his hand. "I live with my cat. Her name's Crackers. A little orange tabby. Best thing I got out of the divorce." She gave him a sideways glance. "She didn't care for my ex-husband at all."

"A good judge of character?"

She laughed. "Actually, she doesn't like men in general."

"I see. And what do you do when you're not turning your cat against men?"

"I read. A lot. Like to spend time outdoors." She gave a nervous sigh. "This is sounding like a personal ad."

"Except you never answered my original question."

"How I make a living?"

He nodded, wondering why she was being so evasive. After she'd called the Phoenix FBI office two days ago, he'd taken some time to conduct a preliminary background check on her. Her profession was listed ambiguously as "self-employed."

"I guess you'd find out anyway," she said, then chewed her bottom lip. "Though I would've preferred a few more days."

This piqued his interest.

"I help people."

"A therapist?"

"Not exactly. I concentrate more on a person's energy … their spiritual side."

"You're a psychic?" he said incredulously.

She glared at him, her eyes darkening. "I hate it when people say that. No, I'm not a psychic. Not in the way you're thinking. That term has so many negative connotations. I don't do ten-dollar palm readings at the fair, hold séances to speak with dead relatives or claim to predict the winning lottery numbers on TV."

"So, what *do* you do?"

She took a deep breath. "Ever since I can remember, I've had … feelings. Saw things. Heard things. When I was young, I tried to push them away. Tried to be normal. Like everyone else. I got married. That's what good girls do, right?"

He nodded, not knowing where she was going with this.

"My self-esteem was at an all time low after the divorce. It took me a few years to get myself together. To change my life. I wasn't going to ignore my inner spirit anymore. I was going to embrace it." She nodded toward the passing scenery. "In that regard, Sedona's the right place for me."

"Okay, but you still haven't told me—"

A deep breath. "I've spent the last five years of my life learning the art of Reiki and Angelic healing...."

"Angelic healing?"

"I talk with angels."

Ransom swallowed hard.

What had he gotten himself into?

Chapter 16

"Angels? The ones with wings?" He looked at her. "As in Michael the archangel and all that?" he said, thinking back to his days sitting in church with his parents.

"Yeah, him too." She turned away and looked out the window. "I didn't want to tell you because I didn't want you thinking I was some crackpot and ignore the evidence—"

"Evidence?"

"Okay. Information might be a better word. The semantics don't matter. I'm proud of what I do, even if you don't believe in it."

He stared straight ahead, the white lines on the black pavement streaming by. What was he going to tell Phillips when he got back to Phoenix? He wasn't working the Longley case because he went to Sedona to look into a murder-suicide that his gut had told him didn't add up? *No, the local police didn't ask for help—in fact they were downright hostile about my presence. Oh, and the woman who called and made accusations of a local cover-up? Well ... she's a psychic you see. Yes, she's the one I'm getting most of my leads from....*

Oh, that would go well. If he was lucky, he'd be sent to the office in Alaska and not fired.

She let out a heavy sigh. "Gabe told me your spirit isn't ready for this. Not yet."

"This is the same Gabe who told you Evan Parker was Craig's lover?"

She nodded. "Gabriel is the messenger angel. He helps with communication and children. Delivers spiritual messages."

"Angels," he scoffed.

"They're here, all around us. They love us. Want to help us ... if only we'd allow it."

"They love us?" he said, unable to stop his voice from rising

"Yes." Hesitant.

His hands clutched the steering wheel so hard, he feared he might twist it into knots. "And if we'd only allow it, they'd help us?"

"Yes ..."

"So," he said between clenched teeth, "where were they when I was holding my dying nine-year-old son in my arms ... asking God, the angels, anyone who would listen, for help? I sure could've used their help right then. I was begging for it. And they did nothing!"

"I ... I didn't know," she said, her voice soft. Sympathetic.

It didn't matter. His anger was overpowering. "What? Didn't the angel of, of whatever, tell you he let my son die?"

"No—"

He was screaming now. "Tell Gabriel ... Gabe ... or whoever you're talking to, if letting my son die is their idea of helping me, I don't want their help!"

She didn't respond, just looked at him. Reading his eyes. Seeing the hurt behind the fury, waiting for his anger to ebb.

And it did. More rapidly than he expected. He took a few calming breaths. "Sorry. It's not your fault. It's mine. I lost all my faith the day Trevor died."

"Faith? In God or—"

"In everything." And that was true. He'd lost his faith in everything. Including himself.

He pretended to concentrate on the road, embarrassed by his outburst. And his sudden revelation to someone he barely knew. It had taken his therapist over a year to dig that little gem out of him.

When he looked back, she was staring at him as if she knew what he was thinking. "I know this is something you don't want to hear right now," she said, "something you probably can't accept, but I believe we're on earth to learn lessons. As we strive to become higher beings, we must discover life's lessons—and some of them are difficult. Your spirit chose what you would learn in this life."

He shook his head. Disbelieving. "What are you saying? My son was destined to die and there was nothing I could do about it?"

"Maybe yes, maybe no. We decide which lessons we want to learn, not exactly how. If it wasn't your son, you would've found some other way to learn the lesson you'd signed up for."

"And what lesson might that be?"

She studied him for a long time before she spoke. "Forgiveness. I'm seeing that you're here to learn about forgiveness."

A chill the size of a California earthquake swept through his body. As if someone … or *something* … had just thrown cold water on his very soul. A wake-up call saying *pay attention.*

But how could she know?

She'd said she helped people. He could tell she was good at it. No, he didn't believe in all this speaking-with-angels stuff, but he did believe in gut feelings. Intuition. That's what had brought him here. Maybe she had a more developed sense of it.

They drove the remaining few miles to Howard Adams' home in silence, except for Laura giving him directions. The house was an older ranch style. Small. Maybe 1500 square feet. But the location was outstanding. Set about halfway up a rolling hill, Ransom could see Sedona spread out behind him. Other homes, some larger, some smaller, sprinkled the red rock hills, each having about a half acre of land.

He said, "Nice view."

"Yeah. It was a big change when we moved here."

"From California?"

She nodded. "There's very few Sedona natives. My grandfather on my mother's side was a lawyer in LA. Has a couple of properties around the country. Gave this one to my mom … thinking, well, thinking it might help. And after she died, it went to my dad."

This time he did ask. "How did she die?"

"Ovarian cancer."

"I'm sorry."

"Yeah, ten's too young to put someone you love in the grave."

It doesn't get any easier with age. "And your father decided to stay here?"

"Mom's death hit him hard. He's semi-retired now, but he worked as a craftsman in California. Installing cabinetry. He was able to find good work here, so we stayed."

"No other family around?"

She shook her head. "Craig was my only sibling. All my grandparents are dead. I've got an aunt and two uncles on my mother's side who live back east, but I'm not close to them. Dad's about all I've got left."

The tires rolled to a stop next to the front door. Ransom wondered what a blue-collar craftsman thought of his daughter's career choice.

Laura turned to him and as though reading his mind, said, "And no, he doesn't agree with my new age beliefs."

A tall fit-looking man opened the door. Howard Adams. Judging from Laura's age, he should easily be in his late fifties, but looked ten years younger. He had a full head of dark hair, with a few gray streaks near the temples.

The man stepped out from the shadows under the entryway, giving Ransom a closer look at red-rimmed eyes, a tight jaw and deep grief lines crossing his face. Ransom imagined that's what *he* looked like after Trevor's death. When he'd looked at himself in the mirror this morning, much of that sadness was still there almost two years later.

As he stepped out of the car, Howard Adams' eyes locked onto his.

And Ransom knew this wasn't going to be a friendly visit.

Chapter 17

"You Agent Ransom?" The man's eyes were hard steel.

Ransom nodded. He offered his hand, but Adams refused to shake it.

"I just got off the phone with Chief Parker. My son's house burned to the ground? What the hell did you do?"

"He didn't do anything, Dad," Laura said as she edged around the opposite side of the car.

Her father's eyes snapped to meet her. "Laura! Are you okay? Parker said you were trapped inside when the fire started."

She stood next to Ransom. "I'm fine. I just smell like an old campfire, that's all."

Adams nodded, then turned to Ransom, "When Parker called … told me about the fire … that Laura … for a minute, I'd thought I'd lost her too. After what happened with Craig, I'm not sure I could handle it."

"I understand," Ransom said.

At that, Howard Adams' mouth tightened. "I don't think you do, Agent Ransom."

"You're wrong, Dad. Stuart—" Laura started, but Ransom touched her arm and said, "I'm sorry for your loss, Mr. Adams. I don't want to make this any more painful than it already is."

Adams expelled a deep breath. "You're right … this business with Craig … it's driving me crazy."

When he didn't offer any more, Ransom said, "You called me. Wanted to talk to me about something?"

Ransom's voice seemed to bring him out of his stupor. "Yes. Right." He glanced at Laura, a slight hesitation, then back. "I wanted to talk to you about Craig."

Ransom gave Laura a questioning look. Something wasn't right between them. "My father and I have a disagreement about Craig … and other things," she said.

Adams didn't seem to hear her. Or didn't want to. "He was a good boy. A good son. Sometimes when the phone rings I think it's going to be him on the other end, telling me it was all some kind of sick joke."

He looked at Ransom. Maybe he was seeing if Ransom would confirm the joke. Or looking to Ransom for strength. Neither of which Ransom could offer.

Adams lowered his head. "I keep thinking … that I could've done something…."

Ransom didn't know if he was talking about what his son was accused of, or the suicide. He said, "You can't blame yourself." And he wished he believed it.

"It was his time to die," Laura said. "His death was for a reason."

Howard Adams' eyes flared. "What reason?"

"I … don't know. But I have to believe—"

"Don't start with that new age angel crap," he said, pointing a finger at his daughter. "You know I don't want to hear it."

Laura obediently fell silent.

Adams' face looked like a man who had lost his faith. A look Ransom had seven hundred and nine days ago. Ransom didn't want to be here. To feel this man's grief. It was like someone was throwing salt in his own wound.

Adams took a deep breath and said, "I've got to accept it. My son is gone … and he committed a terrible crime—"

Laura stiffened. "No! He didn't—"

Adams gave her a sharp look. "I haven't been able to sleep for days. Was my son the brutal murderer Parker and the evidence indicates? Or the pawn of some unknown plot as my daughter believes?" His eyes pierced Ransom's. "What do you think?"

"Well … sir …" Ransom thought of why he'd gone back to Craig's house this morning. *How do you tell someone that his son might have been a serial killer?* "That's what I'm here to find out," he answered, hoping an ambiguous answer would satisfy.

"Well, it doesn't matter anymore. The evidence all points—"

"But—"

"Let me finish!" he snapped at Laura. "And Parker, who I not only consider a friend, but a fine police officer, believes Craig did those things. He wouldn't tell me that unless he was absolutely sure."

"No, Dad—"

"The parents with abducted children say the one thing worse than finding out their child is dead, is not knowing…. The years of looking into everyone's face, trying to spot their missing child. Day after day having their hopes crushed. I decided I wasn't going through that…." He pulled in a deep breath, as if what he was about to say would hurt him physically. "I don't know how or why he became what he was, but I can't ignore the facts—and the facts say that Craig *was* a monster."

"You can't believe that!" Laura shouted. "You can't give up on your own son. Not now!"

His face pinched, the pain etched in lines around his eyes. "He's dead, Laura. It's too late to save his soul now."

Her face flushed, and she opened her mouth, but words refused to form. Then she stormed back to the car, opened the door, climbed inside and slammed it shut. Howard Adams motioned for Ransom to come closer, then in a soft voice said, "Don't get me wrong, I still love and miss my son. Nothing will ever change that. I just want this ordeal to end. That's why I called you this morning. Although I've come to accept what Craig did, Laura still refuses." He shook his head. "Do you know she believes angels talk to her?"

Ransom nodded.

"She's been brainwashed by that new age crap. It's like a cult, and she's not right in the head. And I don't want *you* feeding her strange beliefs. Parker told me that this is an open-and-shut case. I don't need someone creating false hope. I don't want to be one of those parents who are strung out for years, holding onto the thinnest thread of hope. I *need* closure." His voice was trembling now. "Let Parker finish his investigation. He's a good man. And a top cop. If he finds something, he'll pursue it."

"Mr. Adams, I can't—"

"Please. I'm asking you as a father … take Laura home, then go back to Phoenix. Let her figure this out by herself. She needs to learn to accept it. Only then can the healing truly begin." Without allowing Ransom to respond, he turned and walked back into his house.

Ransom stared at the closed door. He knew Adams was right about needing closure. But closure didn't necessarily mean the same thing to Ransom. Unlike Adams, he wasn't ready to accept Parker's word. Not yet.

Something strange was going on. Something not quite right. But he didn't convey these thoughts to Adams. Ransom didn't have any proof. Adams had talked about false hope. No, he didn't want to give that to the broken man. He would keep his thoughts to himself.

For now.

He turned back to the car and wondered how he was going to deal with Laura. She was convinced her brother was innocent … and who could argue against angels anyway? He edged up to the car and opened his door. Laura was on her cell phone.

"Okay, okay, I'll tell him," she said nodding eagerly, then clicked the phone shut, all of her previous anger vanishing.

"Tell me what?"

She held out her cell phone as if it were evidence. "That was Hildy. He got a call from a friend of his on the police force up in Flagstaff."

"Flagstaff?"

"A man abducted a young woman last night, but she managed to escape. It's the same guy who killed Amanda and framed my brother."

Chapter 18

"What?" Ransom blurted. "How do you know—?"

Laura leaned over and grabbed his arm. "Come on, we've got to get to Flagstaff."

He got in the car, and Laura, perched on the passenger's seat, relayed everything Hilderman had told her, which wasn't much more than a guy had abducted a woman, raped her, then tried to bury her in the forest somewhere northwest of Flagstaff.

"It's him," Laura said, "I'm sure of it."

Ransom thought about it. Maybe the killer would dismember the women, then bury their pieces in the forest. It was possible …

He started the car. "Why didn't Hilderman call me?"

"He was at his office. If Parker found out he was calling you, he'd be in big trouble. He knew I was with you, would pass it along."

Ransom angled out of the driveway, headed toward Flagstaff. It was ten minutes before she spoke again. "I just can't understand why Dad's not fighting back. Why he's so quick to accept what Parker tells him."

"A loss of a child is the hardest thing a parent can go through," Ransom said. "It's like a part of your very soul's ripped away." He felt his grip tighten on the steering wheel again. "With nothing but emptiness in its place. It can make you say and do strange things." *He* still lashed out in anger for no reason. And he cried when he thought too hard about Trevor's death. And that had been almost two years ago.

She reached out and touched his shoulder as if she'd done it a thousand times. "What happened? To your son, I mean?"

As she spoke, he held his breath, readied himself for the surge of anger that always accompanied a stranger asking about Trevor. *How dare they?* his mind would scream. They didn't know him. They didn't love him like he did. He always felt they were violating some private space—a special bond between him and Trevor. Always.

Until now.

He waited several heartbeats, but the anger never came. The calm he felt was so foreign to him, he couldn't speak.

"Are you okay?" Laura asked.

"Yes … no … I don't know," he answered truthfully. He was used to blowing up, rage and guilt exploding at the innocent interrogator. But for some reason he didn't understand, now he felt compelled to talk about this dark portion of his life, as if it would somehow help his healing.

"You don't have to answer," she said.

"It's okay. I'm ... just not used to this."

"Used to what?"

"Sharing Trevor with anyone."

"Trevor? That was your son's name?"

He nodded. "Yeah, Trev. He was nine. He died seven hundred and nine days ago. In an automobile accident." He found he was breathing fast and took a minute to slow down. This was the hardest part. "And it was all my fault."

"It was a Saturday night. Trevor's friend from school was having a birthday party at Peter Piper Pizza. I was working...." He took a few gulps of air. "My wife, she has … had … a drinking problem. I knew about it, but was too busy to be aware of the full extent of it. She wanted me to pick Trev up, but I said I had to work." He pounded the steering wheel. "Work, work, work … just too damn busy! She'd been drinking, but I let her pick him up anyway. Thankfully, Morgan was at a friend's house."

"Morgan?"

"My daughter." He recalled the email she'd sent him earlier wanting to know if she was staying with him this weekend. And his response. *Sorry, I'm working.* Just like before. He used to think he was a good father, until he let his drunk wife drive his son home from a birthday party. *What in the hell had I been thinking? And why do I keep making the same mistakes?* he asked himself for the millionth time.

Laura touched his shoulder again, a signal telling him she was there.

"Anyway," he said, regaining his composure. "My wife lost control of the car and slammed into a telephone pole. Hit square on the back door where Trev sat." A long pause. "He spent two days in a coma before he finally died."

"I'm so sorry," Laura said.

Again, he was surprised. Not that she'd said she was sorry. That's what everyone said. But he truly believed she was.

"And your wife? Did she survive?"

His body went rigid. "Minor cuts and bruises. That's all."

"And you two …?"

He shook his head.

"Divorced?"

"I'm not able to forgive her for killing my son."

"Or yourself," she said as if she'd known all along.

"I'm as much—or more to blame as her.…" He let his words hang in the thick silence. This is where most people tried to console him, tell him he really wasn't to blame, etc., etc. Which he *hated.* He knew he was to blame and so did they. Saw it in their eyes.

He waited for Laura to begin the obligatory speech. Instead, she said, "Tell me about Trevor."

No one had ever asked that before. Maybe they thought it would be too painful, and they probably would have been right. But once again, he was surprised that he felt like sharing what he previously thought were memories too intimate for others.

"In twenty-one days, it'll be two years since his death. And a minute doesn't go by in which I don't think of him. I stopped by his gravesite on the way up here. Stood by his grave for a long time. Told him I was sorry … asked for his forgiveness—"

"No," she said gently, "tell me about *him.*"

He sucked in a deep breath, then he did. About how he ate only macaroni and cheese and pancakes for about six months. How he liked to watch the old Scooby Doo cartoons they'd bought on DVD. How his hair had a pesky cowlick in the back. About the time he jumped out from behind his sister's dresser to scare her and she broke her little toe as she raced from her bedroom screaming. It spilled out like someone had opened the floodgates on the Hoover Dam. And except for an occasional tender touch or laugh when he told her a funny story, Laura didn't say a word.

He noticed his voice becoming hoarse about the time they passed the I-40 exit and made their way into Flagstaff. He had no idea how he'd driven there and managed to talk for over thirty minutes.

He turned to her. "Thank you."

"For what?"

"Listening." His guilt and anger over the past two years had left him feeling as though he'd been buried alive under a thousand tons of granite. And each day, another ton seemed added to the pile. Now it felt as though some of that heavy weight had been lifted. Not much, but he felt lighter than recent memory could recall.

With the smallest sliver of hope that the rest of his life might not be destined to be filled with pain, he said, "Now, let's go see if we can find your killer."

Chapter 19

Ransom's greeting at the Flagstaff Police Department wasn't diametrically opposite than that of Sedona's, but it was close. He knew one of the commanders and a few other officers from a few years ago, when he helped them shut down a major drug-trafficking ring.

"Stuart," Commander Flynn said with a slight southern drawl and a wide grin as they were ushered into his office. "Sheeeit. It's been what … two years?"

Ransom knew Flynn came here from Atlanta and tried to hide his southern accent, but sometimes it slipped out. "Three," Ransom said, shaking his hand.

Flynn's face turned serious. "Sorry about your son."

"Thank you," he replied as he'd done a thousand times before, shocked that he didn't feel the familiar anger surface.

Flynn asked what had brought him up to the high country.

"We're interested in the woman who was abducted last night," Ransom said. He introduced Laura and gave Flynn a two-minute brief on the possible Sedona connection. Laura added she thought this guy could have set up her brother.

Flynn motioned toward a couple of chairs, then settled his lanky frame into onto the edge of his desk. "Yeah, I heard about that. Bad business down there."

"Think it could be the same guy?" Laura asked.

Flynn rubbed his chin. "Hard to tell."

Ransom said, "What can you tell us about the case?"

He tapped a few keys on a sleek black laptop sitting on his desk. "I was just writing my report. Let's see, a little after eight p.m. last night, a Flagstaff female NAU student named Kristen Tovar was abducted at knifepoint near the old train depot. The guy—" his eyes swept back to the laptop's screen, "a white, middle-aged man, wearing glasses, dark clothes and driving a dark-colored sedan drives her out in the forest, rapes her, then beats her unconscious. She wakes up as he's digging her grave, runs into the forest and is found by a group of campers the next morning."

Laura asked, "How's she doing?"

"A broken arm, exposure, beaten and bruised … then there's the trauma, both physical and mental, from the guy raping her … and watching him dig her grave." A deep sigh. "But she's young. Strong. She'll do okay."

Laura said, "Do you think he could have been planning to dismember her out there in the woods, take a few trophies, then bury the rest?"

"It's possible. But what connection would this guy have to your brother?" Flynn wondered aloud.

"Maybe Craig arrested him once. Pissed him off, and the guy wanted the ultimate revenge," she said.

"We won't know for sure until we catch the guy."

"And how's that going?" Ransom asked.

Flynn let out a deep breath. "The victim got a good look at the guy and his car, but that's about it. Not anyone she recognized, so it was opportunistic abduction."

"You're keeping a tight lid on it?" Ransom asked.

"As best we can, for at least forty-eight hours. I don't want this guy to know that Kristen survived. I want him to think she's still out there somewhere. Have him still looking for her. He needs to find her. He knows she can identify him."

"What's your plan?"

"I've alerted the Department of Public Safety, put out a statewide bulletin. We're scouring the forest northwest of town, but she'd been running around all night. All we've got to go on is the location the campers found her. We figured she could have run up to five miles. That makes a circular area of about seventy-five square miles to search. Lots of old forest roads out there."

"And he could be long gone by now," Ransom said. "Given up searching for her, making a run for it."

Flynn frowned. "I sure hope not."

The two men went silent for a moment.

"Can we talk to her?" This from Laura.

"Kristen?"

Laura nodded.

Flynn thought for a moment. "I think she'll agree to talk to you, but she's sleeping right now. She was beyond exhaustion when the campers found her. You can head down to the hospital if you like, but I don't want her disturbed. You're going to have to wait until she wakes up."

"Fair enough," Ransom said.

They said their thanks and drove to the hospital. Kristen didn't wake up until almost 6:30 in the evening, and except for a quick trip to the hospital cafeteria for a snack, Laura and Ransom spent most of the time outside her door.

After the nurses were through administering her medicine, Kristen agreed to talk. She sat upright in the hospital bed, her arm in a fresh cast, wrists bandaged, face and arms covered in scratches.

"I'm doing okay," she said when Ransom asked how she was feeling. Nervous eyes watching him as though he were there to arrest her.

Laura gave her a warm smile. "Do you have any family nearby?"

"My parents are driving up from Sierra Vista. Should be here soon." She brushed a lock of blonde hair from her eyes. "They want me to move back in with them. They say Flagstaff is too big—they think it's like a mini-LA or New York."

"Parents can be so protective," Laura reached out and touched her hand. "They just want what's best." She gave her a wink. "But you do what's right for you and they'll stand by you."

The girl seemed to visibly relax, her eyes not as suspicious. Laura's good, Ransom thought. Real good.

"Can you tell us what happened?" Laura asked.

And she did. It came out in short, fast bursts. Tears ran down her cheeks as she described her ordeal. Laura sat on the edge of the bed, holding her hand, supporting her while she told her tale.

The girl answered all of their questions, but after about half an hour Ransom could tell she was becoming tired.

"Thank you," he said putting his card on the bedside table. "I think you've given us all the information we need for now. If you think of anything—"

When Ransom's cell phone rang, Kristen almost jumped out of the bed.

Ransom hit the button to silence it and put it to his ear.

"Meet me down at the visitor's center," Flynn's voice called out. "We might have found the perp's car ... and possibly the man himself."

The city was shrouded in twilight by the time Ransom's headlights reflected off the black asphalt in the visitor center's parking lot. Four cruisers huddled near the building, their interiors dark and lifeless. Ransom switched off his headlights and killed the engine. As he and Laura emerged from the car, a murky shape materialized from the building's shadows.

"Here," Flynn's voice called out in a low whisper.

He and Laura trotted over, rubbing their arms to ward off the wintry chill. Flynn pulled them behind a rough stone wall. "You made it just in time. We're just about ready to go in," he said.

"You think he's here?" Laura said, seemingly astounded at their luck. "He came back to where he abducted Kristen?"

"Not that unusual," Ransom answered. "Perps often go back to the scene of the crime."

Flynn edged out from the corner of the building and pointed at a pair of dilapidated buildings across the train tracks. A lone yellow floodlight flickered above each entrance, but most of the building's details were lost in the gloom. "See those two cars parked in front of the building on the right?"

Ransom nodded.

"One of them matches Kristen's description."

"Tags?"

"Stolen off a Toyota Camry."

"Get a VIN?"

"No. Didn't want to spook him by getting that close."

"And the other?"

"California plates. A Hector Juarez from Orange County."

Ransom reached into his pocket, felt the worry stone's smoothness between his fingers. "Wonder what our boy's doing?"

"Maybe the other car has nothing to do with him. Maybe just some tourists visiting a few bars in the historical district."

Ransom rubbed the stone. Maybe.

"My officers just got into place. I've got three ready to go in the front, and another three covering the rear and sides."

"The buildings, they're abandoned?" Laura asked.

Flynn nodded. "Old warehouses used by the freight lines when the trains stopped here. Now they blow by here doing thirty-five, every fifteen minutes or so. Sometimes, during the summer, we have to kick out a few of the homeless or some crackheads who bust through the boarded-up windows and use one of the rooms for a smoke house. But most of those guys have moved on to warmer climates by this time of the year."

His radio beeped twice. "Okay, everyone's in place. Two minutes before we go in."

"I'd like—" Ransom began.

Flynn shook his head. "I need you to watch her," he said, pointing at Laura. "The captain would have my ass if a civie got hurt. The only reason I'm allowing her to be this close is because I can trust you to not let her get hurt."

He started to walk away, then over his shoulder he called back in a rough whisper, "Don't worry, we'll bring him out soon enough." And then he was gone.

Laura's hand grasped his as they watched Flynn cross the tracks and melt into the building's shadow. Ransom counted to thirty, then started to follow Flynn, whispering, "We don't want him to have all the fun, do we—?"

His' hand snapped backward as Laura refused to budge. He turned and saw she wasn't even looking at him. She stared across the tracks at the spot where Flynn was hidden. No. That wasn't quite right. She appeared to be looking beyond the deserted building, beyond Flagstaff, beyond *everything*. He felt a shiver work through her and radiate into his arm.

"What is it?" he asked.

A train's distant horn wailed a warning.

No answer.

"Laura?"

Without blinking or moving her eyes to him, she said, "This is wrong. All wrong."

A flash of movement under the floodlight. Flynn and two officers breaking down the door. Shouts indicating they were the police and anyone inside should get down on the floor with their hands over their heads.

"What—?"

The sound of breaking wood as the door gave way.

Finally, she looked up at him, her eyes dark and grave. "This is a mistake," she said. "Bad things—"

Then the first gunshots echoed through the night.

Chapter 20

"Damn it!" He tried to pull away from Laura, but she held on.

"I'm going with you," she said in a tone that left no questions.

Shouts pierced the air. Another gunshot. He didn't have time to argue. "Stay behind me," he said.

She let go of his hand and followed him across the tracks. As they raced between the cars, three long air horn blasts sounded. Much closer this time. He felt a slight rumbling under his feet.

They reached the side of the building and melted into a long shadow. He pulled his Glock from his holster. Stopped to listen. The building went eerily quiet. The front door lay discarded on the ground beneath the yellow light. Nothing but darkness inside the building, the exterior light unable to penetrate more than a few feet into the dim cavern.

He resisted the urge to run headlong through the front door and into the fray. Any rash moves were likely to get him or Laura shot, probably by friendly fire. And he could mistake one of Flynn's men for a bad guy. Better for everyone if he stayed calm and cautious.

He inched closer to the door, focusing on taking regular, deep breaths.

His ears picked up a faint scraping sound. He edged up next to the opening. Drew in a breath and peeked around the corner.

Nothing.

Ssshwwwsssshh.

Something was in there. It sounded like someone was sliding a heavy object across bare concrete.

He gripped the Glock tighter, eyes searching for movement.

Ssshwwwsssshh.

Whatever it was, it was close. Couldn't be more than ten feet away. Then why couldn't he see anything?

Ssshwwwsssshh.

He wished he'd brought a flashlight.

Ssshwwwsssshh.

One of the shadows seemed to shift. Maybe—

Breaking glass, a shout, then two quick gunshots … but this time they didn't come from inside the building. These came from his right, between the two buildings. Outside. A tug on his arm.

But he couldn't tear his eyes away from the inside of the building. He cupped a hand over his eyes, shielding them from the overhead exterior light. As his eyes grew accustomed to the darkness, the shadows grew lighter. He saw that the door led into a small foyer with graffiti-covered walls.

Ssshwwwsssshh.

He aimed his Glock at where he thought the sound was coming from.

Ssshwwwsssshh.

The sound was closer. Damn, where in the hell was Flynn?

Three earsplitting blasts fractured the silence, and it felt as though the entire earth was shaking.

The train.

Another tug on his arm. This time the urgency made him twist his head around. His eyes followed Laura's gaze.

A man threw open the black car's door and hurled himself inside.

Shit! He was getting away.

By the time Ransom could rotate his body a hundred and eighty degrees and bring his Glock to bear on the car, its engine had roared to life.

The twin flashes from his Glock momentarily blinded him, but he knew he'd missed even before he pulled the trigger. When his eyes readjusted, the car was moving.

Fast.

It rocketed backward. Ransom thought it was going to slam into the building, but at the last second the driver spun the wheel to the left. Sparks flew as the rear bumper struck, then scraped against the building's rough surface.

It didn't stop.

The car was heading straight for them.

It took Ransom a millisecond to make his decision. The car was fifteen feet away. Even if he could kill the driver with an almost impossible shot, the car would still crush them against the building.

He grabbed Laura and shoved her through the doorway, dove in after her, but was a half second too late. The bumper caught his foot and threw him to the concrete floor. Fiery tendrils of pain tore through his leg.

The terrible scraping noise abated as the car stopped. The driver's window was now parallel to the opening. Ransom struggled to see through the heavy tinting, but couldn't make out more than a shape behind the dark glass. Somehow he'd managed to hold onto the Glock, and he fought to aim it. The car started moving again. This time forward.

Then it was gone.

Grabbing hold of the doorframe for support, Ransom rose to his feet, but was unable to put any weight on his left foot.

A bright spotlight illuminated the back half of the parking lot. At first he thought it was a police helicopter, but there was no wind, and the tremendous rumbling he felt wasn't the distinctive *thump-thump-thump* of a helicopter's blade cutting through the air.

Then he remembered. The train.

Its tremendous shape seemed to fill the entire sky to his left, the single headlamp like a blinding white light.

His eyes caught sight of the car. It sped through the parking lot, attempting to outrun time itself.

The train's whistle screamed as the engineer realized what was happening. The car was almost to the tracks, the train bearing down on it.

It was going to be close.

Ransom fired, the gun's roar deafening inside the small room. He watched the car's rear window disappear, but it didn't slow down. The car seemed to shudder as the front tires jumped over the steel tracks.

He was going to make it!

The shrill whistle was so loud now that it had a physical presence. He felt the sound waves reverberate on his body.

As the car's rear wheels hit the tracks it fishtailed sideways, right into the oncoming steel giant.

With a shriek of tortured metal, the seventy-five-ton steel monster tore into the car's soft skin. The impact spun the car like a top, the front end twisting around and ending up under the engine's immense drive wheels. In an effortless display of the power of mass, the locomotive crushed the car in a shower of sparks.

The engine rumbled past, its steel wheels screeching as it dragged pieces of the car under its frame. Its mass cut off Ransom's view of the car. Holding his breath as the train slowed, he counted twenty cars before it finally came to rest and the night went silent again.

Ssshwwwsssshh.

That sound again. From behind him.

He whirled, his pistol thrust out in front of him.

A shadowy figure rounding the corner of the foyer. Ransom immediately recognized the police uniform, the lanky outline.

Flynn.

He was dragging something.

Shit. It was one of the other officers.

Laura ran over and helped Flynn drag the fallen officer into the light. The man's pants were thick with blood seeping from a gunshot wound just above his knee.

"Anyone else hurt inside?" Ransom asked.

"None of mine."

"Any bad guys left?"

"We got one of them. Another took off. I think he was trying to find a back door."

"He found it."

Flynn looked out the door. "Did you get the son-of-a-bitch?" he asked through gritted teeth.

"I think so." Ransom wondered if the guy in the car could have survived the accident.

"Find out," Flynn said. "I'll take care of Jameson." When Flynn turned to start working on the fallen man, a fresh stream of blood flowed down his arm. Ransom had thought the blood on Flynn had come from Jameson's wounds. But he was wrong.

"What about you?" Laura asked.

Flynn turned back and flashed a toothy smile. "Sheeit. A couple'a stitches and a weeks' worth of sympathy from my wife, that's about all. Now go. Make sure we've got that son-of-a-bitch."

Laura sidled up under Ransom's arm and helped him limp into the parking lot. Two officers appeared from around the building's corner. One was coughing and holding his gut. Ransom identified himself and asked if they needed assistance.

The officer shook his head. "Took two in the vest, but I'll be okay."

Shouting from the other side of the tracks drew his attention away. The train's crew had found the crushed car.

With Laura and the unwounded officer's help, they made their way to the front of the train. What was left was barely recognizable as a car. The entire front was crushed and under the wheels. Only a small portion of the trunk was identifiable. A small gathering of people gawked not at the car, but something under the train. They pushed their way through the crowd and the officer illuminated the spot with his flashlight.

Laura gasped and turned away.

A man—or the top half of him—lay face up between the tracks. His upper torso, face and one arm seemed untouched. His left arm and everything below the ribcage had been cleanly severed. Dark rivers of blood flowed from his core, pooling between the rusted iron rails.

Sirens wailed. Blue and red strobes reflected off the grimy train's boxcars. The man had black hair, and skin the color of tea. Hispanic or Native American.

"It's not him," Laura whispered, disappointment heavy in her voice.

Ransom nodded his head in agreement. She was right. It wasn't him.

Then who in the hell is it?

Chapter 21

"Ray Montoya," Flynn said. "That's the perp's name." He stood next to his cruiser in the visitor center's parking lot and tugged at the bandage the EMTs had wrapped on his arm. They'd told him if he didn't get it stitched up soon, the wound was going to leave one hell of a scar. "The bigger, the better," he'd said with a tight grin. "My wife thinks they're sexy."

"He stole the car yesterday in Nogales," Flynn now said to Ransom. "Took it from some tourists going across the border for a day of fun shopping. Loaded the trunk up with coke and made his way here."

"Handing it off to LA dealers?" Ransom said. He was sitting in the passenger's seat, his ankle, wrapped in gauze and tape, sticking out the open door. His ankle was bruised, but not broken. Should be all better in a couple of days. That's what the ambulance crew told him, though they thought he should get it looked at anyway. "Just wrap it up," he'd said. Flynn had given him a wry grin as though they were in a competition.

"Right. We're still counting it, but it looks like about half a million dollars in cash laid out inside."

"No wonder it was like you'd walked into a hornet's nest."

"So, we still don't know who abducted Kristen?" Laura said, stating the obvious.

"It wasn't Mr. Montoya. That much I'm sure. The stolen car is similar to what Kristen described, but he was dealing drugs, not picking up girls."

"What are you going to do now?" she asked.

"Clean up this mess," he said. "I've got two wounded officers, not including myself...." He pointed to the train. A crane had arrived and was busy pulling the wrecked car from the tracks. "And the railroad's screaming at me to reopen the tracks."

"What about—?" she began.

"Don't worry," he said. "We're still looking for him. But my bet is that he's hundreds of miles from here by now."

She turned to Ransom. "And what are you going to do?"

He looked at his watch. "It's almost ten o'clock. I smell like a used ashtray, my ankle hurts like hell, and I've only had one real meal today. Let's get back to Sedona, grab some dinner. I've still got to find a place to stay since I was kicked out of Kokopelli Inn."

Flynn gave him a curious look.

He returned it with one that said *don't ask*. "And I'm sure Flynn will let us know as soon as they find anything."

"You bet. You've caused enough damage in my town to last a couple of years," he teased. "I don't want to have to kick you out."

If he only knew.

They said their goodbyes, and Laura helped Ransom limp over to his car. She took the keys from his hand. "I'll drive."

He put up a token resistance, but knew it was the smart thing to do.

She slid behind the wheel and cranked the engine over.

"You know this is against FBI regulations. We could get into serious trouble," he said in a deadpan voice.

"Then you've got a tough decision, G-man," she said with a sideways glance. "Either arrest me, or sit back, shut up and let me do the driving."

He chose the latter.

She drove away from the flashing lights and headed south toward Sedona.

He closed his eyes, attempted to let the day's stress drain from him. He was exhausted. More tired than he'd been for months. It seemed that Murphy was on his back again. Everything that could have gone wrong had. If he could just sleep for—

The ring of his cell phone made him that fantasy disappear.

What now?

He flipped it open. "Ransom."

"Where are you?"

It took him a few seconds to recognize Hilderman's voice.

"Flagstaff. On our way down there, maybe thirty minutes away."

"Good."

A long pause.

"What's up?"

Another pause. "Uhhh, there's someone here that wants to talk with you."

He heard a muted shuffle as the phone was passed to someone else.

"Hey, Dad," his daughter's familiar voice called out cheerfully. "Thought I'd come up and spend the weekend with you."

He snapped the phone shut and stared at it, as if it were an alien artifact capable of untold power.

"Your daughter?" Laura asked.

He nodded and clipped the phone back on his belt.

"She's in Sedona?"

He nodded again.

Laura went silent, knowing when not to press. She would wait for him to make up his mind if he wanted to talk about Morgan.

What in the hell was she doing there?

But he already knew the answer. It was her weekend. She wasn't going to let a little thing like him being in another city on assignment stop her. Shit, she was only eighteen. Her self-determination scared the hell out of him.

He looked over at Laura. She flashed him a reassuring smile. One that radiated safety and didn't pressure.

"She lives with her mother," he said, making the decision. "But I have her one weekend a month."

"That's not much," she said. Her voice held no accusatory tone, just a hint of sadness.

"Yeah," he agreed, but he felt too ashamed to tell her that he could have more … if he wanted to. Both Morgan and his ex had told him that.

It wasn't that he didn't love her. He did. Deep down. But he refused to let it surface. He lived in constant fear that she could be taken away from him as easily as Trevor had been. And that was just too painful.

"Who does she take after? You or her mother?" Laura asked.

He didn't even need to think about it. "Her mother," he said. Another reason it was so hard being with her.

"What's she like?"

"Smart. Independent. Confident."

"Sounds like a great person."

"She is. And I guess that's what originally attracted me to her mother. She can also be stubborn and ruthlessly honest." He sighed. "But I have no idea where she gets that from."

In the dashboard lights he saw her smile. "I wonder."

He looked out the window. They were off the interstate now, driving through a forest of tall pine trees along Highway 89A. "And … she's strong." He hesitated. "Not physically … well, I guess she could be, but I meant emotionally."

"Don't worry, I caught that."

He took a deep breath. "After Trev died, the only one in the family who held it together was Morgan. She was sad, yes, but she didn't dwell on it. Didn't let it eat her up on the inside. She grieved, then moved on. Jesus, she was so strong. And she was just sixteen."

"What about your wife?"

"She went off the deep end until she found God. She's made her peace and found forgiveness in religion."

"Good for her. And you?"

"Not so lucky. I'm still looking for it," he said, trying to lighten up the mood.

"I meant, what happened to you after your son died?"

He shrugged. "I went into a deep depression that lasted … oh, hell, I'm still depressed. I feel I'm running on a circular treadmill, unable to get off. That I'm going to be stuck inside it forever."

She took his hand in hers. "Gabriel tells me change is coming."

He didn't say anything about her reference to the angel. Didn't want her to pull away. Her hand was warm and felt nice in his. "Change is good, right?" He said, resorting to jokes to hide his fear.

"Sometimes," she said in a low whisper, as if not wanting him to hear the truth.

But he knew firsthand how brutal change could be. It had been seven hundred and nine days since he learned that lesson.

Hilderman and Morgan were waiting for them in the parking lot when they pulled up to the police station. The big man hovered next to

Ransom's daughter like a mother bear with her cub. Ransom slid the window down as Laura rolled to a stop.

Despite the cool weather, Morgan was dressed in shorts and an old gold-and-maroon Mountain Ridge High School t-shirt. Her long black hair was tied into a ponytail and it surprised Ransom, as it always did, that his little girl wasn't little anymore. She had become a beautiful woman. Just like her mother had been when he'd first met her.

Morgan looked inside the car, did a double take between Laura and Ransom. Then her eyes went to Laura and with a playful smile she said, "You're going to have to tell me how you got him to let you drive, he's usually a male chauvinist when it comes to those things."

Laura smiled back and pointed to his wrapped up ankle. "Physical abuse seems to do the trick quite well."

Morgan took in the medical tape and her eyes widened. "Dad?"

"It's just a little bruise," he said.

Hilderman, who was snacking on a half-eaten burrito, put his massive head in the window, spilling a few pieces of tortilla onto Ransom's lap. "Hi, Laura," he said, his face heavy with concern. "Are you okay?"

She nodded.

"You weren't involved with that drug dealer being crushed by that train—?"

Ransom shot him a look that said *later*.

"Dad?"

"It's no big deal, Morgan." Time to change the subject. "What are you doing here?"

"It's my weekend," she said, then her nose wrinkled in confusion. "You smell like charcoal."

"I told you I was working," he said.

"I called your office in Phoenix," she said. "They didn't know you were in Sedona."

Great. What the hell was he going to tell the SAC?

"Don't worry. I covered for you."

Even better. His own daughter was having to cover for him at work.

She looked at Laura again. "Aren't you going to introduce me?"

"Oh, sorry," he said, then made the introductions.

Morgan reached through the window and shook Laura's hand.

"And I see you've already met Officer Hilderman," he said.

"Yeah, Hildy was kind enough to show me around while we tracked you down." She lowered her voice. "You're not a real popular guy around here, are you?"

Ransom gave Hilderman a questioning look.

Hilderman shrugged. "We ran into Chief Parker. Robert Pearce was with him. He was making an official complaint about your presence here."

"Wonderful." It just kept getting better and better.

"What's going on?" Morgan asked.

"Nothing," he said a bit too sharply.

The inevitable silence that had engulfed their relationship for the past two years moved in. Laura, seeing it was up to her to break through it, said to Morgan, "We haven't had dinner yet. What about you? Are you hungry?"

"Starved." Morgan angled a thumb toward Hilderman. "Hildy offered me half of his fatty cow meat burrito, but I passed."

Ransom said, "Morgan's a vegetarian."

"Good for you," Laura said. "I make a killer salad."

"You got ranch?"

"Hidden Valley."

"Sold."

Ransom looked at Laura. "I thought—"

"Not a lot open this time of night." Laura said.

"And she cooks a killer chili," Hilderman mumbled between bites.

"I'm thinking more like grilled ham-and-cheese and chicken soup," she turned to Morgan. "No offense."

Morgan shrugged. "You want to eat something that had a face, that's your choice. I'll just drop off my bags at the hotel—"

"Uhhh," Ransom started. He'd forgotten he didn't have a place to stay yet. "I checked out this morning and haven't had a chance to—"

Laura said, "You've got to drop me off at my house anyway. I don't have a car. We dropped it off at my house after the fire, remember?"

"Fire? What—?" Morgan said.

He put up his hand.

"Just follow us to my house," Laura said. "I've got a pullout couch in the living room and a spare bedroom."

"But," Ransom began to protest.

Laura gave him a playful jab with her elbow. "You guys can decide who gets what later."

"Come on, Dad," Morgan said. "Hotels suck."

He sighed in defeat. "Okay, okay. For one night."

Morgan gave them a four-fingered waved and headed for her car.

Hilderman leaned closer. "I told the chief your daughter was here to make sure you went home."

"He believe you?"

Hilderman shook his head. "He told me if I saw you to make sure you … and I quote, 'get your ass back to Phoenix.'" His hot breath smelled like onions and jalapeños. "He doesn't want you interfering with his big meeting tomorrow," Hilderman added.

"Meeting?"

"Oh, shit," Hilderman said with a lopsided grin. "I wasn't supposed to let that slip."

Ransom wondered how many times Hilderman had said that before.

Hilderman turned serious. "You didn't hear it from me, but I think the 'chief's gonna announce he's finished with the investigation. That Craig was responsible for the murder of Amanda Pearce, then killed himself."

"What?" Laura said, "He can't—"

"Don't worry," Ransom said, "I'll talk to him. See what I can do."

She visibly relaxed. More than Ransom felt comfortable with. He hadn't done anything to deserve that much trust and he was suddenly terrified he'd let her down.

"Are you sure about this?" Ransom asked.

Hilderman shrugged. "That's the rumor going around." He pointed the burrito at Ransom's chest. "The one thing I do know is he doesn't want you there."

"Sounds like an invitation to me," Ransom said.

"And you wonder where your daughter gets her stubbornness from?" Laura said.

"It's scheduled for noon. Just in case you happen to be in the neighborhood." Hilderman stifled a yawn. "But right now, I'm going home. Gotta get my beauty sleep."

"See you tomorrow," Ransom said as he watched Hilderman walk away. It wasn't too long before a car drew up behind them. He craned his neck around and Morgan gave him a playful honk and revved her engine. Shaking his head, he gave her a wave. How had she talked him into buying her that little sports car?

What in the hell had I been thinking?

Trying to buy his way out of his guilt. As if a car could do that.

Laura pulled away from the curb, Morgan following in her bright red Mazda Miata.

Thirty seconds after the two cars turned onto highway 89A, a third car rumbled to life and pulled out after them.

Chapter 22

Laura's house was a wood-sided bungalow on a modest-sized lot in an older section of Sedona. An old-fashioned porch, complete with two wooden benches, was attached to the front of the house. Morgan carried their luggage through the door while Laura helped Ransom limp into the living room. It was furnished in comfortable earth-toned furniture, and had polished walnut floors. Reproductions of Ansel Adams' black and white pictures hung from the walls. A small kitchen and dining room sat off to his left. Thankfully, no weird voodoo objects or sacrificial chickens hanging on the walls. He was pleasantly surprised the place had an open, relaxed feel to it.

"That's a pull-out. It's got a thick mattress," Laura said motioning to the couch. "And the guest bedroom's over there."

Morgan walked over and patted the couch's thick cushions. "I don't mind sleeping on the couch."

"I'll take it," Ransom said in a tone that made it clear it wasn't up for discussion.

"Okay," Morgan said, putting her hands up in mock surrender. "It's all yours."

He let out a deep sigh. What was wrong with sleeping in Laura's spare bedroom? It would feel like he was … company … a family friend … or maybe more. And as much as he liked the idea, it also scared the hell out of him. He nodded toward an open door. "It's closer to the bathroom." He wiggled his bandaged ankle. "In case I need to use it during the night."

"Good idea," Morgan said, putting his suitcases down. She hadn't fallen for his excuse, but she was smart enough not to pursue the real reason. That was Morgan. Always the practical one.

"Okay," Laura said, "let's get dinner going."

He sat at the dining room table while Laura and Morgan worked on dinner. The two hit it off as if they'd been friends for years, Morgan showing a genuine interest in Laura's new age beliefs and Laura curious about Morgan's life. After about ten minutes, the women carried a grilled ham-and-cheese sandwich on a plate and a bowl of soup over to him.

He smiled. "It's good to be king."

Laura told him not to get used to it. "I've got a soft spot for the sick and injured."

"He's both." This from Morgan.

He took a bite from the sandwich to hide his smile. Jesus, it was so hard to keep his heart closed. Exactly the reason he ended up being busy or out of town during Morgan's weekends. She had told him over a year ago that she was keen to his "screwed up plan to isolate himself from her"—never one to mince words—and that she would wait until "his mental anguish over Trevor's death subsided enough to straighten up and get his life back to normal."

Morgan sat down and speared a clump of greens covered with ranch dressing with her fork. After she finished chewing, she pointed her empty fork at him. "Sedona? That's a new place to run away to."

"I'm not—"

She shook her fork at him but addressed Laura. "Something always seems to come up during my weekends. Busy with a case, sick or out of town—"

"I—"

"I know he loves me," she said, talking to Laura as if he wasn't there. "As much as he loved Trevor. Trevor was my brother. He died in an accident about two years ago."

Laura nodded. "He told me."

Morgan's eyebrows arched in surprise. "Wow."

"Morgan," he began, but she wouldn't be silenced.

"He must really like you. He doesn't ever talk about Trevor … or me for that matter. He's just scared I'm going to die too. I mean, that could happen, but you can't live your life in fear, right?"

Laura nodded again.

He put his head down and concentrated on his soup.

"I know thinking about Trevor's death hurts him. It hurts me too. A day doesn't go by when I don't think about that little squirt … and I miss him, terribly." She took a deep breath. "But we've got to move on, right?"

Laura twirled her fork in her salad bowl, looked at him for a few heartbeats, as if deciding on the right words. "And he's still with you. His spirit is forever connected with you."

Ransom's spoon froze in mid-swing, his eyes cutting to Laura. She wasn't looking at him anymore … at least not directly at him. Instead, she seemed to be focused on something over his right shoulder. So intense was her stare, he had the odd feeling that someone was standing behind him. Watching over him. He felt a shiver race through him.

After what seemed hours, Laura gave an almost imperceptible nod, then shifted her eyes back to his. "Gabriel's talked with Trevor. He wants you to know that he misses you, but the afterlife is—and I quote—pretty awesome. And he doesn't want you to be sad anymore. He said he's enjoying his time with Papa and someone named Mollie."

Ransom's spoon fell from his fingers, hitting the side of the bowl with a loud *clank*. He could see Morgan's eyes were as wide as saucers.

Laura had just named Trevor's deceased grandfather and an old family pet.

Chapter 23

"Do you know those people?" Laura asked.

Morgan recovered more quickly than he did. "'Papa' is what we used to call Grandpa Ransom." A glimmer of sadness swept over her. "But … he died a few years ago."

"And Mollie? Is that your grandmother?"

She shook her head. "No, Grandma's 'name is Martha, and she's still alive. Mollie was our dog … well, really Trevor's. She died last January."

Laura gave Ransom a wary glance. He was still in shock, still hadn't taken a breath since she'd spoken the name of Trevor's deceased grandfather—*his* father.

"Gabriel said that they go fishing quite a bit and Papa's taught him how to play poker." She said this as if it were the most common thing in the world. Then she laughed. "And that he's kicking Papa's butt."

The air in the room seemed to suddenly go still for Ransom. He could remember playing poker with his father when he was young.

"Is he here now?" Morgan asked, her head swiveling back and forth in an effort to see her dead brother.

Laura studied the area over Ransom's shoulder for a moment again, then smiled. "Gabriel says he's sitting right there." She pointed to the chair between Ransom and Morgan.

Ransom's heart stopped. His eyes leapt to the chair, wishing beyond all reason that he would see Trevor actually sitting there.

The chair was empty.

"I don't see anything," Morgan said.

"Believe me. He's there."

"You can see him?"

Laura shook her head. "It's not like the movies. Spirits don't appear in their human forms … usually."

Ransom shook his head, unwilling to believe. He couldn't understand how she had known about his dad and Mollie, but it just couldn't be true.

"Gabriel says that Trevor's been trying to contact you. Leaving you clues. And you've been too bull-headed—Papa's term—to recognize them."

His mind went to Trevor's picture he carried in his wallet. Its seemingly magic power to appear at the strangest times. *Could it...? No.*

He let out the stale air from his lungs and all he could manage was a shallow breath. All his beliefs, the science, the logic, everything seemed to be in question. His whole world spinning. He felt light headed as if he might faint. He took another breath, deeper this time.

"Clues?" he managed to croak out. "What kind of clues?"

Laura turned her hands palm up. "Maybe a favorite toy switching on when you walk by, or his favorite song coming on the radio whenever you think about him. Sometimes their old cell phone number keeps appearing as "missed calls" on your cell phone. Things like that." Her green eyes focused on his. "Anything like that happen to you?"

He shook his head. The pictures ... that was just coincidence. As much as he wanted to, he just couldn't accept that his dead son was trying to contact him. He was afraid that doing so would inflame the sadness he worked so hard to quell.

"My TV!" Morgan shouted. "It must be him. I thought I was going crazy. The little squirt always liked sports. I remember Dad and him watching baseball, football and everything else. We used to fight over the remote control, remember?"

Ransom's head moved up and down in slow motion.

"A few times a month, the TV I'm watching suddenly switches channels to some sports show. Doesn't matter what TV or which channel. It's been driving me nuts." She turned to Ransom, "Remember me telling you about it?"

He didn't say anything, but he remembered.

Laura chuckled. "Spirits can be playful. Especially children. They don't lose their personalities, only their bodies on this world."

Morgan was ginning from ear to ear. "Have Gabriel tell the little squirt to knock it off ... and tell him that I love him and miss him."

Laura focused over his shoulder for a few seconds, then nodded. Her attention shifted to Ransom. He quickly looked down at his bowl of soup.

"Want to say anything to Trevor?" she asked.

He shook his head back and forth, almost violently. He wanted to. Wanted so badly to tell Trevor that he loved and missed him too. Wanted to believe Laura. Wanted to know that Trevor was happy. But it was too much.

"He understands," she said. "But he wants you to know that he'll be with you always. He …"

She went silent. Ransom waited, still staring at his chicken noodle soup. After a long moment, he looked up, unsure what he was going to see.

Laura was once again focused on something beyond him, but instead of a smile, she wore a rare frown.

"What is it?" Morgan asked.

"I don't understand," Laura said quietly. He wasn't sure if it was meant for them, or whatever she was seeing over his shoulder. Then she closed her eyes and in the same low voice said, "I will. Thank you, Gabriel."

She didn't immediately open her eyes to address them. Time seemed to stop as he waited.

"What is it?" he asked.

At last, she looked at them. "Trevor wanted Gabriel to pass on the following information: Be strong. Find Dad."

Ransom said, "That doesn't make any sense to me. My dad's dead—"

Laura said, "I don't think the message was meant for you."

"What?"

"I think it was meant for Morgan."

Chapter 24

"Morgan?" Ransom said.

Morgan stared at Laura "But … I don't understand it either. Dad's right here."

Laura shrugged. "Translations aren't perfect. Gabriel doesn't actually *talk* to me. Not in the sense you might be thinking. Sometimes I just get a feeling … or a name … or words that pop into my head. And sometimes we don't understand the message until later. When it becomes important."

They sat in silence for a few minutes, each picking at their food, contemplating what had happened over the past ten minutes. Ransom felt like a leaf in a windstorm, unable to control the direction of his emotions. In one hand he wanted so much to believe that Laura was talking to Trevor—at least indirectly—and that Trevor was happy in his afterlife. Admitting this might help alleviate some of his anger and guilt.

But those feelings were like an old jacket. Familiar and comfortable. And hard to get rid of. He'd lived with them for so long, he felt naked without them.

Morgan broke the silence, "Well, that was a little creepy." She put her fork down and proclaimed she was done. "You *do* make a good salad, I think—" Then her eyes shifted to the right.

He saw it too. A shadow flicker through the doorway.

His chair screeched against the wood floor as he kicked back with his feet, startling Laura. She was facing the wrong way and hadn't seen the shadow. Her head spun around in the direction he was looking.

For an instant, the silhouette grew larger, almost filling the doorway. "Morgan," he called out in warning, his hand finding his gun.

"No!" Laura yelled.

Then the form shrank as it came into the light. A small orange tabby strolled through the doorway.

Jesus, he was jumpy. He put both hands on the table and took a deep breath. Waited for his heart to stop trying to blast through his chest. With everything that had happened today … and all the talk about Trevor had put him on edge.

The cat's huge green eyes cautiously surveyed the room's occupants. Going from Laura, to Morgan and finally coming to rest on him. His imagination must be working overtime, because he could've sworn the cat's eyes narrowed when they met his.

"This is Crackers," Laura said. She took a piece of cheese from her sandwich and put it on the floor. "Come here, girl."

Crackers sauntered over to Laura, rubbed against her ankles and snatched up the offering. Laura stroked her fur and Cracker's back arched in cat ecstasy. After a few moments, the cat sat down under Laura's chair and began cleaning its face.

Morgan, who'd been viewing the scene by bending over and looking under the table, lifted her head. "What a beautiful cat. Can I pet her?"

Laura nodded. "Give her a call. See if she'll come to you."

Morgan did so, but the cat refused to budge from under her protective cover. Laura handed her a piece of cheese. This time, the cat warily made her way to Morgan, sniffed the treat, then took it from her hand. Soon the cat was doing figure eights between her legs, rubbing each one with fervor.

"Well done," Laura said, then she turned to Ransom. "Now, it's your turn."

He gave her a dubious look. "Didn't you say she doesn't like men?"

Laura nodded. "The only one she liked was my brother."

"Great."

"Go on. Maybe she'll like you."

"And why would you think that?"

Laura handed him a piece of cheese. "Because *I* like you."

He took the cheese and held it out for the cat. "And you didn't like your ex-husband?" he asked, never taking his eyes off the tabby.

"Not much," she said matter-of-factly. "You'll find that although I can talk with angels, I seem to ignore them when it comes to men and have made some bad choices in the past." Her green eyes locked onto his. "Hopefully, not this time."

What did she mean by that?

But she didn't give him a chance to respond. "Now don't be a wuss, call her over."

He took a deep breath. "Here kitty, kitty," he called half-heartedly.

Morgan laughed. "You have to do better than that, Dad."

He gave her a sideways glance, and she giggled. He almost dropped the cheese. For an instant his heart seemed to burst with … with a feeling he hadn't experienced in a long, long time. In that fraction of a second he had almost forgotten that he'd lost Trevor … and everything else. It had felt like he was whole again. That he was part of a family. Albeit, a different one. But a family nonetheless.

"Crackers … here kitty," he called out. This time like he meant it.

And the cat responded too. Slowly, cautiously, she made her way to him. He held out the cheese … and his breath. Crackers stopped a few inches from his outstretched hand and sniffed the air suspiciously.

"Come on," he whispered.

She eyed the treat, weighing her options: to trust or not. Ransom kept statue still. Another sniff of the air and he saw the shift in her eyes.

She had made her choice.

The resulting yowl cut through the room like a sonic boom and he knew he didn't have a chance.

He pulled his hand back, but she was too fast; her claws tearing through his skin.

"Yeoouch!" It felt like razors raking his hand.

Crackers followed the attack with a menacing hiss that clearly meant her actions were not a random act of violence. She gave him one last hateful glance, then scampered off to the living room, considering her job done.

"I'm so sorry," Laura was saying, doing well to control her amusement.

Morgan, on the other hand, was having no such luck. She was doubled over in her chair, laughing hysterically. Laura came to his side and held his hand up for inspection. Three parallel crimson lines ran along the back of his hand from his wrist to his fingers.

"I getting the feeling I'm not the one who's going to change her mind about men," he said.

"Doesn't appear so," Laura replied as she took a napkin and began dabbing at the blood seeping from the scratches, "though I had such high hopes."

Thirty minutes and a shower later, he lay on the pullout couch looking at his bandaged ankle and hand. Quite possibly the day had been a new low in his seemingly eroding career. Once again, he toyed with the idea of throwing in the towel and taking over his father's plumbing business. But he knew it was a fantasy. He didn't know shit about the plumbing business. No, he would stick it out for as long as the FBI would have him, which by the way things were going, wouldn't be long.

The SAC was expecting him to have an answer on the Longely case by Monday, Wednesday at the latest. And here he was in Sedona, investigating a murder-suicide which wasn't going anywhere except pissing everyone off. Including the chief of police. Which usually he wouldn't have thought twice about, but he wasn't supposed to be here. And if Parker pressed the issue, he could be unplugging toilets sooner than he thought.

Yep. He was neck deep in the cesspool … and it was filling up fast.

He hated to admit it, but the only bright spot had been Morgan's surprise visit. And Laura. What had she meant when she'd said she hoped she wasn't making a mistake *this* time? Did she really mean Ransom and her?

They'd known each other for less than twenty-four hours—and most of that time had been spent dodging bricks or fighting fires. He thought he felt a connection, but he'd been out of the singles game for so long, he couldn't be sure it wasn't just heartburn.

And what in the hell could she see in him anyway? A used-up FBI agent with a past he couldn't escape. Now, there's a future for a smart and beautiful woman if he ever heard of one. If her angels had any sense at all, they'd be telling her to run away. Far away.

But … he had seen the look in her emerald eyes. Although he couldn't understand it, he *had* seen the future in those eyes.

He turned off the reading lamp and closed his eyes. He wasn't sure, but he thought he felt something in his heart he'd thought he'd lost seven hundred and nine days ago.

Hope.

Chapter 25

The pale light filtering through the living room windows told Ransom dawn was approaching.

About time.

Although the Hide-A-Bed had been comfortable, it hadn't been a great night: four hours of sleep at best. No surprise there. His ankle still throbbed, but the pain was a dull ache compared to the night before. And his mind wouldn't stop thinking about the possibility that Trevor had communicated with him. Through Laura. Then there was Laura herself … and the chance there might be some chemistry between them.

It was the classic yin and yang battle. A part of him, buried deep beneath his anger and shame, wanted to be with her. Longed to be with her. And that was just on an emotional level. Physically? That was more like a hunger. It had been a long time since he'd been with a woman. Way too long. And he couldn't help thinking about those emerald-green eyes.

Intermingled with all of this, he couldn't stop thinking about Amanda Pearce's murder. It was amazing he'd slept at all.

He rolled to his side and gently placed both feet on the floor. Testing. Not too bad. Slowly, he stood up, using his good leg to support his weight. He took a deep breath, then shifted his weight to the right. A slight increase in pain. Much better than expected.

Surveying the room, he saw no sign of Crackers. Good. He didn't want to be ambushed. Full of confidence, he took a step forward.

Jolts of pain shot through his leg. He gritted his teeth and breathed through it. After a few seconds, the ache subsided. Nothing that a few hundred ibuprofen couldn't fix. But first things first.

He hobbled into the kitchen and pilfered through the cabinets until he found some coffee. While the coffee brewed, he used the bathroom.

Inside, he found a bottle of ibuprofen and swallowed four. Then he shaved, ran a comb through his hair and brushed his teeth. He dressed in his last pair of clean pants and a navy-blue shirt.

When he opened the door, he half expected to see Morgan and Laura waiting for him. Neither had emerged from their bedroom.

On his way back to the kitchen, he folded up the Hide-A-Bed, grabbed his keys and wallet off the coffee table. He paused as he shoved his wallet into his pocket. Thought about Trevor's picture, what Laura had said about Trevor communicating with him.

Slowly, he unfolded it. His hands shook, unsure of what he was going to find. Unsure of what he *wanted* to find. He knew where he'd put it the other night: behind his credit cards. But, if what Laura said last night was true …

The billfold seemed to weigh a thousand pounds, unfolding it was like lifting a heavy casket lid. His heart blasted in his chest as he flipped through the credit cards.

Disappointment, much harsher than he expected, coursed through him. Trevor's picture was still tucked neatly behind his Mastercard. He had wanted to believe. More than he would ever admit. Even to himself.

Still, he pulled the photo out and stared at it. "Trev," he whispered. "Can you hear me?"

Trevor's picture looked back at him, but made no effort to speak. His ears listened for any response. A faint voice. Something.

Tears rolled down his cheeks. "Why can't I hear you?"

Nothing.

He shook his head. *Angels! Trev playing poker with his grandfather. Speaking with the dead.* He must have been utterly exhausted last night. Or maybe he was losing his mind. His shrink had warned him that if he didn't deal with his *issues* in a positive manner, he might just slid off into insanity. Was he starting down that slippery slope?

He slid the billfold into his pocket and made his way back to the kitchen. Sitting at the table, he sipped his coffee slowly, thinking, waiting.

When the stove's clock read 7:37, he started to get anxious. At 7:46 Crackers came into the kitchen and gave him a hateful glare. At 7:50 he began to wonder if they were ever going to get up. Laura's door was open a few inches and he couldn't see inside. Morgan's door was closed. Shouldn't she be up by now? What time did she get up in the morning? He wondered. Then it hit him that he didn't know. Jesus, he'd shut her out so completely he really didn't know her anymore. And the thought that terrified him even more was that he was so far down that road, he might never get her back—even if he wanted to.

By the time he finished his coffee, the medicine had kicked in and his ankle was feeling reasonably sound. Time to go. He found a piece of scrap paper and scribbled:

Laura,
I'm going to see if I can talk with Evan.

Morgan,
How about dinner? 5:30? My treat. Tell Laura where you want to go and we'll meet you there.

He looked at the note. Thought about signing it. But what was he going to write? *Love, Dad?* He hadn't said that for two years. Just *Stuart?* Seemed cold, even for him. He left it unsigned and slid it under his coffee cup.

He wondered what Morgan would think about his dinner invitation. Would she believe him? He hadn't reached out to her for so long. Should he tear it up and start over?

No. Maybe this was a first step in trying to reconnect. Before he could change his mind, he rose to his feet and limped out the door.

Ransom called Hilderman from his car. Evan Parker worked at Robert Pearce's Bell Rock Jeep Tours. The company led tourists on a variety of scenic trails through Sedona's famous red rocks country. Big business for Sedona. They employed about one hundred people, fifty of which were driver/guides, and had over forty bright-yellow Jeeps in their inventory. The company was one of the largest employers in Sedona, making Pearce a multimillionaire and a very powerful man.

Ransom pulled up in front of Bell Rock Jeep Tour's office in downtown Sedona and waited five minutes for the door to open at 8 am. A family of four beat him to the counter and made reservations for an afternoon ride.

The attractive woman behind the counter smiled brightly when his turn came. "May I help you?" she asked, showcasing a set of perfect teeth.

"Got any tours available this morning?" he asked.

"I think I can fit you in."

"A friend of mine recommended a driver by the name of Evan Parker, does he have any openings?"

The woman's smile faltered for a moment. "Sure," she said, her smile making a valiant reappearance, but it was only window dressing this time. "Let me see." The computer's mouse clicked a couple of times. "He's part of a group of three Jeeps going out to Broken Arrow this morning at 8:30."

"Broken Arrow?"

"It's our most popular tour," she said, then leaned closer and whispered, "but I'd recommend riding with Ricky, he's the best driver we've got."

He rubbed his chin as though considering her suggestion. "How long's the tour?"

"About two hours."

"That's not so long, I'll stick with Evan."

She shrugged in resignation, gave him a ticket, told him where to meet, then turned to help the others who'd started lining up behind him.

As he walked out the door he thought about the woman's reaction when he'd mentioned Evan. Something about Evan rubbed her the wrong way. But what? He remembered seeing Evan sitting at the table in George's. His face had been full of anger. Not a happy camper for sure. Could it be that simple? Evan just didn't have the demeanor to be a good guide?

Possibly.

But he couldn't help think there was something else … something darker behind it.

Evan Parker killed him as he took the ticket. At least his eyes did. If it were possible for a look to have physical qualities, Ransom knew he would have been ripped apart.

The bright-yellow Jeep had been modified to seat six passengers and Ransom climbed into the rear seat. His ankle wasn't happy about it, but he bore the pain with a smile.

A man with white hair and a wide-brimmed straw hat gave him a friendly nod. "Ever take one of these tours before?"

Ransom shook his head. "First time."

"You'll love it," he said slapping Ransom's knee. "If you don't get scared too easily."

"Scared?"

The man grinned at the passenger next to him, an older woman Ransom assumed to be his wife. "The Steps. They'll get your heart rate going the first time you go down 'em. Some of the good drivers even get a scream or two out of the young ones."

"I promise not to scream," Ransom said.

The woman laughed. "That's his favorite part of the ride."

The last of the tour group loaded onto the Jeep and the three Jeeps roared to life. Evan angled in behind the first two and they began weaving their way through Sedona's morning traffic for the trailhead. Evan introduced himself, then made a few sporadic comments on Sedona's history in a gruff tone. After a few minutes, they turned onto a rock-strewn dirt road, if it could be called a road, leading through Sedona's red rocks. Although the scenery was beautiful, Evan's narration was sharp and lacked any sense of the splendor around them.

The old man elbowed Ransom in the ribs and leaned over close. "Who pissed in this guy's cornflakes this morning? He's the worst driver I've ever had … and I've been on a bunch of these."

Ransom would have liked to focus on the striking salmon-colored scenery, but he kept going over what Laura had said.

Gabe said that Evan was Craig's lover.

An *angel* had told her this. And here he was, looking for an opportunity to confront the guy. All on the word of a new age angelic healer he'd just met. Jesus, maybe he should just let the SAC fire him now, make it easy for him. If the SAC knew what he was doing, he'd be pink-slipped quicker than shit through a goose.

Evan announced they were going to get out for a few minutes at a place called Chicken Point, a spot where four-wheelers could opt, or chicken out of going down the Steps. Evan pulled up next to the other yellow Jeeps sitting high on top of a huge rock outcropping. Even with his mind on Evan, Ransom's breath caught at the sight.

Tall spires of multicolored rocks rose hundreds of feet on either side, and in front of them, the water had cut a narrow canyon that wove through the green scrub oak trees, making this one of the most spectacular places Ransom had ever seen.

"This is what I come here for," the older woman said as she made her way from the Jeep.

Ransom exited last, sidling up to Evan, who was leaning against the Jeep's massive front bumper looking out in the distance.

"I'd like to talk to you for a minute," Ransom said.

"Fuck you," Evan said not even bothering to face Ransom.

"It's about Craig."

Evan said nothing.

"I know about you and Craig. I know you were his lover," Ransom said.

Evan turned to face him, eyes bright with rage. "I've got nothing to say to you."

Maybe throw a little water on that fire. "If you don't want to talk, fine. I'll just go have one with your father."

Ransom watched the color drain from Evan's face, the cold water of reality hitting home. Ransom surveyed the slickrock, nodded toward an unoccupied spot near a boulder about the size of a compact car. "Let's go someplace a little more private."

Evan hesitated, kicked the Jeep's front tire, then stomped off behind him.

The boulder sat on the edge of the precipice. Ransom looked down. The canyon floor was about one hundred feet below, a group of hikers strolled along a narrow trail that twisted through the pinyon trees.

"Where did you hear that?" Evan asked.

"A friend," Ransom said vaguely.

"Your friend lied."

"Yeah?"

"We were just friends, that's all."

"Friends?"

"Yeah." Evan pointed an accusing finger at him. "You got any friends?"

He nodded, though, once again, it was difficult to come up with specific names.

Evan chuffed as though he were surprised Ransom had any friends. "Some of them men?"

A shrug.

"Are you gay?"

He raised his eyebrows.

"Just because I hung out with Craig, doesn't mean I'm gay. And you can tell my father the same fucking thing."

"I'm not here to judge yours or Craig's or anyone else's choice of lifestyle. I'm just here to find out what really happened."

"What happened? Haven't you talked to my father?" he said, his jaw muscles so tight they looked ready to snap. "He'll tell you exactly what happened. Craig went fucking nuts, killed the girl, then himself. Open and shut."

"But that's not what you believe?"

Evan's face was now the color of overripe plums. "It doesn't matter what I believe. Or are you so fucking stupid you haven't figured that out by now?" Evan pressed closer. "Mr. Pearce runs this shithole of a town, and my father does his bidding—even if it means covering up the truth."

"And the brick? What was that for?"

"I … I don't know what you're talking about."

"Now who's hiding behind their lies?"

"You … you … just don't understand."

"What I don't understand is why you're lying."

Evan said nothing.

"From what I heard, he and you were getting along so well, he wanted to come out of the closet, so to speak."

"Craig …" Evan clamped his mouth shut.

"Unless … you didn't want him to expose your relationship."

"What—?"

"Maybe you killed your lover to keep him from telling your secret."

"No!" Evan screamed, eyes brimming with rage.

And Ransom knew he'd made a mistake. Pressed him too far. Before he could react, Evan gave him a shove.

On any other day, it wouldn't have been lethal. Except at that moment, he was only a few feet from the cliff's edge and his ankle had seen better days. As he took a step backward, his ankle buckled. Then Stuart Ransom felt himself tumble off the edge and plunge into nothingness.

Chapter 26

Blue. A deep cerulean blue. A truly dazzling sky.

That's all he could see as he lost his footing and tilted backward. His arms began flailing, finding nothing but a mixture of nitrogen and oxygen. In the microsecond it took for him to realize he was going to die, his thoughts turned to Trevor. Surprisingly, he felt no panic, no terror … only a strange combination of hope and anxiety.

Am I finally going to be with Trevor again?

"Dad …"

Trevor—?

Then the tendons keeping his shoulder neatly tucked into its socket felt as though they were being ripped apart. His body jerked to a stop, his good foot finding solid rock.

What in the hell …?

He looked at his outstretched arm in confusion. A strong hand had found his wrist. Evan. Keeping him from plummeting to the rocky floor below.

But it was close. He felt himself teetering. On the edge. If he leaned back just a little more, he could join Trevor.

Forever.

Just a little bit …

"Shit, mister!" Evan screamed.

A second hand grabbed his arm. One of the other drivers. Then he was yanked back to safety.

He collapsed to his knees, his breaths coming in rapid gasps, fear and shock finally surfacing.

"Are you okay?" the other man was saying, but to Ransom, it sounded as though he were speaking in a hollow drum. His ears were straining. He could have sworn he'd heard Trevor call out to him.

Evan moved in closer, his eyes wide with terror. "I thought … it looked like … you *wanted* to fall."

Ransom thought for a moment. For a few heartbeats, he had.

Then there was a crowd around him, pulling him to his feet, everyone asking if he was okay. He nodded, said he was fine, but he didn't know for sure.

What was happening to him? Had he really just heard his dead son calling to him? And had he almost committed suicide? Jesus, maybe his damn shrink was right. He was finally losing it.

He'd better make another appointment when he got back to Phoenix. Or maybe two. At this rate, he didn't even know if he'd make it back to Phoenix before they carted him off to some loony bin.

"Come on," the other driver said, offering him a shoulder. "You can ride with me."

Ransom wondered if he'd seen his confrontation with Evan. He looked at the circle of faces around him. Evan's wasn't among them.

"Sure," he said. It was clear that bullying Evan wasn't getting him anywhere.

He didn't leave the Jeep for the remainder of the tour. And the Steps? Some of the other passengers screamed, but compared to what he'd already been through today, they were a piece of cake.

The throbbing in his ankle had started to settle down by the time the Jeep pulled into Bell Rock Jeep Tour's parking lot. As long as he didn't get into any more shoving matches, he thought he'd be okay.

Maybe today wasn't going to be so bad after all.

Then he saw Laura. What was she doing here? Her eyes caught his … and in that instant he knew it was bad news.

"What is it?" he said.

"It's Morgan," she said, eyes dark with concern. "She's missing."

Chapter 27

"Missing?" Ransom said, almost leaping out of the Jeep.

"Her car's still in the driveway, but I haven't seen her all morning."

"I'll follow you back to your house," he said, walking as fast as he could to his car, hardly noticing his ankle. He tried calling her cell phone, but she didn't answer.

No …

They flew back to Laura's and sure enough, her car was in the drive. Right where it had been when he'd left a few hours ago. He forced down the panic blossoming in his gut.

Where could she be?

He tried not to think about it. Tried not to imagine what could have happened to her. The image of Amanda Pearce's horror-stricken face flashed before him.

No! he told himself. Morgan was fine.

He was two steps behind Laura as she threw open the front door— then stopped dead.

He craned his neck around Laura, unable to keep the ghastly visions away any longer.

"What's up?" This came from Morgan, who was sitting on the couch, a half-eaten orange in her hand. She must have caught the anxious looks in their eyes, then added, "Not supposed to be eating in the living room?"

"No … no," Laura sputtered. "We … we just didn't know where you were."

"I wanted some fruit for breakfast. It was such a nice morning I decided to walk to the store."

Ransom edged past Laura. "You didn't think to leave a note?" he said, regaining his voice: all angry.

"You were already gone," she said, her own voice becoming sharp. "Who was I supposed to leave a note for?"

Without thinking, he cut his eyes to Laura.

"Uh, no offense, but she's not responsible for me," Morgan said in a tone that told Ransom it was questionable *he* was even responsible for her. "I—".

"You're right," Laura said, cutting him off. "And, no offense taken. We were just worried, that's all."

Morgan looked from Laura to him. Then all the fight seemed to flow right out of her. "Okay, Sorry. I should've left a note."

Ransom made his voice calm. "I tried to call you on your cell."

She shrugged. "I left it in the car."

He shook his head and turned to Laura for help.

Laura said, "You need to be careful, with what's been going on around here and all."

A smile. "She's good, Dad. Don't let her go."

He glanced at Laura. She raised her eyebrows. He turned back to Morgan. "Don't change the subject. You need to be careful."

Morgan's eyes met his. "Why *are* you here?"

"My job."

"No shit?"

"Morgan—"

"She deserves to know," Laura said.

He flexed his fingers, uncurling them from the tight fists he'd been holding at his sides. "Laura ..." he started, but by the look in Morgan's eyes, he knew she was right. Maybe Morgan would be a little more careful if she knew what was happening.

He and Laura sat next to her on the couch and filled her in. Not all of it, of course. He left out some of the more gruesome details, but still provided enough to make it clear someone bad, really bad, might still be around.

"Okay," Morgan said, holding her hands up in surrender. "I'll make sure I leave a note next time."

He stared at her.

"And take my cell phone with me."

He closed his eyes. Took a deep breath. Clearly, she didn't grasp the situation. Or maybe *he* was overreacting. It was possible that Amanda's murderer had already put a bullet through his brain. Or maybe it was the guy who had abducted Kristen Tovar, and he was long gone by now.

Maybe.

But his gut told him different.

A knock on the door stopped his heart cold. Like the grim reaper calling, they came in rapid succession. *Bam-bam-bam.*

Spooked by the story just told to Morgan, no one moved.

The knock came again.

Bam-bam-bam.

Then a voice called out. "Laura, it's me."

It was Laura's father. Ransom let out a sigh of relief, feeling a little foolish for allowing his business to get him so worked up.

Laura went to the door and opened it. Her father entered the kitchen, but his demeanor made it clear he wasn't going to stay long. "Laura, I'm so sorry. I was out of line yesterday. All of this is driving me crazy. It seems like days since I've had any sleep. I'm not doing so good."

From what Ransom could see, the man was right. He looked five years older than he did yesterday. His hair was unkempt, day-old stubble lined his chin, and his shirt was so wrinkled, it looked like he'd slept in it.

"It's okay," Laura said, stepping aside. "Come on in. I'll fix you some lunch."

It was then that his eyes caught Ransom's. They flashed with something close to hatred, telling Ransom in no uncertain terms that he didn't approve. Then they went back to his daughter. "No, that's okay. I just came by to tell you I'm going away."

"You're leaving?"

"I … I just need to put this all behind me. Get away," he said in a way that hinted there was a finality in his decision.

"I don't understand. How can you … when are you—?"

"Please, Laura. I can't take this anymore. It's too hard. It's eating me up inside. I'm just going to drive—"

"Where?"

"Phoenix … or Tucson. Maybe back to California. As long as it's away from here."

From his solemn tone, Ransom didn't think the man was planning on coming back.

He turned to leave. Gave her a kiss on the cheek. "I'll call you in a couple of days. Let you know where I ended up."

Then he was gone.

She closed the door, but made no effort to move away. Ransom came up to her. "Your father ... I'm sorry—"

Without looking up at him, she said, "He's done this before. When Mom died. He's not real good at handling stress, but this time ... this time ... I don't think he's coming back."

Chapter 28

Ransom edged his car out of Laura's drive. He drove quickly. Parker's big meeting was less than thirty minutes away, and he wanted to talk to Parker first.

Laura sat in silence beside him. She'd put on a good face as she'd made lunch, but he knew she was hurting. Her world was crumbling around her. Her brother was dead, accused of a horrible crime, which it looked like the police were closing the book on. Now, her father, unable to take the stress, appeared to be abandoning her. He wondered if Laura had picked up on her father's suicidal undertones. Most likely. She seemed more perceptive about those things than he was.

They shared a quiet meal with Morgan. No one mentioned her father's visit, each captive to their own thoughts.

And right now, he was thinking about Evan Parker. His face glowing with rage as he shoved Ransom off the precipice at Chicken Point. An accident?

Probably.

Maybe.

One thing he did know. Evan had been Craig's lover. Not because Gabriel had said so. Ransom was a good enough interrogator to see the lies behind Evan's fury. He didn't need angelic help for that.

Now, the only question was: Did Evan know anything? He sure knew more than he was telling Ransom, but that could be of a more personal nature, having nothing to do with Amanda Pearce's murder.

But why be so secretive? Announcing you're gay in today's society wasn't supposed to be a big deal. Wasn't it even considered stylish nowadays? Then why didn't he come clean? Was it because of his father? Parker might not think it so fashionable.

But was hiding behind your sexuality enough to murder someone? Murder your lover if he threatened to reveal your secret? Or his sister, because she was going to find something incriminating in his house?

Ransom took a right onto the city's main drag and—

—a Sedona police cruiser flew by him in the opposite direction. He wouldn't have thought anything of it, except that another cruiser raced passed by seconds later.

"Someone's in a hurry," Laura said.

He nodded. "I've got a bad feeling about this."

She gave him a peculiar look. "Don't tell me the G-man's starting to have visions of his own?"

"If you call gut instinct prophecy, then I guess I've had a few."

"They are," she said with a straight face. "It's your angels telling you something. Listen to them."

"Then they—my gut's telling me wherever those cops are rushing off to is bad. Not someplace I want to be."

A third cruiser, this one followed by an ambulance ablaze in red and blue lights and its siren screaming, raced by. Shit. It was too much to ignore.

Taking advantage of the break in traffic left in the ambulance's wake, he spun the wheel hard to the left. Not a textbook one-eighty, but close enough.

"Chasing ambulances now?"

"Something big's happening."

"What about 'not someplace I want to be?'"

He jammed the accelerator to the floor.

"Ignoring angelic advice usually isn't in your best interest. I ought to know, I've done it enough," Laura said.

He flashed her a grin. "Then we make a good team, because I've never been good at listening to the voice of authority either."

The ambulance led them down Back O Beyond Road, toward Cathedral Rock. Exquisite million-dollar homes nested in the secluded red rock foothills passed by on either side.

"Nice digs," Ransom said.

Laura scowled. "Money doesn't make it a home."

"Doesn't hurt," he said, thinking about his little one-bedroom apartment back in Phoenix.

"Sure. If you're into faux logs and rock." She waved her hand at a mansion atop a hill that was all glass and stonework. "These big homes have no character."

"Still, it must be nice—"

The ambulance suddenly angled into a wide driveway. His eyes caught the name on the ornate mailbox.

"It must be nice … for a cop."

Three police cruisers, lights still ablaze, were already parked in the drive. If Ransom didn't feel like he'd just swallowed a dozen cannon balls, he would have been impressed by the home's size. It had to be five thousand square feet, covered in salmon-colored flagstone and huge windows.

"Sedona must be paying its police force more than the average wage," he said as he rolled to a stop.

"Parker's wife is a realtor," Laura said. "She and Pearce's wife run one of Sedona's largest realties."

"It looks like they've been successful."

He switched off the engine and they watched as the ambulance disgorged two paramedics who raced inside.

"This isn't going to be good," he said.

"Good to know all that G-man training isn't going to waste."

"*Something's* wrecking havoc in my gut."

"Your angels."

"Whatever it is—or whoever they are—they must be having a party down there."

"They're trying to tell you something."

"All they're telling me is that I might be getting sick."

She put her hand on his. "We can leave. Ignore this."

"What about your brother? Clearing his name. Finding the truth." He pointed to the police cruisers and ambulance. "This has something to do with whatever's going on here. You don't need FBI training, gut instincts or angels to tell you that."

"We could just go away."

"If we pass this up, you might never find out what really happened to your brother. Can you live without knowing for sure?"

Her eyes searched his for a long time. "I think so. I know he didn't kill Amanda. Maybe that's good enough." She looked out the window, took a deep breath. "I used to think that clearing Craig's name meant everything, but now I'm not so sure. Is that worth someone else's life …?"

"Mine?" he said.

She nodded. "My brother's already dead. Nothing I can do about that. But … what if the brick wasn't meant for me? What if it was a warning for you?"

"Laura," he said, though he'd been thinking the same thing.

"I brought you here … and if you were hurt, or …"

"I'm a big boy. I can make my own decisions. Many of them aren't the right ones, but they're mine and I take full responsibility for them."

"Guilt or no guilt," she said, "we have to ask ourselves if finding out what happened to my brother is worth your death … or anyone's."

He thought for a moment. "We have to think about this: if your brother didn't kill Amanda, who did? And will he kill again? Probably." He balled his hands into tight fists. "I can't let that happen. Not just because it's my job. We can talk all we want about guilt, but I know I couldn't live with myself if we left, and whoever murdered Amanda kills again."

After a few seconds, she said, "Me either."

"Okay, that's settled. Now, why doesn't my stomach agree with my decision?"

"They're trying to protect you. That's a big part of their job."

"Why don't they just tell me who the bad guy is and be done with it? Then I wouldn't need their protection."

She laughed. "That would make life a lot easier. But that's not their job. You, me … everyone, we're all students."

"Students?"

"Think of earth as a big classroom. Our angels are here to help guide us, but not give us the answers. By telling you the name of the murderer, it would be like they were helping you cheat on an exam. We all have something to learn during our time here. Some of these are hard lessons, lessons we don't want to learn."

"Like algebra?"

She narrowed her eyes at him. "Let's take Amanda as an example. Young, innocent. Why wouldn't her angels tell her not to walk home that night?"

"Maybe they did? Sort of like that bad feeling in my stomach right now."

"Sure, they might have. Or any other not-so-subtle hints. And if she had heeded them, she might be alive today." She held up a finger. "But, sooner or later, she would have died in a similar fashion."

"Why? What message could she learn from being murdered?"

"Maybe what it felt like to be a victim. She could have been a serial murderer in another life and had to learn what her victims had gone through."

"Sort of like angelic karma?"

"Perhaps. Or it could've been something as simple as needing to feel empathy for others. Being tortured might lead to that."

"That's a tough final exam."

She nodded. "No one said life was easy, right? The lessons we're here to learn can be extremely difficult."

"And what are you here to learn?"

"Sometimes I wish I knew. Before Craig was killed, I thought it had to do with teaching people about angels, but now I'm not so sure."

"And Gabe? He isn't helping?"

"He is. In his own way. Sometimes … many times, we don't understand how they guide us. They may give us information … or not tell us things … all to help guide us toward what we're here to learn. Sometimes leading us to bad things."

"You're saying that Amanda's angels might not have given her any clue to what was going to happen because she was *supposed* to be brutally murdered?"

"It was part of her lesson."

"So we have no choices in life. It's all destiny?"

"No. Not entirely. Your spirit does choose what lesson they want to learn in this lifetime. How that's accomplished … or not accomplished … is up to you."

He shook his head. "Sorry, this is just a little out there for me."

She smiled. "I know. But don't worry. It's like a fungus. It grows on you."

He laughed. "Okay, whatever it is. We're not going to find the answers out here." He nodded to the house in front of them. "Let's see what's making my stomach feel like it's in a vise."

Chapter 29

Morgan watched TV from the couch, one of Laura's soft quilts covering her. Okay, *watched* wasn't the correct term. The TV was on and she could see it, hear it, but none of it was getting through. She was too busy thinking about what had been and about what was to come.

She remembered her life before the accident. Not perfect. Not even close.

Her father had been a workaholic, her mother a vodka-alcoholic. But neither was cruel. There was no abuse. When her father hadn't been working, he'd been a good dad. And her mother? She was a friendly drunk. Morgan hadn't even known how big of a problem the alcohol was before Trevor's death.

No one did. And only after the little squirt died did her parents deal with it. Unfortunately, in different ways. Her mother positively, through forgiveness, religion and healing. Her father through anger and guilt.

She knew Dad blamed himself more for Trevor's death than he blamed her mother. But there was still a great deal of anger there.

At first, Morgan had tried to keep them together. But she was a smart girl and it didn't take long before she knew it was a lost cause. Better to concentrate on battles she could win.

Like keeping her father sane. Alive.

She could see the pain in his eyes. See the guilt. The unbridled fury. He was walking on a razor's edge. His mind unsteady. Unbalanced. A breath away from tumbling off into a black abyss he might never recover.

So, she had to be strong. For her father. He tried to keep his distance. Afraid to be hurt again.

She drew in a deep breath. She would ultimately prevail. The words of her mantra came to her.

Time.

Strength.

It was all she needed to bring him back.

Time.

Strength.

She told herself for the millionth time.

Time. The healer of all things. Time would bring her father back to her. *Strength.* A strong will could overcome all obstacles. She had to be strong. For her father.

But it was hard. She doubted if he knew how she had cried, off by herself, for months after Trevor's death. How she cried sometimes at night, even now. How she missed that little twerp.

She thought about what Laura had said last night. That Trevor was with them. Would always be with them. And she believed her. Sometimes she thought she could *feel* Trevor close by.

She remembered the look in her father's eyes. What had she seen? A small glimmer of hope? Maybe. Whatever it was, what had been clear to her was how Laura was making a difference.

She was good for him. Showing him there were avenues other than anger and guilt. He might not believe in Laura's new age mumbo-jumbo, but she thought she saw a small spark of life inside him. Something other than sadness and despair.

He wasn't happy. Not by any stretch of the imagination. But she could feel a shift in him. He was climbing out of his depression.

It wasn't going to be easy. *Time. Strength.* Not easy at all.

She turned to see Crackers jump onto the back of the couch and stretch out, her green eyes watching with an indifferent look only a cat can master. She put her hand out for the cat to sniff. Crackers ignored her, seemingly bored with her attempts to become friends. She ran her hand along the cat's back.

No reaction.

She did it again. This time, Crackers closed her eyes and raised her hind end. Morgan scratched her just in front of her tail, said, "You're a good girl, aren't you?"

Crackers responded with a soft meow. Morgan heard a faint purr rumble through the cat's chest.

She continued to stroke the cat, explaining, "My dad's not so bad, you just need—"

Then Crackers stiffened. Her purring stopped as if someone had pulled the plug on an electrical appliance. Her head turned toward the front door, ears twitching.

"What is it, girl?"

Crackers didn't move. Eyes locked on the front door. Ears listening.

Hissing, she shot off the couch, a small, fur-covered missile heading for Laura's bedroom.

Then someone knocked on the door.

The paramedics had left the hand-carved front door ajar and when he pushed it open, he felt a waft of cold air on his face. Refrigerator cold.

He entered and cautiously sniffed the air, expecting the unmistakable smell of death, but he caught a faint floral scent instead.

Voices. To his left.

He guided Laura through a vast living room, aiming for a hallway he guessed led to the bedrooms. He turned into the hallway and—

Crashed into a tall, well-dressed woman.

She jumped back in surprise. "Who the hell are you?"

He introduced himself.

The woman looked from him to Laura. "The angelic healer and the FBI agent?" Her voice was sharp and accusatory.

He nodded. The woman's face turned the color of red chilies. "You!" she screamed.

He raised his hands in a gesture of capitulation. Now was not the time for provocation.

"All because of you!" Her finger jabbed at his chest.

He took a few steps backward, felt the fabric of a couch against his legs. *Out of maneuvering room.*

Hate, scorching hot and untamed, filled her eyes. "You!" she screamed again. "You killed Evan!" Then she went for Ransom's throat.

Ransom easily deflected the woman's arms, spun her around and tossed her over the back of the couch. It had been a gentle throw and she landed, unhurt, on the soft cushions, surprise adding to the rage in her eyes.

She rose to come at him again, but then two officers were next to her, one saying, "Take it easy, Mrs. Parker. Don't kill him."

Her words finally caught up with Ransom. "Evan … he's … dead?" he managed to spit out.

The woman, Evan's mother and Parker's wife, buried her head in her hands.

"We don't know for sure," the officer said, "the paramedics think there's a chance he'll survive."

As if on cue, two paramedics pushed a gurney around the corner.

A body was on the gurney.

Evan Parker's body.

Mrs. Parker rushed to her son's side, took a limp hand in hers. "Evan … you're going to be okay," she said.

"Ma'am," the lead paramedic said, "we've got to get him to the hospital, now!"

She nodded, started to follow the paramedics, then turned to Ransom, her fingers pointing between Ransom's eyes. "Arrest that man for attempted murder!"

The gurney's wheels clicked along the tile floor as the paramedics, Mrs. Parker and two officers rushed outside. The door closed behind them, leaving them alone with the lone officer.

Ransom turned to the officer, whose nametag read, *K. Williams.* "What happened?"

"Tried to commit suicide. Took an overdose of sleeping pills. The chief's wife found him in his bedroom. Barely breathing."

"Then why's she blaming him?" Laura asked, nodding toward Ransom.

"Evan left a note," Williams' eyes narrowed on Ransom. "Said something about how this FBI agent was harassing him, wanting to talk to him about Craig Adams … spreading lies."

"What lies?" Ransom asked.

A shrug. "Didn't say."

"Can I see the note?"

An acid laugh escaped Williams' throat. "Sure. Just ask the chief."

"Speaking of Parker," Ransom said. "Where is he?"

Williams didn't say anything.

"If it were my son, I'd be here—"

The man's eyes flashed red. "I don't think he knows," he said defending his boss. "We haven't been able to get a hold of him yet."

Ransom's eyebrow arched upward. "Isn't that strange?"

"It happens," Williams said, with a smile that told Ransom it wasn't any of his business.

He looked down the hall from which the paramedics had come. "Evan was found down there?"

Williams crossed his arms over his chest. "I'm sure the chief doesn't want you traipsing around his house."

"Evan lives at home?"

No answer.

"Come on, it's not like it's classified information."

Williams pressed his lips together, then said, "He moved back home about a year ago. Guess things in California didn't work out."

"Can I see his room?"

"Not a chance."

Ransom gave it some thought, then shrugged. "Then I guess we'll be going," he said, starting for the door.

Williams put his hand up, blocking his path. "Why don't you have a seat? I'm sure the chief will want to talk to you about all of this."

Ransom gave him an incredulous look. "You're not going to let us leave?"

"I think it's best for you to stay put."

Laura asked, "Are we under arrest?"

"Not you."

"Am I under arrest?" Ransom said, moving into Williams' personal space, his own anger flaring.

"Mrs. Parker—"

Ransom edged closer, his face inches from Williams'. "I don't give a shit what she said, she's lucky *she's* not under arrest for striking a federal agent—"

"But—"

"Attempted suicide is not attempted murder. And if you don't get the hell out of our way," Ransom poked his finger at the officer's chest, "you can kiss that pretty little shield of yours goodbye."

Williams stood his ground.

For about two seconds.

He had enough self-preservation to do the right thing. Throwing a few choice swear words out for good measure, he sidestepped and let them pass.

Once they were back in the car, Ransom took a deep breath. He didn't think the cop was going to try and arrest him, but then again, this town was getting so paranoid, that he guessed it wouldn't have surprised him that much.

"I can't believe it," Laura said. "Did Evan seem suicidal when you talked with him this morning?"

"Pissed, yes. Suicidal, no. I'd have bet he'd have come after me in a dark parking lot with a crowbar before trying to commit suicide."

"You're right. He's always had a temper, just like his father—" Laura's mouth froze open. For a moment time seemed to stop, then she swallowed hard. "What if he *didn't* commit suicide?"

"You think someone tried to kill him and make it look like suicide?"

Laura nodded her head vigorously. "Just like Craig."

"Whoa," Ransom said, "slow down. Faking a suicide with a handgun is difficult, but with sleeping pills—that's almost impossible."

"Right," she said, undeterred. "And they might've bungled the job. Evan might survive."

"Evan might have bungled the job."

"Come on. You said yourself that it looked like Evan was more angry than depressed."

"Okay, say you're right. What's the motive?"

"To keep people from finding out he was Craig's lover."

Ransom rubbed the knot on the back of his head. "There's a few problems with that theory. One, I don't see how his relationship with Craig would make a difference in the case against your brother—"

"But you said gay people don't commit those types of crimes."

"I said, they *usually* don't. Again, it's not any hard evidence. And two, the only person who cared whether Evan was gay was Evan."

"And his father," she threw out.

He remembered Evan's reaction when he'd mentioned his father. "I can't believe it. A father murdering his own son to keep his sexual preference a secret?"

"What about all those things you said at dinner the other night? A father sexually abusing his own daughter, mother's setting their children on fire."

"Sure, it's possible—"

She grabbed his hand in a vice-like grip. "Please. Don't throw it away. I just got a little nudge from Gabe. Like we're getting warmer."

He shook his head. *Angels*. "I don't think—"

"Okay, forget I said that. Think about it. That's all I'm asking."

"Fair enough," he said. "I'll check it out, see if I can talk with Evan."

"If he can confirm someone tried to murder him—and who—it might just point us to who killed Craig and Amanda."

"I don't think he's in any condition to talk to us right now."

"So what now?"

"That's a good question." He let out a deep breath. "One I wish I had an answer to."

She pursed her lips in thought. "What about Hildy? He might already have the inside scoop on what happened."

He looked around, finally noting Hilderman's absence. "I'm surprised he's not here."

"Me too," she said, "maybe he's taking a long lunch." She made a half-hearted attempt at a smile but wasn't able to mask the concern in her eyes.

He started the engine, put the transmission into gear. "Okay, first order of business: find Hilderman."

He pulled out of Parker's driveway and headed for town, trying not to dwell on what might have happened to Hilderman.

What could have caused him not to be here?

Or Parker for that matter.

Chapter 30

Their first stop was city hall. Ransom asked the desk clerk if Hilderman was in. A negative response. Short, not so sweet. Same for Parker. No mention of the big meeting or press conference. If there had been one, Parker had obviously canceled it.

He'd expected as much, but when he asked if he could leave Hilderman a message, the clerk's eyes darted from side to side before once again saying no.

It should have been a no-brainer. "Sure, no problem," was the correct answer. But the clerk's eyes had sought help. Something wasn't right.

Five minutes of further inquiries and badgering, the officer left him no closer to the answer. Where *was* Hilderman? The desk cop refused to budge, kept repeating, "I'm not allowed to give out information, even to the FBI. You'll have to talk with Chief Parker."

But they wouldn't tell him where Parker was either.

All of this could be Parker's revenge on him, but he doubted it. Something had happened to Hilderman.

As soon as they emerged into the sunshine, he was calling Hilderman's cell phone.

No answer.

Laura knew where Hilderman lived. Their knocks on his door went unanswered.

"Damn," he said, "where the hell is he?"

She shrugged. "Maybe he's at the hospital?"

"I doubt it. Parker's probably there by now, and they don't seem to be the best of friends at this point."

"Something's not right," she said, echoing his own concerns.

"Maybe he's at his brother's?"

Her face brightened. "Taking a long lunch?"

"Right."

The drive to George's took less than five minutes. The lunch rush was over and only two cars sat in the front parking lot: a bright red Ford Focus and a brand new SUV. No police cruisers.

Ransom hadn't seen anything else. "What's he drive? His personal car." Ransom said.

"Last I knew, he was driving an old cop car he bought at the city auction."

Definitely not one of the cars in the parking lot. They spent another twenty minutes driving around town, and just as they were ready to give up, Ransom's phone chirped. He pulled into a Circle K's parking lot and snapped open his phone. "Ransom."

"You called?" A familiar voice answered back. Hilderman. But the tone was all wrong. Distant. Cold.

"You okay?" It had been two hours since they'd first tried to reach him.

"Peachy."

"We need to talk to you."

A long hesitation. "I'm a little busy."

What's wrong with him?

"It's important," Ransom said.

Another long pause. "Meet me at George's in half an hour," he said, and the line went dead.

"What's wrong?" Laura asked.

"I don't know. He sounded strange. Distracted." Ransom pulled back onto the road. "Let's go find out why."

They grabbed a corner booth at George's, ordered a couple of iced teas and fifteen minutes later, Hilderman walked in. He was dressed in jeans and a black western shirt instead of his usual uniform. The sight gave Ransom a brief shock. He'd never seen Hilderman out of uniform. It was like seeing your grandmother in a red thong and Wonderbra. Unsettling.

Hilderman acknowledged them, though his customary smile was missing.

"You okay, Hildy?" Laura asked as he slid into the booth across from them.

He merely cycled his huge shoulders up and down. The waitress came over and he ordered two burritos.

They said nothing.

Hilderman blew out a big breath. "Guess I eat too much when I get upset."

Laura leaned forward, grabbed his meaty hand. "What's wrong, Hildy?"

He didn't say anything at first, then he turned from Laura to Ransom, his big eyes somber. "Got any openings at the FBI down there in Phoenix?"

"Parker fired you?" Laura asked.

"Administrative leave," Hilderman said. "But that's just a formality. I have to go in front of a board of inquiry within two weeks, but the Devil's made his deal ... I'm gone."

"What for?"

A sheepish grin. "Multiple offenses. Leaking official information, spoiling a crime scene and ..." he looked down at the table. "And a bunch of other bullshit."

"And the real reason?"

"Parker thinks I'm helping you instead of escorting 'your sorry ass'—his words—out of town. He's pissed that you're still here causing trouble."

Laura said, "And after what happened with Evan—"

"Evan? Evan Parker?" A thin smile spread across Hilderman's face. "You didn't hurt him during your little four-wheel drive adventure, did you?"

"He tried to commit suicide," Ransom said.

Hilderman's face fell and the smile vanished. "Jesus. When?"

"A couple of hours ago. Sleeping pills. He's at the hospital. Don't know if he's going to make it or not."

"Why'd he do it?"

"Evan's blaming Ransom," Laura said. "He—"

"I did have a little talk with him out at Chicken Point. Only I didn't hurt him. He got upset, gave me a push and almost sent me sailing off the edge."

Hilderman's two burritos came and he dug in. "He's always been a hothead."

"Right. It doesn't make sense," Laura said, then turned to Ransom for approval. He shrugged. "I don't think he committed suicide," she continued. "I think the same person who set up Craig tried to kill Evan."

"Why?" Hilderman asked again.

Laura looked from side to side, confirmed no one was in earshot, then in a low voice said, "Craig and Evan were gay. lovers."

Hilderman looked as though he'd just eaten a plate full of jalapeño peppers. "Craig was gay?"

"Evan too."

"I can't believe it."

"Evan denied it, but I could see the truth in his eyes," Ransom said.

"Jesus. If his father ever finds out … man, he would go through the roof."

Ransom said, "Parker's not a fan of alternate lifestyles?"

Hilderman blew out a tremendous breath, half laugh, half snort. "Officially, he walks the PC line. Unofficially, he'll find a way to boot them off the force."

After a minute, Ransom said, "Maybe that's what came between him and Craig a month ago. Somehow, Parker found out he was gay."

"And the chief started riding Craig's ass, writing him up for any small infraction. Hoping Craig would quit," Hilderman said.

"But Parker doesn't know that Evan was Craig's lover," Ransom said.

"*Didn't*," Laura said. "Maybe Evan was afraid you'd tell his father, and wanted to do it himself. He confesses all after he gets back from the Jeep tour, his father goes nuts and …"

Hilderman shook his huge head. "If you're thinking he's got something to do with Evan's suicide attempt, think again. From what I've seen, he loved Evan. Even his hatred of homosexuals wouldn't allow him to harm his son. No, if the chief's up to something, it doesn't have anything to do with his son, it's got to do with Robert Pearce."

"Amanda's father? He seems to have his hands in everything around here," Ransom said.

Hilderman nodded. "He's Mr. Big in Sedona. Kept Evan working as a driver, even though he was one of the worst he had. But …"

"What?" Ransom said.

"He's the one person who scares me more than the chief."

Ransom thought of how Pearce had stormed into the hotel's lobby the other morning and nodded.

"Mr. Pearce," Hilderman continued. "He did a few months in the big house when he was younger. Aggravated assault, that kind of stuff."

"But now?"

"The chief keeps him in line. He and Pearce are tight."

"Friends?"

"More than that. Political business allies. Business partners. At least their wives are."

Laura said, "And what does this have to do with Craig?"

Hilderman pushed away the empty plate that had contained the first burrito and started on the second. After a few bites, he said, "The chief threatened me with everything from desk duty to jail time if I said anything." He shrugged. "I guess—since I'm not officially on the force anymore...."

Ransom thought about saying, *When has that stopped you before?* Instead, he leaned closer. "What weren't you supposed to tell me?"

"Mr. Pearce was at Craig's house the night he died."

Chapter 31

Ransom's jaw tightened. He thought about the pizza boxes. The two plates. He'd known someone had been having dinner with Craig the night he died. Now he knew who. "And why didn't he feel it necessary to share that little gem with me?"

"The goddamn FBI will treat Pearce as a suspect," Hilderman said in a passable rendition of Parker. "He already has to deal with the death of his daughter, he doesn't need any FBI agent-wannabe asking him twenty questions."

Ransom asked, "And my first would be, what was he doing there?"

"Don't know. The chief never told me."

A waitress strolled over, asked if they needed anything else. Ransom and Laura shook their heads. Hilderman said he'd take a piece of apple pie with vanilla ice cream on top for dessert.

Ransom said, "Who else knows about this?"

Hilderman thought for a minute. "Besides me and the chief? I think Jim was in the room—"

"Jim?"

"Sorry, Officer Mosner," Hilderman said. "He was at Craig's house when you arrived, remember?"

Ransom remembered, and knew he didn't like the man.

"He's also Parker's nephew," Hilderman added.

More reasons not to like him. "Anyone else?"

"There could have been another few officers … if someone opened their big mouth."

Ransom gave Hilderman a skeptical look.

"Not me, boss. You're the first ones to hear this from my lips."

Ransom continued staring at him for a moment. "Anything else Parker doesn't want me to know?"

A nervous chuckle. "I'm sure he doesn't want you to know he once got the shit beat out of him by a juiced-up fifteen-year-old girl carrying a hockey stick and—"

"About this case."

"Can't think of anything,"

Ransom studied the big man's face, knowing he wasn't good at lying. Or at least hadn't seemed to be. Although he couldn't see any signs of deceit, he had to wonder if Hilderman suddenly held a winning poker hand. Hilderman just grinned back at him, a picture of ignorant bliss.

Laura broke the silence. "Now it looks like we've got a pair of suspects."

"And who might they be?"

"Parker—he's mad at Craig because he's gay, might know he's seeing his son. Confronts Craig, tells him to go away. Craig tells him to pound sand. So Parker kills him, makes it look like a suicide. Who better to commit the crime than the person in charge of the investigation?"

"And what about Amanda?" Ransom asked. "Parker abducted her weeks earlier, just to give a viable reason for Craig's suicide? The daughter of a friend, a man he's trying to protect?"

Laura frowned. "I don't know. What about Pearce? He was at Craig's house the night he was killed. Maybe he found Amanda's body in Craig's basement. He went crazy and—"

"Then who killed Amanda?"

She opened her mouth to say something, then changed her mind. "I don't know," she said.

"Okay, so what do we have? We've got a police chief lying to protect his friend, and the father of a murdered girl eating pizza at the house of the accused killer. Why?" He shook his head. "Neither has motive for both crimes. So we're back to square one, with all the evidence pointing back to a murder-suicide."

"Craig didn't—"

"I know," Ransom said. "My gut's screaming at me, telling me there's something strange going on."

Laura nodded, gave him a look that said *I told you so.*

"What now, boss?" Hilderman said.

"It's time to take off the kid gloves. We go talk to Pearce. Find out what he was doing at Craig's house ... and why Sedona's chief of police would lie about it."

Ransom and Laura found Robert Pearce in his office at Bell Rock Jeep Tours. At least that's where his receptionist said he was, though it had been more than thirty minutes and they were still waiting to see him.

The receptionist, a gray-haired woman of about fifty, who looked like she'd seen everything life could throw at a person, sat behind her desk, typing on her keyboard, humming to the soft music coming from her computer's speakers.

She had disappeared into Pearce's office when Ransom first asked to see him.

"He's busy right now," she'd said, "have a seat, he'll be with you shortly."

He looked at his watch again. Thirty-five minutes.

Ransom had started off playing nice. Polite. Willing to wait.

Not anymore.

He lifted himself out of an overstuffed chair and walked up to the receptionist's desk. He put both hands on the polished wood surface. "It's very important that I speak with Mr. Pearce," he said.

She looked up from her typing and gave him a condescending smile. "I'm sure it is."

"You told him this has to do with his daughter's murder."

"He knows."

She went to turn back to the computer monitor, but he reached in and yanked her keyboard away.

Her eyes popped open in surprise. Maybe she *hadn't* seen everything.

"Tell Mr. Pearce we need to talk to him now," he said with quiet authority. He didn't bother with what the consequences would be if she didn't, his tone made it clear she wouldn't like them.

Pearce burst out of his office less than thirty seconds later. His face was red, eyes blazing. He strode toward Ransom, aiming a thick finger at his head. "I told you to butt out. That you aren't welcome here."

Again with the unwelcome crap. Ransom was getting tired of hearing that line. Damn tired.

Pearce's eyes went to Laura. "And you. Your brother killed my little girl, so stop spreading lies. Take your FBI boyfriend and get your rocks off some other place."

By the time Pearce's eyes shifted back, Ransom's fist was an inch away from his jaw and moving fast. Ransom felt the blow in the bones of his arm and shoulder. That's how he knew it was a decent hit.

Pearce stumbled backward, but didn't fall. He was a big guy. It was going to take more than one good punch to put him down.

Ransom took two steps forward, moving in close, and sent a second rage-induced fist into Pearce's gut. A satisfying explosion of air rushed out of Pearce's lungs as he crumpled to the floor.

After a long minute, Pearce pulled himself up to a sitting position. Blood streamed down his chin from a split bottom lip. He pointed a beefy finger at Ransom, then, taking large gasps of air, said, "I'm … going … to … have … your … fucking … job."

Chapter 32

Ransom wasn't impressed. He leaned over and whispered in Pearce's ear, "Is that before or after we talk about what you were doing at Craig Adams' house the night of his supposed suicide?"

Another sharp rush of air, this one *into* his lungs. His eyes locked onto Ransom's, fear replacing anger. He used the doorframe to help him stand, then turned to his receptionist cowering behind her desk. "Get me a cold washcloth. I need to talk with Mr. Ransom and Ms. Adams for a few minutes."

She nodded and rushed from the room like a rat escaping a sinking ship.

Pearce motioned them to follow him inside his office. Blonde wood paneling decorated with pictures of yellow Jeeps on top of red slickrock, awards and copies of magazine articles covered the walls. He pointed toward two chairs sitting in front of a massive oak desk as his receptionist handed him a damp towel. Ransom and Laura each took a seat.

Pearce settled into his leather chair, took a minute to wipe the blood from his chin, then said, "Should I be calling my lawyer?"

"Not unless you've got something to hide," Ransom said.

"I didn't do anything wrong."

"If that's the case, you've got nothing to fear. If you tell me everything, don't leave anything out, I'll keep our conversation just between us. If you go the lawyer route, I'll make this public so fast it'll make your head swim." He made an exaggerated gesture toward all the pictures on the wall. "I'm guessing that won't be so good for business."

Pearce thought about it, held the towel against his lip. "Parker told me I didn't have to say anything. Not unless you asked me directly."

"I'm asking you directly."

He took a deep breath and leaned back in his chair. "Craig called me the morning Amanda was found."

Ransom made a mental note. Phone records could be easily verified.

"What did he want?"

"He wanted to talk to me about Amanda. Ask me some questions."

"Did he say anything specific about her?"

Angry eyes flared. "Like he had her fucking head down in his basement?"

"Mr. Pearce—"

"Okay, okay," he said. "No. He wanted to talk in person, after he got home from work."

"Tell me what happened when you got there."

"He was still dressed in his uniform, anxious as hell. His eyes kept going to the door as if Parker was going to burst through and arrest him any moment."

"Did he say why he was so nervous?"

Pearce shook his head.

"Then what?"

"He started asking questions about Amanda."

"What kind of questions?"

"Like he was looking into her disappearance. Asking about the night she went missing. Personal questions. Playing detective." His eyes narrowed, shifted to Laura and back again. "Instead of a coldblooded killer."

Laura said nothing.

"Did he seem to concentrate on anything specific?" Ransom asked.

Pearce thought for a minute, then scowled. "The necklace."

Ransom remembered picking up the delicate chain and the small gold angel when he'd been in the ME's room. "The one she'd been wearing when she disappeared?"

"Yes," he said. Short and curt. He didn't offer anything more.

Why was he upset about her necklace?

Ransom pushed ahead, "What did he want to know about it?"

He pressed his lips together. "Where she got it. How long had she had it. Those kind of questions."

Ransom didn't say anything. Waited.

Pearce rose from his seat and started to pace. "Her mother bought it for her ninth birthday." He looked at Laura. "I don't get into all that crap. Vortex's, crystals, angels—all bullshit." He shook his head. "But

… she had to have one. All her girlfriends had them. They were the in thing back then. And she loved it. I'd never seen her without it since the first time she'd put it on."

"Did she wear any other jewelry? Rings? Bracelets?"

"No rings," Pearce said, "she hated rings. But she would wear bracelets sometimes. She wasn't wearing one the night Craig abducted her. At least that's what her girlfriends said."

Ransom chewed on the inside of his lip for a moment. "What I can't figure out is why was he asking you this? Didn't you give that information to the police already?"

He nodded. "When I asked him if he was working with Parker, he said some bullshit about not trusting him."

"Did he say why?"

"No. But I'm guessing he didn't want Parker to know what was down in his basement."

"What else?"

Pearce shrugged. "He asked me not to say anything about our talk. That's it. We talked for about ten minutes, then I left."

"You never went down to his basement."

Pearce's glare told Ransom the answer.

"What about the pizza?"

"Pizza?"

"I saw a box of pizza on the dining room table. Two plates. Two unfinished bottles of beer."

"Oh, I forgot about that. Craig offered me a piece when I arrived. But neither of us was very hungry."

Ransom drummed his fingers on Pearce's desk. "So … why call you? Why have you come to his house?"

"Guilt. Because he killed my daughter!"

Ransom just stared at the man, but that didn't stop Pearce. He was on a roll.

"The son-of-a-bitch felt guilty about what he did to my little girl. His suicide proves that. Shit, he was nervous as hell. I think he wanted me to figure it out and kill him right then and there. So he wouldn't have to do it." Pearce had worked himself up into a fury again. Blood still trickled from his lip. "And I would've too … if I'd been smart enough to see through his little guilt play. But I just would've strangled the son-of-a-bitch with my bare hands, not took the time to make it look like a suicide, if that's what you're thinking."

Ransom watched the bull of a man pace back and forth, barely able to control his rage. He thought about what Hilderman had said. That Pearce had spent some time in jail for assault. And Ransom could see he had a temper. He wondered if Pearce's temper would have allowed him to delay his wrath. Take the time to set up the whole suicide scene. Or would he have gone after Craig right then and there?

Ransom got up to leave. "Parker should know better than to have told you not to say anything unless asked. At a minimum, I could have him investigated for obstructing an investigation."

"Leave Parker out of this. He's a good, honest man," Pearce said. He pointed a finger at Laura. "That's more than I can say for her family."

"Craig didn't do it!" Laura shot back.

"You seem to be the only one in town who believes that," Pearce said. "Even your father knows the truth."

Laura didn't say anything.

"Speaking of your old man, where the hell is he? He won't return my calls."

"He's ... out of town," Laura said.

"Smart man," Pearce said. "You should follow his lead."

Ransom resisted the urge to pound the guy in the face again, choosing to leave instead. Once they got in the car, Laura turned to him and asked, "Why do you think Craig called Pearce? Asked all those questions about Amanda?"

He started the car, put it in gear. "I don't think it was guilt. I think Craig found out something about Amanda's disappearance that scared the hell out of him. Something he wasn't supposed to know."

"The necklace?"

"Maybe. Pearce said that Craig seemed to concentrate on it. And it was the only item of Amanda's left with the remains."

"Do you think he knew who the killer was?"

He shook his head. "At best, he suspected. If he had any real evidence, he would've gone to Parker."

"And Pearce?"

"Sounds like your brother was pumping him for information."

"Or looking for confirmation?" Laura said.

"Pearce killed his own daughter?"

"You said it yourself, humans have the capacity of unimaginable evil."

He nodded. She was right. He couldn't rule out Pearce as a suspect just because he was Amanda's father. But, still … "What about motive? Why would Pearce kill his daughter?"

She furrowed her brow in thought for a long moment, then shrugged. "I don't know. Maybe it has something to do with her drinking, getting in trouble …"

He gave her a skeptical look.

"I know it's a long shot, but something feels right about it."

"What?" he said. Although she hadn't said anything about angels this time, he knew that was what she was thinking.

Another shrug. "I don't know … something … something." Then she waved her hand in front of her. "Okay, enough of this weirdness. Why would Craig be so scared?"

"Maybe he was getting close to the killer. And the killer knew it. And Craig didn't know who to trust. Look, he didn't even call you or Hilderman," he said. "That's how freaked out he was. And that means someone local."

"But he supposedly trusted Pearce?"

"I guess so. But he was scared. And that meant it was someone he knew well. Someone he used to trust."

He saw Laura stiffen at his words. Her head swiveled left and right, surveying the parking lot.

"What is it?" he asked.

"If Craig knew and trusted him. I probably do too."

Chapter 33

They spent the next thirty minutes in the parking lot discussing people Laura knew in common with her brother. This original list was long, so they kept chiseling it down until only the twenty most probable suspects remained.

Twenty names. Twenty suspects. Still way too long. They needed to do some fieldwork to narrow it down. The list was like a who's-who of Sedona. There was Parker, Evan and Pearce of course, some other high-ranking police officers, city employees, prominent businessmen, family members and friends.

At the bottom of the list was Hilderman. Laura had argued against it, but Ransom said—friend or not—he fit most of the factors they had come up with to make the list. So his name stayed.

He placed the list on the dash. "Okay, where do you want to start?"

She didn't even look at the names. "Parker and Evan."

"The hardest first?"

She shook her head. "The most likely."

He looked at his watch. It was almost 4:00. An hour and a half until they were to meet Morgan. He took his cell phone out, punched in Morgan's number.

Laura gave him a look that said, *If you're checking up on Morgan, you're going to be in big trouble.*

He put the phone against his ear and gave her palms up. He *needed* to do this.

After the fourth ring went unanswered, he felt his stomach tense. When her voice mail picked up, his stomach felt as tight as a fifty-year-old rusted bolt.

Laura saw the look on his face. "She's probably out for another walk. Left her phone in her car."

"But she promised to take it with her."

"She's a teenager."

He took a deep breath. Told himself Laura was right. He remembered how scatterbrained he'd been at her age. And after his overreaction this morning, he would feel silly doing it again so soon.

"Don't worry. She'll show up." She said in a perky voice, though deep down, he could tell she was concerned too.

He went to put his phone away, but she snatched it from his hand. "Now, I've got to make a call."

She called the hospital, asked for a nurse named Katie Gibbons. While she was on hold, she told Ransom that Katie was one of the few people in town who hadn't shunned her for Craig's supposed atrocities.

She asked Katie about Evan and his father. From Laura's responses, he could tell that things looked good for Evan. And that Parker had finally showed up and was still there.

Fifteen minutes later, they were standing outside Evan's room. Ransom could hear Parker talking on the phone, but couldn't make out the words. When Parker's voice went silent, he knocked on the door.

To his surprise, when Parker saw him, there was no anger in his face. Instead it was something even more troubling: an *I own your ass* look.

"Mr. Ransom," he said. It was the first time he hadn't used *Agent. This can't be good.*

"Coming to check on my boy?" he said, smiling. Yes. Parker had something up his sleeve, but he wanted to savor it.

"I heard he's going to make it," Ransom said, refusing to bite.

He nodded. "No thanks to you."

"I'm just glad he's doing better."

"He's a strong kid," Parker said, his smile never fading. "But I'm sure you're not here to talk to me about Evan's health, right?"

Parker definitely thought he was holding a winning hand. But what was it? He had no clue, so he might as well jump right in. "I need to talk to you—"

Parker held up his hand. "I'm sorry *Mr.* Ransom, but I don't think you're in a position to be asking any questions anymore." The shit-eating grin doubled in size. "I just got off the phone with your boss. You're not supposed to be here, are you?"

Damn.

Chapter 34

"Mr. Big FBI Agent doing some freelance work? Sounds like your boss isn't too keen on the idea. And from his tone, I'm gathering you're not one of his favorite agents." His smile turned into a snarl. "If you were one of mine, you'd be out on your ass so fast it'd make your head spin."

Ransom didn't blink at the news. Didn't even flinch. He played the part of the stoic general being told he was surrounded, but didn't give a damn. Inside, however, his intestines had just turned to dust. He was in deep shit. So deep, he didn't see a way to dig himself out. But Parker didn't need to know that.

"Then I'm glad I'm not one of yours," he said using his entire brain capacity to keep his voice confident and even. "Phillips and I go way back. Had our share of spats. But we always work it out."

"Sounds like you guys are fucking married,"

"Hardly. We might work a little differently, but all he really cares about are results. We'll be drinking buddies by next weekend."

Parker shook his head. "I don't think so. Not this time. The only results you've managed is to get your ass in a sling."

"No," he said, "I think Phillips will be more than willing to forgive my *freelancing* when I tell him I've got a chief of police who's not only steering a murder investigation to suit his own agenda, but covering up evidence that suggests his friend and wife's business partner is a suspect."

For a moment, Parker's self-assurance seemed to evaporate. Figuring it was better to stay on the offensive, Ransom surged into Parker's personal face. "When I hand him *your* ass on a platter, he'll be more than happy to forgive my minor indulgences. Hell, I expect to get a promotion."

Most other men would have crumbled, but Parker didn't get to where he was by being weak. He recovered in less than a second. "Your threats don't mean shit. As far as I'm concerned, you have no official jurisdiction here. Until I receive an official letter from your boss saying otherwise, you're nothing more than a pain-in-the-ass civilian. And if I even catch you speeding, your ass will be in jail—"

"So fast it'll make my head spin," Ransom finished.

Parker turned to Laura for the first time. "And the same goes for you. I've had it with all your talking-with-angels bullshit. You aren't welcome here anymore. It's bad for business. I suggest you find some other place to hole up."

Ransom didn't immediately respond. He gave Parker five seconds, then said, "Now that we're both done with our threats, I need to ask you—"

Parker shook his head. "Don't you get it? Are you this fucking dumb? You have no authority here."

Ransom shrugged. "Stubborn, yes. Dumb, no. I don't think Craig killed Amanda … or himself. If you would put on your detective hat instead of being in CYA mode, you'd be able to see that. With me, or against me, it doesn't matter. I'm going to find out the truth."

He grabbed Laura's hand and went to leave.

"You wouldn't know the truth if it bit you on the ass," Parker said with a bitter laugh.

Ransom turned around. "The truth? The truth? Ask your son about the truth. Ask him about his relationship with Craig Adams. Why he was so terrified I was going to tell you about it. Then ask yourself how is it that a man so perceptive didn't know the truth about his own son. His gay son."

For a heartbeat Parker's face showed nothing. Then, the changes were fast and furious. Disbelief. Shock. Anger. And finally, fear as his face fell like a building collapsing.

He envisioned Parker going through all the clues Evan had left throughout his adult life. Clues which now made sense. And it terrified Parker.

"Go talk to Evan," Ransom said, his voice becoming soft. "Tell him you love him. Tell him you don't care if he's gay or a three-headed purple people eater."

Parker didn't move, didn't say a word. Just stared back with empty eyes.

"Trust me," Ransom said. "If you love your son, don't let this get in the way of that. Because someday, he could be taken away from you

… for good. I know what that's like … and it's much worse than what you're going through right now."

As he spoke the words, Morgan's image flashed in his mind. *You give great advice*, he told himself. *Too bad you don't take it yourself.*

What the hell *had* he been doing over the last two years? His son's taken from him, so he pushes his daughter away? All screwed up. That's what it was. That's what he was. Deep down, he'd known it all along, but his confrontation with Parker and the whole woo-woo stuff at Laura's house last night had finally broken him free.

Or maybe he'd finally hit rock bottom. And now, his career—the only thing that seemed to hold him together—was in dire jeopardy.

Time to shit or get off the pot, his father, the eternal plumber, always said.

Right. He was getting off the pot. Time to start living life again.

He would start tonight. At dinner. With Laura and Morgan.

"That went well," Laura said as she slid back into the car.

"Look at it this way," he replied with a grin, "at least I wasn't attacked or shoved off a cliff, and didn't bruise my knuckles on some jerk's face. I'd call it a big success."

"What about your boss?"

"Phillips?" His grin faded. "That's going to be a problem."

"And those lines you fed Parker?"

"BS."

"All of it?"

"Most of it," he said, then shrugged. "I haven't been the best agent in the world since my son died. He's had to cover for me more times than I'd like to admit. And as they say, this might be the last straw."

"What about giving him Parker?"

"We don't have squat on Parker. Remember, I'm not here in an official capacity, so it doesn't matter if he held anything from me."

"But, if we could prove he's somehow involved?"

Ransom thought about it for a moment. "We have to move fast. I've got twenty-four hours at best. First, Phillips will call me. Order me to come back to Phoenix. He might let me state my case, but like Hilderman, it's just a formality. It'll take him a day to gather the paperwork on my past slip-ups to make a case. Once he gets the green light from his boss and human resources, I'm gone."

As if on queue, his phone rang. He looked at the Caller ID. Recognized the number. Phillips. He didn't answer it.

When the phone went silent, Laura said, "I'm sorry. Sorry I dragged you into all of this. If you go back, apologize—"

He shook his head. "Won't do any good. The only way I can save my job is to find out what's going on around here fast. And then it's still a big maybe."

"Okay, you're a G-man for another day. Then we have to make those hours count, right?"

"Right," he said without enthusiasm.

"But …"

"I haven't a clue where to start," he said.

Chapter 35

Morgan clawed the trunk's lining. Kicked the release mechanism. Screamed. Banged her fists on the back of the rear seat.

Nothing worked. She was trapped.

But it didn't surprise her. She'd known that after her initial search revealed that the trunk's safety release had been removed. He wasn't taking any chances.

She took a few deep breaths. Told herself to relax. Keep the claustrophobic panic at bay. She touched the side of her head where he'd hit her with the pipe. Although the force of the blow had nearly knocked her unconscious, it hadn't been a lethal strike. She had remained awake—though in an impaired state—as she was dragged to a car and forced into the trunk.

He could have used his gun, shot her dead, but she guessed he wanted her alive. Why? She had no idea.

She continued her deep breathing as the car rumbled along. It was hard to tell how long in the dark confines of the trunk. Ten minutes? Twenty?

Then she heard the engine stop. She tensed.

The trunk was flung open and she caught a glimpse of open sky and trees. She was no longer in the city.

He came for her and she went for his eyes. An awkward strike. Her bruised brain was still having trouble controlling her body. The man showed no mercy for her impaired state and the pipe struck again. A wicked blow on the meaty part of her thigh. It'd felt like she'd been hit by twenty-pound sledgehammer.

And she couldn't stop him from forcing a pillowcase over her head and taping it around her neck. Next, her hands and ankles were bound and the trunk was slammed shut.

The car didn't start again. So she waited. Waited for the trunk lid to open. What would happen when it did, she didn't exactly know. But she knew it wasn't going to be good.

She listened with dread for the click of the trunk's release.

It never came.

So she started counting to herself. Trying to count the minutes. Trying to keep herself sane.

It was then she noticed that the pillowcase over her head smelled like a spring rain. At least the dryer sheet manufacturer's representation of a spring rain. And until now, it had been a scent she enjoyed.

Not anymore.

After thirty cycles from one to sixty, she almost began to wish the trunk would open. Breathe fresh air. She had never been claustrophobic before now. As a child, she always won playing hide-and-seek, being able to hide in small cabinets, under beds and even once in the dryer. Now, bound with a pillowcase over her head in the cramped trunk, it was a different story. Fear, terror, panic. It all flooded through her.

After another thirty cycles, she started screaming again. Screaming for him to let her out. Banging her feet against the side of the trunk.

Was he going to just leave her there? Let her starve to death? Bury her alive?

She didn't know how long she screamed, but when her voice started going hoarse, she forced herself to stop. No one was going to hear her anyway.

She needed to calm down. To be strong. Her mantra came back to her.

Time.

Strength.

She began to repeat it over and over in her head. Time seemed to stand still as if she were already dead, buried forever in a steel coffin.

Time.

Strength.

Again and again she said to them herself. Two words. The same two words that had gotten her through her brother's death would save her now.

Or would they? This was different. One of the words was working against her: Time.

The click of the trunk's lock opening sounded like a bomb blast in the silent tomb.

Time.

She was running out of it.

They were still sitting in Ransom's car five minutes later when his cell phone rang again. Probably Phillips again. He looked at the Caller ID to confirm his suspicion.

Not Phillips' number. Or Morgan's either.

Two rings.

He stared at the LCD screen. It was a number he didn't recognize.

Three rings. One more and it would go to voice mail.

"Ransom," he said as he snapped it open.

"Sheeeit," the familiar voice of Commander Flynn came through. "I was starting to think you didn't want to talk to me."

"I'm all ears."

"I've got good news," Flynn said.

Ransom's heart leapt. "You found the man in the black car?"

"No. That would have been great news."

"Okay. I'll settle for good news."

"We got lucky. One of my men was out scouring the area where Kristen Tovar was found. He talked to a group of hunters who remember seeing a dark-colored car drive by their campsite the night of Kristen's abduction. A lone man was driving. He's been back and forth a couple of times. Always alone. They thought it was a little strange."

"They get his plate number?"

"Not exactly."

"Then how's this help us?" Ransom asked, trying not to sound too frustrated.

"They don't remember seeing him come out after the last time he drove by."

"But—"

"The road is an out-and-back."

"Out-and-back?"

"One way in, one way out," Flynn said. "It leads to an old Forest Service cabin."

"Think he's still out there?"

"The hunters aren't sure. But I've got units already heading there and I'm leaving as soon as I get off the phone with you. Thought you might want to tag along."

"Just tell me where," he said, then wrote down the directions on his notepad. "I'll see you in forty-five minutes."

He clicked the phone shut and looked at Laura. "I think we might have him."

Strong hands pulled her from the trunk and for a fraction of a second she thought—fantasized—they were her father's. Rescuing her. She tried to see through the pillowcase, but the dark material didn't allow her to see more than blocky shapes.

The hands stood her next to the car. Her legs, cramped and sore from being curled up for so long, buckled under her. She sank down to her knees.

The hands helped her stand up again. Held her in place. Not rough. Tender. Maybe it *was*—

"I'm sorry," the voice said. "I should've known better."

No. It wasn't anyone to help her. It was *him.*

For a long moment he just held her, like a father holding his young daughter when she scraped her knee. Except her hands were bound and her head covered with a pillowcase. She could feel his breath through the fabric, hot against her cheek.

She resisted the urge to start screaming again. Instead, with all the strength she could muster, she asked, "What do you want?"

It was a stupid question. What kind of answer did she expect? And what was she going to do when he said, "Cut you up in little pieces"?

He didn't answer immediately, and she used the time to steel herself against his answer.

But when he answered, she found herself not ready. Not at all.

In a voice that held no anger or deception, he said, "I want you to love me."

Ransom was doing just over one hundred as they made their way west of Flagstaff on I-40. Tall pine trees ticked by like the posts of a picket fence. The engine roared in protest as they climbed a steep grade. He white-knuckled the steering wheel and squinted against the setting sun.

It was going to be night soon. When it got dark, their chances of finding the killer were cut by half—at best.

Laura, who had said she wanted to think during their drive up from Sedona, looked over at him and said, "Pearce told us that Craig was nervous. Scared. That he didn't trust Parker."

"Right."

"He was a good cop," she said. "Craig, I mean. Not Parker. He was careful. You know, always wore his bulletproof vest, didn't take chances."

"Okay," he answered, unsure where she was going with this.

"So if we agree he was careful and scared, where did he go wrong? How did he end up dead?"

"He made a mistake."

"Yes, but what was it?"

"He was surprised. Let his guard down and something unexpected happened," Ransom answered.

"That's what I'm thinking." She looked out at the dark trees flashing by.

Now Ransom knew where she was headed. "There was no sign of forced entry, so, whoever killed him, it was someone he let into the house—willingly. And that means it was someone he trusted."

She took a big breath. "Now the question is *who* did he trust?"

Neither spoke, but both knew that Laura was on the top of the list of people her brother would trust. Friends, family: that's who people put their faith in when things went bad. Unfortunately, it looked like one of those people had betrayed him.

He slowed down to make the off-ramp at Bellemont. The sun was now just above the tops of the trees. It was another eleven miles to where he was meeting Flynn. On dirt roads. The sun would set in twenty minutes. It was going to be close. He flew by the stop sign to Forest Road 171 as if it weren't there.

"This is scaring the hell out of me," Laura said.

"My driving?"

She shook her head. "That we might be making the same mistake Craig did."

Chapter 36

The stench took a while to permeate the pillowcase's sweet fragrance. Musty, foul air in the beginning. Then a hint of … She couldn't place it at first, but after an hour of smelling it, thinking about it, gagging on it, she was positive she knew what it was: rotting flesh.

A shiver coursed through her. Now, she was almost thankful for the pillowcase and its capacity to hide whatever horrors might be next to her.

Almost.

She didn't want to see what smelled so bad, but she had to see to have any chance at escape.

Escape.

She had added the word to her mantra.

Time.

Strength.

Escape.

Three words now. It felt right.

As she was dragged from the car and into her new prison, she'd decided not to throw *time* out of her mantra.

She had to buy *time* and be *strong* until she could *escape*.

She was alone now. He'd taken her shoes and socks, then left with the unmistakable sound of a solid door closing, the lock being thrown. She still lay on her side where he'd left her, the floor beneath her cold and hard. Concrete.

Time.

Strength.

Escape.

Another shiver. The air inside her prison was cold. She needed to do something to keep warm.

Using her bound hands, she hauled herself up into a sitting position. Bare feet solid against the floor, knees bent, she pushed. Three times she slid across the floor until she bumped into a wall. Leaned her back against it. Rested.

She worked at her bindings for a while. If she could get her hands free …

No use. The tape was too strong, too tight. But she had to do *something*. She thought for a moment. What could she do? Her hands and ankles were bound and she couldn't see. She felt the wall behind her and had an idea.

Using the same technique of pushing herself across the floor with her feet, she slid backwards along the wall until she bumped into a corner. A starting point.

Okay, let's see what size this prison is.

She aligned herself parallel with one wall and started pushing with her feet again. She guessed the length of each stroke to be about a foot. After fourteen, she hit the far wall.

She repeated the process three more times. The room was roughly square, twelve to fifteen feet on each side.

She rested in the corner, breathing hard from exertion. She hadn't bumped into anything other than the four walls. No tables, no furniture, no bed, no toilet.

And no door.

She had to have missed it. She remembered being dragged through it. She could either search for the door or trace a couple of lines through the room's interior to see if there was anything in the center. She doubted it. The room felt empty. She chose to look for the door.

During her second, more careful inspection of the walls, she found it.

She tested it with her knuckles. Wood. Solid. She tried to dig her fingernails into the crack, but it was too narrow. She needed a knife or screwdriver. Maybe then she might be able to pry it open.

That wasn't going to happen until she could see. She was just wasting her energy until then. She slid off to a corner to rest.

And wait.

Wait for him to return.

Wondering what he was going to do with her when he did.

The sun had almost set by the time Ransom and Laura found Flynn. One wrong turn at a forest road, and Ransom had to backtrack almost four miles.

They pulled up next to a pale green SUV with Forest Service markings on the door.

"Let's go," Flynn said, pointing to the back seat, a white bandage covering a portion of his arm.

Ransom looked at the SUV. It had seen some rough years. Maybe decades. "I'll follow you," he said. "A car can make it, right?"

Flynn nodded. "But we'll move faster in this."

Ransom wasn't sure he would trust it to take him to the corner store, never mind miles back into desolate forest.

"Come on, get in," Flynn said. He patted the door, which rattled as if it were on the verge of falling off. "She's got a few hundred thousand miles left on her. Besides, if we need to go off-road, we won't be forced to leave you behind."

That was enough of a nudge to get Ransom going. Flynn sure as hell wasn't going to leave him behind anywhere.

Flynn sat in the passenger seat while Ransom and Laura piled in the back. Then they were off, tires spitting gravel, two more trucks following behind them. Flynn introduced the driver as Luis Salazar, a friend from the Forest Service.

"ETA?" Ransom asked.

Flynn looked at his watch. "Twenty minutes. Fifteen if we're lucky."

"Do we know if he's still there?"

"I sent two trucks ahead of us to check it out." He held up a small radio. "They called a few minutes ago to let me know they'd reached the gate."

"The gate?"

Salazar spoke up. "It's about a mile from the old Bar-T cabin. We lock it up around mid-September, don't want to have to clear the road all winter."

"If the gate's locked …?" Laura said.

"It wasn't," Flynn replied.

"But—"

"Someone cut the lock off."

"What about your men, they're aren't going in without us?" Ransom asked.

"I told them to leave the trucks, proceed the rest of the way on foot. Sneak up and surround the cabin if they can. Then wait 'til we get there to go in."

For the next few minutes, Salazar worked the old SUV like a favorite musical instrument as he drove down the curving forest road, up and down rolling hills. With a growing sense of urgency, Ransom noticed that the trees' shadows were visibly darker than when they'd started. They had half an hour at best before it got full dark. They needed to get the guy before then. If somehow they lost him, he would almost be impossible to find in the dark forest.

It was silent inside the SUV until Flynn's radio crackled to life.

"We're there," an out-of-breath voice called out in a half-whisper.

"Do you see him?"

"No, the door's shut and the windows boarded for the winter. But a car's parked outside."

"Bingo," Flynn said to Ransom with a grin. "Stay put," he called back on the radio. "Make sure he doesn't leave. We'll be there shortly."

He clipped the radio back to his belt. "I think we've got him this time."

She heard the footsteps a few seconds before the door's lock clicked. Instinctively, she turned her head in the direction of the sound. But she couldn't see anything. And it wasn't just because of the pillowcase over her head.

The room was dark. Sealed tight.

Then, she felt a change in the room's air pressure.

He was coming in.

"Hello, my beautiful," he said. A gentle, kind voice.

A bright light flashed in her eyes. A flashlight.

She drew up as small she could in the corner.

"What's your name?"

She said nothing. Pulled her knees up against her chest. The light intensified. His footsteps on the concrete. He was coming closer.

"I would really like to know your name."

Time.

Strength.

Escape.

She jumped as his hand touched her knee.

Time.

Strength.

Escape.

She repeated her mantra over and over in her head.

After a few moments, he pulled his hand away. "I'll make you a deal. You tell me your name and I'll take off that terrible pillowcase. I know it must be frightening and I don't want you to be scared. Not of me." A deep breath. "And I want to see you. See your beautiful face."

It didn't take her long to make the decision. She needed the pillowcase off if she had any chance for escape. Besides, what would be the harm in him knowing her name? "Morgan," she said.

"Good, good," he said. "What a beautiful name. For a beautiful girl."

The light dimmed and she heard a metallic *clink* as he set the flashlight down. She felt a hand on her neck. A cold sharp blade against her skin.

Jesus, no …

Cool metal. Pressure.

Then the sound of fabric and tape being cut. A second later, the pillowcase was lifted from her head. The flashlight was still on the floor, its beam aimed at the wall behind her.

He was kneeling down next to her. His face, dark with shadows, was smiling at her. Only his teeth shone in the unearthly light, giving the illusion that he was part skeleton. She wanted to turn away, not look at him any longer.

She knew who he was. But a portion of her mind refused to accept it.

He was just staring at her. Grinning. As if she were a long-lost friend.

No. That wasn't quite right. It was more like she were a … a … long-lost *lover.*

There was no doubt about it.

There was lust in his eyes.

And then she knew—at least in part—the answer to her first question: what he wanted with her.

Chapter 37

Salazar made it to the gate in ten minutes and Ransom felt like he just went eight seconds riding a two-thousand-pound bull. If it weren't for the circumstances, he might have thought the fast, wild ride was fun. But all he could think about was getting to the cabin before all the light faded.

Salazar looked to Flynn for guidance.

"Keep going," Flynn said. "With my men surrounding the cabin, he's not going anywhere."

Salazar nodded and the SUV's engine roared as they sped through the gate and past the truck Flynn's advance team had left. The road immediately dipped into a small valley. The forest of wooden trunks grew heavier, overshadowing the tiny road. It was almost as if someone had turned off the light.

Come on, go, go, Ransom thought, *before it gets pitch black.* His earlier estimate had been wrong. It was the trees. Night was coming ten minutes ahead of schedule.

Salazar must have heard Ransom's thoughts. He switched on a set of dim headlights and continued his break-neck race toward the cabin.

Ransom wondered what scared him more, speeding half-blind through a dark forest, slamming into an immovable pine tree and not getting to the cabin at all, or getting there late and missing their chance at grabbing the guy.

He thought about Amanda Pearce and there wasn't a decision at all. He gripped the backrest in front of him a little tighter, put his faith in Salazar's knowledge of the road, and silently urged him to go faster.

"I'm sorry," he said over and over. With a tender touch, he cleaned the blood from her face with a wet towel. The cut was just above her left ear, and he told her it wasn't too bad, not even enough for stitches. When he was through, he brought his face right up to hers, sniffed the air. Not like a dog. Like a connoisseur of wine.

"You smell so good," he said, his breath hot against her cheek. "Like Lauren." His fingers caught a thicket of her hair. He stroked the dark mass, held it under his nose. "*Mmmmm.*"

She jerked her head to the side, wrenching her hair from his hand. "Leave me alone."

He recoiled as if stung by a bee, gaining his feet in a flash.

Even in the dim light, she saw the glint of metal. The flare in his eyes.

Oh, God.

The pipe.

In his hands.

A murky shape, barely visible in headlights, streaked across the road in front of the SUV.

What in the hell?

Then another.

Ransom felt Salazar hit the brakes a split second before a massive black form filled the front windshield.

"Shit," someone yelled.

Three events seemed to occur simultaneously. He was thrown into the seat in front of him, the quiet forest erupted with an inhuman shriek, and the windshield exploded in a hurricane of shattered glass.

He didn't hit her. At least, not yet. For a long moment, he just stood there.

Watching her.

Deciding.

She didn't move. Didn't dare breathe. She wanted to curl up in a ball, close her eyes. Pretend he wasn't there.

Time.
Strength.
Escape.

She told herself this again and again while his eyes bored down on her.

Finally, he took a deep breath and his face seemed to relax. "All I want is for you to love me. By your own free will," he said in a quiet voice. "I don't want to have to make you love me."

She said nothing.

He reached down and picked up the flashlight. "I really do love you. You'll see. It'll be just like before."

Before? What was he talking about?

"And I'll be able to let you out of this horrible place." He continued. "But until then, you're going to have to learn to be nice." The pipe hit the concrete with a heavy ring.

"I'm … I'm sorry," she managed to force out through her terror. She held no illusions of the agony the pipe would bring.

Time.
Strength.
Escape.

She would have to wait.

He smiled. A warm, genuine smile of affection. It made her sick to her stomach.

"That's a good girl. You'll see that I can be a giving person," he said. "I'm going to leave your hood off."

"Thank you."

The smile widened. A proud teacher seeing his new student making the grade. "Hungry? Want something to eat?"

Was he kidding? She was supposed to have dinner with this monster? She wanted to spit in his face. Instead, she took a deep breath. "Yes, please," she said. "And I need to use the bathroom." Which was true.

He nodded.

Leaving the flashlight on the floor, he turned and walked to the door, opened it, and pulled something inside. It was boxlike, about sixteen inches square and covered with a flower-print blanket. He slid it across the concrete with his foot until it hit the wall, then pulled the blanket off to reveal one of those self-contained camping toilets.

"Your bathroom," he said. "And something to keep you warm."

He bent down, grabbed her arms and pulled her to her feet. "Stay still," he said, then used a folding knife to cut through the duct tape binding her wrists and ankles.

She shook her hands and feet, thankful for the new freedom. And thought about escape. Making an attempt right then. But the guy wasn't stupid. He stepped backward, positioning himself between her and the door. And he still held the knife.

No, she told herself. Not now.

He clicked the knife shut, slid it back into his pocket and picked up the heavy pipe. "Love," he said, his eyes narrowing. "It's all about trust. Remember that. I'll be back with dinner in a little while."

Then he was gone, the door locking behind him with a solid *thump*.

With his eyes still closed, Ransom used his hands to brush away the glass shards from his face and hair. The night had gone strangely quiet. Gone was the engine's roar, the screech of sheet metal tearing apart.

And the horrible animal-like shriek.

With all the glass cleaned away, he opened his eyes. The inside of the SUV was dark. He could barely see the seat in front of him.

"Laura," he called out.

No answer.

No ... Laura.

He did a quick self-diagnostic. Somehow he'd managed to stay in a seated position and remain unhurt.

A strong scent filled his nostrils. Musty and foul, as if someone had been disemboweled. And he smelled blood. Lots of it. Someone hadn't been so lucky.

He swiveled his head to where Laura had been just seconds ago. The seat was empty.

"Laura," he called out again.

Something moved off to his right.

A bright flash. The truck's interior filled with white light from behind. With one hand, he shielded his eyes from the glare. Then his eyes began to adjust and track toward the movement.

There. Between the fronts seats. A leg slowly came into focus.

He took a sharp intake of breath.
It wasn't Laura's.
In fact, it wasn't human at all.

Chapter 38

She stared at the locked door for what seemed like hours. He was gone. And with him, all his talk about love. Giving. And trust.

She wanted to throw up. Tear his eyes out. Rip the smile from his face. Anything but be *a good girl*.

And what had he meant when he'd said *it would be just like before*? She hadn't a clue. She would worry about that later. Now she had more pressing business to take care of.

He'd left the flashlight with the toilet and blanket. Picking it up, she used the toilet, then made a survey of the room. This time with all her senses intact. Her initial measurements had been accurate. She was in a small, square room, with no furnishings and only the lone door to access the outside world.

She walked over to the door and studied it. Made of solid hardwood, it was flush against the wall. No door handle. No hinges. She pictured how it had looked when he closed the door. It opened outward.

She put her ear to the door. Listened. Was he still here? He said he'd come back with dinner. What did that mean? Did he actually leave, or was he just outside the door pulling something from a cooler? Since she'd been blindfolded when he forced her down a flight of stairs and into the room, she had no idea what was outside the door—a house with a kitchen full of food or some abandoned cabin.

Then she remembered what she had heard—or more exactly, what she hadn't heard—when he'd popped open the trunk. No traffic noises. No city sounds at all. A kind of silence only nature can provide. No, she wasn't in some Sedona subdivision. She was somewhere out in the boonies.

But did that imply he had to leave the house to get food? He could be standing right outside the door. Waiting for her to try to escape.

Playing some sort of game. She remembered his anger and the pipe's cruel attack.

She waited another five minutes. Listening.

Nothing.

She gave the door a quiet, tentative push. It didn't move. No surprise there. She held her breath, straining to hear anything but her own blood coursing through her veins.

Perhaps he had left, and she was alone. Or maybe not. What had he said about love and trust?

She tried to squeeze her fingers in the narrow crack between the door and the frame. If she could pry it open just a little—

Snap.

A fingernail broke off, sending darts of pain through her hand.

Maybe another spot.

With slow, methodical motions, she swept the light along the crack between the door and frame looking for any weakness. A widening of the crack. Some place she could get her fingers—

She stopped. Almost dropped the flashlight.

Halfway up the door, the crack did widen. Just a little. But it wasn't the crack that her eyes had stopped on.

It was the claw marks.

Deep grooves in the wood.

Someone had been in this room before her.

Had tried to claw her way out.

And failed.

Coarse hair, dark and matted with blood, ran down the length of the appendage. It twitched in a series of violent spasms.

"Down here," a soft voice called out.

He took his eyes from the leg and searched the floor space between the front and rear seats. Even with the bright lights blazing outside, the area was still deep in shadow. But he did see more arms and legs. Only these he recognized.

"Laura," he said, reaching for a hand.

"I'm okay," she said, "help me up."

He could see that she was also covered in silver fragments. "Don't open your eyes. You've got glass all over you."

He reached for her hand. Flesh met flesh, and he pulled. Her slight frame unfolded onto the seat next to him. He went to help brush the glass out of her hair when a voice from the front seat suddenly called out. "Get it off! Get it off!"

Flynn.

His head turned, and he took in the strange leg again. It was a familiar shape, but his brain was having trouble keeping up with his eyes.

"I can't breathe," the voice called out again, "it's crushing me."

He was still looking at the leg, trying to process the data. *What in the—?* Then he had it. The leg belonged to a deer. No, bigger than a deer. An elk.

Now he knew what had happened. A herd of elk had raced across the road in front of the SUV—that was the shadows he'd seen—and one didn't make it. The unlucky animal had smashed through the window and landed in the front seat.

On top of Flynn. All one thousand pounds.

Crushing him.

In a flash, he was outside and jerking on Flynn's door.

It was stuck.

He couldn't see Flynn at all; he was hidden beneath a quivering mass of animal fur. Then, others were next to him. Hands prying the door open. Pulling the animal out.

Ransom caught a glimpse of Salazar, slumped against the steering wheel.

Unmoving.

He hadn't been wearing a seatbelt. And the old SUV didn't have airbags.

Now Laura was next to him, helping drag the elk away. With one last jerk, the animal fell free, revealing Flynn, pressed against the seat thick with blood.

She backed away from the door as if it exuded an incurable disease. Felt the panic rising.

The claw marks.

She couldn't pull her eyes from them. Dark channels, dug deep into the pulp. For a moment she wondered what had caused the discoloration, then wished she hadn't.

Blood.

The others before her had worn their fingers down to bloody stumps trying to get out the door. A flood of hopelessness blossomed deep inside her. She wasn't going to get out.

And he wasn't going to let her go.

Ever.

He was the reason her father was in Sedona. He'd killed at least once before, probably more, her father had said.

She had been terrified in the trunk. And when he talked about loving her. But she had always kept a small bit of faith with her, that somehow she would prevail. Outsmart her captor. Get away. Escape.

She thought of her mantra.

Time.

Strength.

Escape.

But the words didn't have the same calming effect. She collapsed into a heap on the floor. Morgan knew the others hadn't found a way out. If they had, he would've been in jail, and she wouldn't be here.

No. They hadn't found the *strength* or *time* to *escape.*

They had died at his hands.

And so would she.

Chapter 39

"I felt like I was suffocating under that thing," Flynn said, nodding toward the bloody heap next to the old SUV.

Ransom and the other officers had pulled Salazar and Flynn out and helped them over to one of the other trucks. Another truck lit the bed with its headlights.

It had been a terrifying few minutes. Ransom remembered his first view of Flynn, who looked as if he'd lost twice his bodyweight in blood. But when Flynn shot up from the seat, uninjured, he realized the blood was the elk's, not Flynn's.

A closer survey of the elk had revealed its neck had almost been completely severed as it crashed through the window, disgorging gallons of blood into the SUV's front seat.

Salazar had also come around. He had a nasty cut above his right eye, but was refusing any first aid other than a bandage.

"I couldn't stop in time," Salazar said with a dazed expression on his face.

"It's okay," Ransom said. "Everyone's okay."

"They came outta nowhere," Salazar said, then he began to repeat himself.

Ransom looked at Flynn, wondering if Salazar's injury might be more than just a cut.

Flynn seemed to understand and put a hand on Salazar's shoulder. "I need you to stay here until the ambulance arrives."

Salazar's head slowly rotated toward Flynn. "What about you?" he asked.

Flynn shook his head. "We've lost ten minutes already. I'm going to the cabin."

Salazar nodded in slow motion, as if Flynn had spoken a foreign language and he had trouble understanding the words.

Flynn pointed to one of his officers. "Stay with him."

The man began to protest, but a stern look from Flynn quashed it. The way Flynn looked right now, Ransom would've backed down too. Although he had used an old towel to wipe off some of the elk's blood, his face was streaked in crimson and his hair, matted and unruly, still dripped the thick liquid. He looked like a ghoul from an old slasher movie who'd just dined on human flesh.

Flynn brought his radio up. "Any change?"

"Nothing," the radio crackled back.

"Make sure he stays inside," Flynn replied. "We're on our way … again."

Ransom, Flynn and Laura climbed into the front seat of the second truck with two officers in the back. Flynn threw the transmission into drive and stepped on the gas.

Once again they were rocketing down the dirt road.

But they were ten minutes late.

Ten minutes.

Ransom had seen cases when ten minutes meant the difference between success and failure. Life and death.

He just hoped this wasn't one of those times.

For a while she lay on the floor as the terror coursed through her. Then she began to sob, her breaths coming in frantic gasps.

There was no way out.

She was going to die.

Just like the others before her.

She felt as though she was teetering on the edge of a great chasm. If she fell in, she wouldn't be coming back. She thought back to when Trevor died. She'd held it together when everyone else around her was falling apart. For two years, she never faltered. Never wavered.

She had gotten through that horror. She could get through this. She repeated her mantra a few times.

Time.

Strength.

Escape.

Her breathing began to slow down. She had to be strong. If she was going to survive.

Slowly, she felt herself regain her balance and pull away from the cliff's edge. She wasn't going to give up. She was going to find a way out.

Escape.

After a while, she felt calm again. She needed to *think*. Was he still here? Doubtful. She'd been alone for long enough to believe he was no longer in the house, that he had to actually leave to get the food.

She picked herself up and walked back to the door. It was the only way out. She had to get through that door. Bust it down, rip it off its hinges, whatever it took, she was going to get out of that room. And without him there, she didn't have to worry about making noise.

She stepped back and kicked out with her foot, just like she'd seen in the movies. Only in real life, the door didn't fly open in a dramatic splintering of wood. The sound of her foot hitting the door echoed in her little prison. She cringed, but heard no footsteps, no unlatching of the lock.

She'd been right. He was gone.

Then she was giving it everything she had. Ramming the door with her shoulders, kicking it, pounding on it. Clawing at the wood.

Anything she could think of.

She wasn't going to be here when he returned.

Ransom squinted, eyes barely able to distinguish the cabin in the gloom. Flynn had turned off his lights and coasted to a stop maybe fifty yards away from it. Set back in a dense stand of pines, it was almost completely hidden in shadow.

Flynn turned off the truck. They sat in silence for a moment. Listening.

A shape materialized from behind a tree. "Over here," it called out in a whisper.

Flynn waved him over as they left the truck, the clicking shut of heavy steel doors sounding like thunder cracks in the silent forest.

"Anything?" Flynn asked as the man trotted up.

"Nothing."

"I want a man on each side of the place," Flynn said, "Anyone tries to come out, you take him down. No repeats of the fiasco at the train depot, got it?"

The man nodded. The two men from the back of the truck joined him, and they disappeared in the darkness around the cabin.

Flynn turned to Ransom. "What do you think?"

Ransom looked at the cabin, dark and silent. "We go in the front door."

After a few minutes, her fingertips began to sting as the rough wood ground them raw. She was breathing hard from her effort and stopped to inspect the door. To see if she'd made any progress.

Her heart fell. All she'd managed to accomplish was add her own blood to the door's marred surface. She wasn't going to get through by brute force. *Think*, she told herself.

She sat down on the toilet's lid. *Don't panic. Use your brain.* She couldn't get out by herself. She could claw and pound on that door for twenty years before it gave way.

She needed help. Someone to unlock it from the other side. And there was only one person she knew who could do that.

Him.

He was going to help her escape.

When he unlocked the door, she would be ready. She didn't hold any illusions that she could overpower him. He'd have that pipe and the knife. Or the gun. She had nothing. No, she didn't want to fight, she wanted to flee.

A plan formed in her mind. Nothing exotic. She wasn't MacGyver, but it was something.

She pushed the toilet to the farthest corner of the room, threw the blanket over it, then set the flashlight on the floor—aimed at the door. If she were lucky—very lucky—with the light in his eyes, he might believe she'd curled up in the corner for a nap.

If she could surprise him, push him into the far corner of the room, it might give her enough time to make it to the door and outrun him. Or maybe she could lock the asshole in his own dungeon.

She smiled at the thought, her on the other side of the door, him pleading with her to let him out, saying that he *loved* her. She fantasized about leaving him locked up until his own flesh rotted off his bones.

See how he likes it.

Morgan was so caught up in her fantasy that she didn't hear the sounds from outside right away. When they finally broke through her internal daydreams, she bolted next to the door and flattened herself against the wall.

Had he returned? Although she didn't immediately hear anything else, she was sure he had. She held her breath while she listened and repeated her mantra to herself.

Time.

Strength.

Escape.

Then she added *luck*. She would need plenty of it if this was going to work.

Another sound. This one closer.

She'd been right.

He was back.

Then another, even more terrifying thought came to her.

Maybe he had never left.

Chapter 40

"What about me?" Laura asked.

"I want you to stay here. We'll let you know when it's secure."

This time she didn't protest. She leaned against the truck. "I'll let you guys do what you do best."

Ransom and Flynn each grabbed a flashlight and unholstered their weapons, then Ransom followed Flynn as he crept toward the front door. They stopped by the car to listen. All quiet. Ransom put his hand on the car's hood. Cold.

Shadows shifted from tree to tree as Flynn's men got into position.

"Ready?" Flynn asked.

Ransom gripped his Glock tighter. "Let's do it."

They covered the remaining ten feet in three strides, each ending up on different sides of the door. No doorknob, just a wooden handle and a heavy-gauge hasp. The padlock was missing, but someone had secured the door by ramming a fat wooden spike through the clasp.

In one silent motion, Flynn wiggled the spike out, then took hold of the handle. Ransom started counting in a hushed whisper.

"One."

He took a deep breath.

"Two."

A crouching stance. Ready to spring. One hand on his Glock, the other on the flashlight.

"Three."

Flynn yanked the handle and the door flew open.

And then Ransom was through.

He hit the flashlight's on button and the room instantly brightened. By the time he felt Flynn come through the door behind him, his eyes had adjusted and had swept the small room.

Empty, except for an old wood table and a couple of tattered camping chairs.

"Shit," Flynn said.

They'd missed him.

Again.

The door slowly swung outward.

She tensed. Ready to make her move.

But nothing happened.

She continued to hold her breath, eyes locked on the door.

What was he doing?

He needed to step *inside* the room for her plan to work.

Just as her lungs were starting to burn from the lack of oxygen, she heard him softly call out, "Morgan?"

She drew in a shallow breath, but didn't dare answer. He needed to think she'd fallen asleep in the corner.

"Morgan?" he called again, this time in a louder voice.

One of his hands broke the door's plane.

Come on. Just another two steps.

He was like a wary animal. Testing the air. She imagined him studying the dark clump in the corner. Wondering.

I'm sleeping, her mind called out, *it's safe. Come a little closer, just to make sure.*

His hand moved and she thought her prayers had been answered, but then another beam of light stabbed through the darkness. It was much brighter than the small flashlight she'd been given and it easily illuminated her trap.

A long silence, then, "Please, I don't want you to be afraid of me. You don't have to hide."

She didn't move. *Come in and find me.*

"I'd thought we'd made such good progress. We had talked about trust being the foundation of love," A deep sigh. "I wanted to trust you. Offered it to you. And this is how you repay me?"

His last words were pointed and full of resentment.

"I brought you dinner," he said as a shadow sailed into the room and thudded against the far wall. Some sort of sandwich, wrapped in green and white fast-food paper, fell to the floor. "And you want to hide, try to escape. Play games. I thought you were going to be different. Like Lauren. But you're not. You're just like the others. And just like the others, you've got to be punished."

Morgan's heart stopped as the pipe's metallic skin glinted in the flashlight's beam.

"You need to be taught a lesson in trust," he said as he stepped through the door.

Chapter 41

The cabin's air was stale and smelled like rotting leaves, and Ransom instantly knew they hadn't been only ten minutes late. He swept his flashlight's beam around the cabin. Shoddy furniture. A stack of old newspapers. Trash. Old bird droppings.

"I don't think he's been here for a few hours," Flynn said.

"Think he's still out there looking for Kristen?" Ransom asked.

"Maybe," Flynn said. "Or, if we're lucky, he's the one who got lost, and some hiker will find his bones in a few years."

Ransom went over and used the tip of his foot to lift up the corner of the topmost newspaper off the pile. A cloud of dust particles blossomed upward into his flashlight's beam. He used a hand to wave them away, and looked at the headline from 1994. NAFTA was coming into effect. Not current reading material.

"Or he ditched the car and found some other way out of here," he said.

Ransom and Flynn made a quick survey of the cabin and found nothing of immediate use.

"Damn," Flynn said, then he brought his radio up and said, "He's not here. I need someone to bring up the trucks and make sure the crime scene techs don't get lost on their way out here."

"I don't think they're going to find anything," Ransom said.

Flynn shook his head. "Me either."

"What about his car?"

Ransom whirled around. Laura was standing in the doorway. So much for staying behind until they told her it was clear.

She angled her thumb behind her. "Can't you find out who the guy is from his car's license plate?"

She was right of course. He'd been so focused on finding the guy *in* the cabin, he'd forgotten about the car.

"The car," Flynn said and began barking orders into his radio.

Morgan stepped into the center of the room, her hands held up, palms out. "I'm sorry," she said. "I didn't mean anything—"

He turned to face her, the flashlight blinding her. "I untied you, gave you a blanket and a light. And what do you do? You try to trick me."

"No, I—"

"Trust." He slammed the end of the pipe on the concrete floor again. "I trusted you."

Then he moved toward her, bringing the pipe up to strike.

All her self-preservation instincts told her to flee. To get as far away from this person as possible.

But there wasn't any place to go.

Then she remembered what she'd been told to do if she was ever confronted by a mountain lion or bear. If you turn to run, you become prey, and they'll chase after you. But if you stand your ground, they might believe you're their equal and not attack.

Fighting an overpowering urge to hide in the corner, she took a step toward him, arms open, non-confrontational. "I'm sorry," she said again. "I'm just so scared." She didn't cry, but her voice cracked with emotion. And it wasn't fake. She *was* scared. Scared shitless. "You understand, don't you? This is so new to me, and, I barely know you." She shielded her eyes from the light and took another step forward.

He was now about three feet from her. Frozen in place. Her boldness had confused him. At least for the moment.

"I was wrong to try to escape. I know that now," she said, winging the entire speech. She just hoped she didn't say anything to trigger his rage. "But trust works both ways. I need to know I can trust you. And trust is something that takes time. If you hurt me now for a little mistake on my part, how am I going to trust you in the future?"

"But you wanted to leave—"

"I don't want to stay with someone who's going to beat me, can't you see that? I want to love someone who loves me back. I can only love someone who's kind and thoughtful." She took another step, the light searing her eyes. "Love the sort of man who brought me a blanket and a toilet," she nodded toward the spilled food, "and a nice dinner."

"You're just saying that!" he screamed, but he made no move to harm her.

She wondered how he was going to take her next words. But she had made it this far by her intuition, so she said, "The others, they never loved you. They tried to escape, didn't they?"

He said nothing.

So she kept going.

"And you beat them for breaking your trust."

"They needed to be taught a lesson."

She took her final leap of faith. "I want to be like Lauren."

He staggered backward as if she'd hit him in the gut. "Lauren …" he said in a soft voice.

"I know you love her," she said, "and I want to be like her … be her. But you have to help me."

His eyes were focused on her, and at the same time, not on her.

"What's another element of love?" she continued.

He didn't answer.

"Forgiveness. We need to learn to forgive if we're ever going to learn to love each other." She took a deep breath to calm her shaking hands. Then she reached out for his arm.

He jumped at her touch. She saw the pipe start its downward arch and knew she'd gone too far.

She wanted to close her eyes. Watching the pipe as it flashed toward her was like watching a movie of your own death. But she couldn't break her gaze. To do so was a sign of weakness, and the big cat would pounce. And it would show a lack of trust. Using more willpower than she ever knew she had, she kept her eyes locked on his. She would meet whatever came with her eyes on him. And he would have to look into hers as she died.

Her hand touching his bare arm, her eyes joined with his, she waited for the pipe's blow. The instant before it connected with her skull, he adjusted the pipe's trajectory and she only felt a cool breeze as it swept by, less than an inch away.

The tip of the pipe clunked against the floor next to her feet and she let out the air she'd been holding in her lungs. She squeezed his arm. "Thank you."

He pulled his arm free and cupped her chin with his hand. He wasn't rough, but she wouldn't have called it a tender touch either.

"I forgive you," he said. "And I do understand. We started off on a bad foot and I'm willing to start over."

"Me too," she said.

He moved closer, brought her chin upward and she thought he was going to kiss her, but he stopped just inches from her face. "But don't ever try to leave me again."

Then he bent over, picked up the sandwich and walked out of the room. The door locked behind him.

She sank to her knees, all of her strength evaporating as relief flooded through her. She had managed to cheat a cruel beating and possibly her own death. But she wasn't out of the woods yet. Not by a long shot.

He was going to come back and make her own up to her words. Expect her to love him. To be like Lauren. And she held no illusions as to what that would involve.

She moved over to the corner and wrapped herself up in the blanket. She wasn't gong to let that happen. Not while she was able to think … and act.

But she had to be careful. The look in his eyes told her he would kill her if he caught her trying to escape again.

She had to make the next one count.

It would be her last chance.

Laura was wrong about the car, but it wasn't her fault. The car turned out to be a rental. Picked up two days ago at a Hertz office on Indian School Rd in Phoenix.

It had taken almost two hours to get the information from the rental car and credit card companies. This was due to Flynn having to relay the information via radio and the multiple favors he had to call in to bypass a warrant for the information.

In the end, it didn't matter.

The name that came back was Robert Kelvin Jenkins. The credit card was new. Active for less than a week. It listed Jenkins' address as one that turned out to be a pawnshop in Phoenix. A search of Arizona's DMV computers showed no Robert Kelvin Jenkins registered in Arizona.

Jenkins, or whatever his real name was, had used a fake ID and credit card. Their only hope in finding out his real name was through any fingerprints or items he'd left behind in the car.

While Ransom watched the crime scene techs work over the car, he didn't hold much hope for either. The guy was smart. He wasn't going to give it to them easily. He looked at his watch: 8:30. Shit. This was going to be the night he was going to start being a real father to Morgan, begin his new life. And he was already blowing it.

Over three hours late for dinner. And no way to call her to explain: no cell phone service this far out. He wondered if she would forgive him for his latest transgression, or if this would be the last straw in their relationship. With the investigation into the man's identity going nowhere fast, he was getting antsy to get back to Sedona and ask for her forgiveness.

He called over to Flynn. "Can I get a ride back to my car?"

Flynn looked up. "Too boring for ya?"

"I'm in deep shit with my daughter. And the longer I stay here, the deeper I dig myself."

"You seem to be jumping from one shithole to another," Flynn said with a wide grin, then called one of his men over and told him to give Ransom and Laura a ride back to their car.

"I'll call you if we come up with anything," Flynn called out as their truck sped away.

Ransom waved, but he doubted he'd be hearing from Flynn anytime soon.

The officer driving out did so at a much more leisurely pace than their ride in, and Ransom kept checking his cell phone for service.

Laura took his hand in hers. "She'll forgive you," she said with enough confidence that he almost believed her.

Forgiveness. He thought about Trevor, and wondered if he would ever be able to forgive his wife. Or himself. A week ago, he would have said there wasn't a chance in hell. But now, after meeting Laura, all her talk about Trevor's spirit, he could see that it was at least a possibility. Before he could concentrate on that, he needed to make amends with Morgan.

As if on cue, his phone beeped to let him know he had service again. He punched in Morgan's cell number. No answer.

Did she see his number on the Caller ID and was ignoring him? He wouldn't have blamed her, but it wasn't like her. The ringing stopped, and the phone switched to her voicemail.

"Morgan, it's … it's …" he stumbled, "it's your dad. I'm sorry." He took a deep breath. "I'm really sorry. I thought we had the guy I've been looking for. I'll make it up to you … I promise. Please call me." Another long pause, then, "I love you."

He clicked the phone shut and stared at it for a long moment. It had been over two years since he'd said those three words to her.

To anyone.

He felt eyes on him and looked up to see they were Laura's. She was smiling. "Not bad, G-man, not bad."

Saying those words made him feel better, but it didn't last long. Where was Morgan? Why hadn't she left a message on his phone? He couldn't stop the sick feeling in the well of his gut from blossoming.

He called Laura's home phone. No one picked up. Another message, this one straight to the point, "Morgan, it's your dad, call me."

He told himself she was okay, that it was like what had happened this morning. She'd just left her cell phone in her car. But something told him this was different. This was really bad.

So he called Hilderman. He didn't answer either.

Where the hell is everyone?

As he was starring at the color LCD screen, his voice mail caught up with him and a screen popped up to say he'd missed four incoming calls. He pressed the button to view the calls.

All the calls had come from the same number. A number he knew well. But it wasn't Morgan's. It was Phillips. Four calls, four messages. Probably just wanting Ransom to come back to Phoenix; his boss had enough savvy not to fire him via voice mail.

He would wait to do that in person.

And Ransom wasn't going to give him the opportunity.

Not tonight.

There would be time for that tomorrow.

He pushed his job-related trouble to the back of his mind and tried to focus on the task at hand. Finding Morgan.

He called her cell phone three more times on their way back to Sedona. Same results.

Ten miles from Sedona, his phone rang.

Finally.

"Morgan," he said, snapping the phone open with a flick of his wrist.

"Sorry, boss," Hilderman's voice sounded, "it's just me."

Not bothering with pleasantries, Ransom asked, "Have you seen Morgan? I can't get hold of her."

"Not since yesterday."

"Where have you been?"

"My brother's."

"You were at the restaurant all this time?" Ransom wondered how much the man ate in one day.

"No," Hilderman said. "He's got an old ranch out in the middle of nowhere near Cottonwood. Just wanted to get away from all this stuff for a while."

"Where are you now?"

"On 89A, heading back into town. Should be there in twenty minutes or so."

"Keep an eye out for Morgan's car, then meet me at Laura's."

"I'm sure she's fine," Hilderman said, "She's probably … shit—" then nothing but silence.

Ransom's hair stood up on its ends. "Hilderman?"

No response.

He stole a quick peek at the phone's display. The call had been cut.

He redialed Hilderman's phone, but it went to straight to voicemail.

First Morgan, now Hilderman.

What the hell is going on?

Chapter 42

When Ransom pulled into Laura's drive, saw the dark house and Morgan's car parked outside, he went into full panic mode. He was right behind Laura as she stormed through the front door.

"Morgan!" he called out.

A heavy silence greeted them.

It didn't take long to confirm his fears. The house was empty.

He collapsed onto one of the dining room chairs. Morgan should be here. She wasn't on a stroll to the store this time. Laura came up behind him and put her arm around his shoulders. She started to say something, but a knock on the door made both of them jump.

For an instant, relief swept through him, then he heard Hilderman's voice. "Hey, boss, you there?"

Laura went to the door and opened it. Hilderman's tremendous frame filled the doorway.

"What happened to you?" Ransom asked.

Hilderman held up his cell phone. "Phone went dead."

"You didn't see—?"

He shook his head. "Didn't see her." He hadn't moved from the door; his eyes were still on Ransom. "By the look on your face, I'm guessing you didn't find the guy in Flagstaff."

Ransom looked at the floor. "We missed him … again."

"What happened?"

Ransom waved his question away with a hand. "Later. We need to find Morgan. Call dispatch and have them—"

"Parker gave me a vacation, remember?" Hilderman said.

"Damn."

"But I've still got friends. I'll make some calls." He turned to Laura. "Can I use your phone?"

She nodded and pointed out a cordless in the living room. Hilderman moved from the doorway and Laura went to shut the door behind him. She stopped halfway and looked back at Hilderman. "You hurt yourself, Hildy?"

"What?" He turned around, a confused look on his face.

"There's blood on the door."

Ransom was on his feet and at the door in two heartbeats. Dark-red blood stained the edge of the door just above the handle. He reached down to touch it. Dry. It was hours old.

Ransom's heart dropped to his gut.

The blood was definitely not Hilderman's.

It had been ten minutes since Hilderman made the call to Parker. Ten frantic minutes. They'd made a thorough search of the house and found nothing out of the ordinary—besides the blood on the door. But outside, it was a different story. Under a flashlight's glare, Ransom found another small spattering of blood near the street. Then, in Morgan's car, he found her phone, all of his messages on it.

She wasn't going to be returning his calls anytime soon.

Morgan! She was gone. This is exactly what he feared most. Jesus, he was barely able to control the fear burning inside him. He resisted the urge to vomit as cold sweat soaked his clothes. He wanted to punch out a window, shout out in anger, curl up in a ball and cry.

But none of those things would get Morgan back. Dwelling on what had happened wouldn't get him any closer to her. He had to control his emotions. Concentrate on positive actions. Be strong.

Somehow, he was going to get her back.

Time.

Strength.

The words came to him, but he had no idea from where.

Time.

Strength.

The words kept repeating themselves like a song stuck in his head.

A police cruiser rolled up, lights on, but no sirens. Ransom stepped up to the car.

Parker rolled down window. "What is it now? If you think—"

"Can it, Parker." Ransom leaned inside the car. "This isn't about you and me. This is about my daughter. She's been abducted."

"Abducted?" Parker's eyes shifted left and right, as if he were watching his stock go down the drain. "By who?"

"If I knew who took her, do you think I'd be talking to you right now?"

Parker shoved open the door and Ransom stepped back to let him out. "How do you know she just didn't decide to go for a late-night walk?"

Ransom explained the situation as he led Parker to Laura's front door. Parker bent down and studied the bloodstains for a long moment.

When he looked up, his eyes met Ransom's. "This isn't some bullshit ploy to stay in town longer, work on the Adams' case?"

If Ransom wasn't so distraught, he would have torn off Parker's head for the comment. Instead, he just shook his head. He needed Parker's help right now. Parker and his officers would be Ransom's best bet at finding Morgan. He couldn't do it alone.

Satisfied, Parker started barking orders into his radio.

Time.

Strength.

Those words. They seemed to comfort him. He didn't know why, but he knew he needed both to get Morgan back.

Morgan didn't sleep at all during the night. At least, she assumed it was night. Inside her dungeon, it was impossible to tell. She had no sense of day or night. No watch or cell phone. All she had to go on was her internal clock, and it told her it was sometime early in the morning. She switched on the flashlight, stretched to work out the kinks in her back and neck from the hours spent on the hard floor, and used the bathroom.

She thought about what she'd told her captor last night. Lies to appease him. Save her skin to fight another day. And *this* was going to be that day. It didn't matter what she said last night, she wasn't going to be Lauren, or any of the others. She knew he'd killed them after he was done having his fun. Just like he would with her.

She wasn't going to be here that long. She was going to escape … or die trying. No way was she going to allow him to do what she knew he wanted to.

No way.

But first things first. Her stomach grumbled. She hadn't eaten in almost twenty-four hours. She felt weak. She needed food and water to bolster her energy. And that meant dealing with him.

The thought made her stomach knot, but she pushed away her revulsion, took a deep breath and knocked softly on the wooden door.

"Hello?" she called out in a pleasant voice. "I'm hungry. And thirsty."

No response.

She knocked a little harder and repeated herself.

Nothing.

She walked back to the toilet, sat down on its lid. She would wait a while, then try again. Banging relentlessly on the door would give him the wrong impression. She wanted him to believe she was willing to stay here under her own free will. His twisted mind would be eager to believe her.

Then, when he let his guard down, she would act.

She just hoped that door would open before he acted on the lust she'd seen in his eyes.

It had been a long, terrifying night. He'd spent most of it cruising around Sedona in his car, searching for Morgan, and coordinating the search with Parker. He'd just returned to Laura's. Empty handed. He looked across her dining room table, which Parker had turned into a makeshift operations center. Parker was talking to one of his officers. After listening to his report, he gave him new orders and the officer left in a rush. Parker turned and saw Ransom eyeing him. He shook his head, but Ransom already knew the bad news.

Morgan had simply vanished.

He wanted to blame Parker, but couldn't. Although they still weren't buddies, he had to admit that Parker was doing everything within his power to find Morgan, including issuing an AMBER Alert. Ransom didn't know if it was because Parker didn't care whose daughter it was, or that another missing, and possibly murdered, girl in his little tourist town was going to be bad for business and might cost him his job.

Ransom didn't care. As long as they found Morgan.

He stared down at his half-filled cup of coffee hoping for a clue to who had taken Morgan, but the dark liquid wasn't giving away any secrets.

The crime tech had taken samples of the blood and confirmed it was Morgan's type. DNA testing would take days or weeks, depending on the backlog. No anomalous fingerprints had been found, and after talking with the neighbors, the only cars seen at Laura's the previous day were those he had already known about: his own, Morgan's, Laura's, Laura's father and Hilderman's.

Did the guy just walk up and take her away? Ransom didn't think so. You couldn't walk down the street with a hostage … or a body over your shoulder. That meant a car. The guy got lucky, slipped in and out without anyone noticing. But that wasn't too surprising. Only three of Laura's neighbors had a good view of her drive and front door, and two of them worked during the day. The third was a mother of two young children. She'd been leaving for afternoon preschool when she noticed Laura's father pulling into the driveway to tell Laura he was going away, and was coming back from picking them up when she saw Hilderman's car in Laura's drive.

Ransom turned his attention to Hilderman, who was helping Laura cook up pancakes for the officers coming and going. Hilderman had said he'd stopped by earlier in the day to see if he could help with anything. No one had been home. He said he'd just figured Morgan and Laura had been with Ransom.

If only.

All his gut instincts told him that the same guy who'd taken Amanda now had Morgan. The thought made him sick, as if his entire being were being sucked into a black hole. It was the same feeling he'd had when Trevor was taken away. But worse. Although Trevor hadn't been killed instantly, Ransom knew he hadn't suffered much.

Then his mind flashed back to the pictures he'd seen of Amanda Pearce. The sheer terror in her eyes. The words scribed with a knife in her skin. She had gone through unspeakable horrors. Before he could stop it, his mind had replaced Amanda's face with Morgan's.

Was she still alive? Or had she already been cut to pieces?

Stop it! he told himself. Laura had told him to think positively. *Concentrate on what you can control. Intend for Morgan to be safe.*

He took a bite from the pancake on his plate. He forced it down with a gulp of coffee.

Another officer came through the door. Mosner. He looked like he'd been up all night, and looked expectantly at the table.

Seeing the hunger in the man's eyes, Ransom picked up his half-eaten plate of pancakes and stood up. "I'm stuffed," he lied. "Sit down and grab a bite."

Mosner took a seat, and Hilderman brought him over a plate stacked with pancakes. Ransom had asked Parker if Hilderman could be temporarily put back on the force, but Parker had refused, saying it was out of his hands until the board of inquiry ruled. Hilderman merely shrugged at the news and continued helping any way he could—in an unofficial capacity.

Parker and Mosner started conversing about the plans for the day and Ransom tried to listen, but he couldn't concentrate. He needed five minutes away from everything. His eyes were tired from countless hours of talking with people, scanning the dark city for any shadows that could have been Morgan or her abductor.

He trudged off to the living room, looking at the couch as a temporary refuge. Crackers lay on the one of the armrests. She opened an eye as he approached. He thought he could sit on the far end, but Crackers made it clear that wasn't an option.

Not wanting to start a fight he knew he couldn't win, he dropped into the reclining chair. He wanted to rest. Just for a minute.

The next thing he knew, someone was touching his hand. His eyes snapped open. Laura was standing over him.

"Sorry," she said, "I didn't mean—"

"How long was I out?" he said jumping to his feet.

"Half an hour."

"Shit. Anything happen?"

She shook her head. "Not really. Parker left for the hospital. Evan woke up. He's going to be okay, might even go home sometime later this morning."

"That's good," he said. And it was, though he felt a tinge of jealousy. Trevor had never been given a second chance. And now, Morgan might be taken from him.

He pushed the thought from his mind. "Who's in charge now?"

"Mosner."

"Great." He liked Mosner less than Parker. "What about Hilderman?" he said as he started for the kitchen.

"He decided to go and look for Morgan."

"That's what I should be doing too," he said.

"Wait a sec," she said, stepping in front of him, "I need to talk to you."

It was the solemn tone of her voice, not her body that stopped him.

"What is it?" he said.

She couldn't meet his eyes.

"What is it?" he repeated, a ripple of fear streaming through him.

"I wanted … to make sure … before I told you, but I still don't know whether I should."

"Tell me what?" He put both hands on her shoulders and she looked up at him.

It took her a few moments to answer. "Do you believe I can talk with angels?"

Now it was his turn to look away. "I'm not sure." He took a deep breath. "I know you aren't some crackpot, reading palms to unsuspecting saps, but … I just don't know…."

"Fair enough," she said. "I didn't expect you to embrace the idea."

"What does this—?"

"Even if you don't believe … do you still want to know what they say?"

"Why not?" he answered.

"Because it might not be good news," she said. Her shoulders slumped and she almost fell into him. He wrapped his arm around her as she began to quietly sob, mumbling the words, "Not good news. Not good news at all."

Chapter 43

He held her for a long time. Her arms were around him too, her body pressed against his, face buried into his shoulder. He liked the way she felt. It was as if they were pieces of a puzzle, connecting for the first time. Under different conditions, it might have been sexual, but at the moment it just felt … right. After a while, her sobs quieted and she gently pulled away.

"I'm sorry," she said, wiping her tears away with her forearm.

"Don't be. It gave me a chance to hold you. And I've been wanting to do that for a long time."

Her eyes opened wide in mock surprise. "So, there are some feelings underneath that cold G-man exterior after all?"

Ransom didn't answer right away. He was still in shock from what had just come out of his mouth. He hadn't planned to say anything like that. The words just spilled out. But that didn't mean they weren't true. They were. And it felt good to say them. He took a deep breath and decided to keep going.

"Laura, listen. I want to be honest with you.…"

"Okay," she said. Hesitant.

"You're the reason I came up here."

"I called you—"

"No, not because of what you told me about Craig— Well, that was part of it. But when I heard your voice … I don't know … I just felt …" He didn't know how to put words to it.

She nodded in agreement, as if she had experienced the same thing.

"When this is all over, I'd like to see you, maybe we could go out to dinner, see a movie.…"

"Are you asking me out on a date?"

"Yeah, I guess I am."

A devilish grin spread across her face. "That's a long drive from Phoenix," she said, having some fun with him.

"I was thinking about staying up here for a while. I don't think I'll have a job to go home to anyway." He could play a little too.

"Hotels in Sedona might be a little expensive for the unemployed."

"I was hoping to stay here," he said, then angled his thumb toward the orange tabby on the couch. "That is, if she'll let me."

Laura moved back into his arms. "She's extremely stubborn, but I think I can talk her into putting up with you for a few days."

His eyes searched hers for a long time. After a few heartbeats, he pulled back to look at her, felt his blood rushing through him in ways he hadn't experienced in years.

"Maybe, you, Morgan and I—"

She jumped as if she'd just touched a cactus. "Morgan," she said, "Morgan … that's what I needed to talk to you about."

"We're going to find her," he said.

She shook her head, looked down at the floor. "I'm going to just come out and tell you. Even if you're not ready to believe me. I can't keep it to myself."

"What is it?" he asked, feeling to cold tendrils of panic creeping into his mind.

She started to cry again. "I saw Gabe … standing over you. And I asked him if everything was going to be all right."

Oh, God.

"He wouldn't answer me directly. He kept saying, 'We are here on earth to learn, Laura.'"

"What about Morgan?" Ransom asked, his chest so tight he was barely able to get out the words.

She shook her head. "Gabe told me some lessons are harder than others."

Ransom didn't say anything. It was as if he'd lost all the air in his lungs. He stared out the living room window for a while. If only Morgan would walk past, come through the door, say it was all a mistake. That she'd gone out and forgot to tell anyone. She would say she was sorry and he'd hug her and everything would be okay. But he knew it wasn't going to happen. She wasn't going to just walk away from this.

He returned his gaze to Laura. "What exactly did Gabe tell you?"

She looked away, unable to meet his eyes anymore. After a few moments, she said, "He talked about lessons. Said we are all here to learn. That lessons can be difficult. Very difficult."

"What lessons?"

"The words *family* and *forgiveness* kept appearing in my mind, he told—"

"Wasn't Trevor enough?" he said, balling his hands into tight fists. "Now, they're after Morgan?"

"No, you don't understand, it wasn't just about you. This is about *me* too. This is my final exam."

"I understand just fine," he said, his anger not allowing him to hear her words. "This is my own personal hell, and they want to take Morgan away from me too."

She sighed, as if giving up on what she'd really wanted to say, and was drawn into his argument. "It isn't up to Gabe, or any other angel either. They're here to help you. That's all."

"Help me?" he roared. "*This* is how they help me? That's what you believe?"

She put a calming hand on his shoulder. "Before you were born, your spirit, your soul, decided which lessons you would learn during this lifetime. Sometimes those lessons are very difficult. Especially if you resist them."

"Are you saying I'm responsible for Trevor's and possibly Morgan's deaths?"

"Of course not. It doesn't work like that. But, if you are here to learn forgiveness, you'll invite situations that tend to teach you what you're supposed to learn. It's similar to people who always expect bad things, then those bad things happen to them."

"Like Ritchie Valens dying in a plane wreck? He was terrified of flying. Dreamed about dying in a crash."

She nodded. "And you'll continue to go down the path you've chosen until you learn why you're here."

He shook his head. Although much of what Laura was saying rang true, he found he couldn't accept it. It was too much. Too new. And, he thought he had learned how to forgive. Hadn't he vowed to work on that last night? Then why had Morgan been taken away from him? Maybe vowing wasn't enough. Maybe he had to actually *do* something.

The image of Trevor's marble headstone flashed before him. He remembered how it had looked just a few days ago when he'd visited his son's grave. The gray headstone was small and insignificant among all the hundreds of others. An inscription in carved black letters read, *Earth has no sorrow that Heaven cannot heal. We entrust you into your angel's loving arms.*

Sorrow. Another understatement. If his wife—

He felt the familiar sensation of anger—flaming rage—begin to burn inside him.

Maybe he would never learn how to truly forgive. Maybe it was already too late.

Morgan tried the door four more times, each about an hour apart and all with a similar lack of response. Still wrapped in the blanket, she surveyed her room again, looking for anything she might have missed. Anything she could use to help her escape.

She started with the door, spent another ten minutes trying to find a way out. But it was no less impenetrable than it had been last night. Disheartened, she turned her attention to the gray cinderblock walls. They looked even more formidable than the door, that's why she hadn't spent much time on them before. Besides, she remembered that he'd dragged her down a small flight of stairs, and so the only thing behind the blocks was tons of dirt.

But right now, all she had was time. Using the flashlight, she went over every inch, every joint, every imperfection.

She was on her hands and knees, face just above the floor when she saw it: a miniscule crack in the joint between two blocks.

She moved in closer and her heart skipped a beat. It wasn't a crack. It was too straight and too regular to be natural. And so fine, if she'd been another foot away, she would've missed it. No wonder she didn't see it last night.

She traced the line with her finger until it stopped at a small slot chiseled along the crack on each end. Her brows furrowed as she pondered its use. Maybe someone could use a small screwdriver—or fingertips—to pry the block away from the wall.

A rush of hope coursed through her as she found the crack outlined the entire block. And the one next to it. And another. She flew across the floor, her knees scraping against the concrete.

Six blocks. Six!

Someone had painstakingly cut through the joints of six blocks. Maybe someone *had* found a way to escape. Somehow they'd dug a tunnel outside.

Greedy hands started prying out one of the center blocks. But she stopped after only a few seconds.

What about him?

He could return any minute. What if he found her trying to escape again?

She knew the answer to that question.

He would kill her. Beat her to death with that damn pipe. No twisting of words on her part would save her this time.

She weighed her options. Act now, or wait until later. He had left her alone for a few hours last night while he slept. Maybe she should wait … No! She wasn't going to be here when he returned.

She jammed her fingertips in the slots on each side of the block and pulled. The heavy block slid out easier than expected. As if someone had done it many times before.

A bad feeling erupted in the pit of her stomach an instant before the smell hit her. The same sour, rancid odor she'd smelled last night, this time ten times stronger, caused her to pull back.

"No, no, no," she whispered as the flashlight reflected off a clear plastic container about the size of a shoebox. Written in black letters on the end was the name, *Amanda Pearce*. It was the girl who had been abducted a few weeks ago. The reason her father was here.

Tenderly, she reached in and pulled the container from its resting place, not wanting to look at it. Peering inside the cavity, she saw the hard packed soil behind the blocks had been carved out with a sharp instrument like a gardening trowel. She swiveled her flashlight left and right. The cavern didn't extend too far back. Maybe sixteen inches. But it was as wide as the six blocks were long. And she could see other plastic containers hidden behind each block. She wondered which one belonged to Lauren.

She felt her stomach turn inside out and had to will herself not to vomit, now thankful she hadn't eaten for almost twenty-four hours.

This was no escape route.

It was a trophy room.

With almost inhuman determination, she returned her attention to the container she'd pulled from the wall. She didn't want to open it, but she had to be sure.

She covered her nose with one hand. Popped open the lid with the other.

Snap.

The smell. God. She breathed through her mouth, sucking the air through her teeth as though they would protect any foreign material from entering her body.

She couldn't do this. She wanted to go back to her corner, close her eyes, go back to sleep. Wake up from this nightmare. She wasn't strong enough. Not for this.

But her hand continued to pry off the lid. She watched as if she were viewing a movie. Pretended she wasn't actually here. Her hand controlled by some actress in a bad horror film.

Then the lid was off and she looked into the container.

"God, no," she managed to rasp. Although she'd suspected what the container held, she wasn't prepared for it. Not even close. Four partially decomposed fingers and a thick mass of straight black hair, toes and other small body parts she didn't recognize lay on the bottom of the container.

What was left of Amanda Pearce. After he got through with her.

She quickly sealed the container and slid it back into its hiding place. Then the block. Brushing away the few remnants of dirt littering the floor, she made sure there was no evidence of her intrusion. He wouldn't be happy with her discovery.

Crawling to the far corner of the room, she brought her knees up to her chest and hugged herself. She couldn't control the primeval terror—the absolute horror—coursing through her. Ending up in a plastic box hidden in a wall as another one of his grisly trophies was beyond any nightmare she could have imagined.

She pictured what the wall would look like with a seventh block excavated. A seventh container hidden in the earthen tomb. The seventh name written on the side:

Her name.

Chapter 44

He came for her about an hour after the batteries in her flashlight died. She was still in the corner, wrapped in the blanket, arms around her knees, when she heard the door unlock.

She took a deep breath and went through her mantra again.

Time.

Strength.

Escape.

It had helped. The panic raging inside her had calmed and her mind was clear. Focused on what she needed to do. Start acting. But not too much. As she saw it, the best way to play it was with cautious receptiveness. If she laid it on too thick, he'd see right through it.

The door opened and her room filled with light, but he didn't enter. He was being cautious, too. Wary of her last attempt to trick him. Although he spoke a good game about trust, he didn't trust her.

Right back at you, asshole, she thought, but she raised her hand and waved in a friendly greeting.

"Good afternoon, Morgan" he said.

Afternoon. *Jesus, time flies when you're having fun.*

She said, "Hello." Her tone wary, but approachable.

"Something to eat?"

"That would be wonderful. I'm starving." She didn't move from her corner. Didn't want to give him the impression that she was going to make for the door.

Using his feet, he scooted two large paper grocery sacks into the room. Next came a powerful lantern.

She blinked at the sudden brightness.

Then he entered, dragging the pipe across the concrete floor, and closed the door.

She shuddered to herself.

For a heartbeat she thought about making her escape attempt right then, but the time wasn't right. She offered him a guarded smile. "What did you bring to eat?"

"Sandwiches," he said. His face brightened at her apparent interest. He reached into one of the bags and pulled out two sandwiches wrapped in Subway paper. "I've got roast beef or turkey, whatever you like—"

He must have seen her face drop. "What is it?"

"I … I'm a vegetarian."

His smile faded. "A vegetarian?" He looked at the sandwiches in his hands. "I didn't know…. I'm sorry. I should've asked. I didn't even think…."

She could see the tendons in his neck starting to bunch and his grip on the pipe tighten. A bad sign.

"How could you? We're just getting to know each other."

"But you're hungry, and now I gone and messed everything up," he said, berating himself.

"It's okay. I deal with this all the time." She spoke in a soothing voice. He was starting to lose control. She needed to calm him down. "You can have the meat and I'll have a veggie-bread sandwich."

"But—"

"It's fine. Really." Keeping the blanket draped around her, she slowly gained her feet. "What else did you bring?"

He stared down into the bags for a long moment, as if deciding if it truly was okay.

"Do you have anything to drink?" she asked. "I'm thirsty too." And she was. But more important, she didn't want him obsessing about the vegetarian thing. She needed to keep him calm and rational. If he went crazy, she knew she'd end up in one of those containers hidden behind the wall.

Thankfully, her question broke his fixation and he looked up at her. "Sure. I've got Coke and diet Sprite"

"Ooooh, Coke. My favorite," she purred, even though she almost never drank the stuff.

His smile came back to his face.

She held out her hand. "How about I get our sandwiches ready while you do the drinks and whatever else you've got in there."

He passed over the two sandwiches. She sat down on top of the toilet and spread the two Subway wrappers on her knees. Then she removed the turkey from one sandwich and stuffed it into the middle of the other. She traded him the roast beef/turkey sandwich for a bag of chips and a Coke.

She took a bite of her sandwich. "Mmmmm," she said.

"Really?" His eyes told her he wanted her to like it.

She nodded and took another bite. The sandwich was nothing but lettuce, tomatoes, onions, cheese, mayo and bread, but given how hungry she was, it tasted wonderful.

She was halfway through the sandwich before she had a drink of Coke and looked up at him. He was still standing by the door, pipe in one hand, sandwich in the other. He hadn't taken a single bite.

"Not hungry?"

He shook his head.

She found his eyes. Watching her. An intense hunger within. But he hadn't lied; he wasn't hungry for his sandwich.

He was hungry for something else entirely.

For her.

She had another bite, her eyes still on him.

His silence was spooking her. Last night, he'd seemed to want to talk, but now he was just staring at her. Watching her. Wanting her.

She needed to get him talking. Get his mind on something other than her. But what in the hell was she supposed to say? *Did you have a good day today, honey? How was work? When are you going to kill me?* Or how about, *I hope you choke to death on your sandwich?*

She felt a cold wind … no, not wind, in fact the air wasn't moving at all … it was more like the temperature dropped for an instant. The hair on her arms stood straight up. It felt as though a storm was building from *inside* the room. The air charged with static electricity.

Something was coming. She could feel it. But what it was, she had no idea. She just knew she needed to be ready when it came. She unwrapped the blanket from her shoulders and let it fall to the ground. The blanket would restrict her actions if she had to move quickly.

Then she saw it was a mistake.

His eyes traveled down her body, hesitating at her breasts and then just below her waist. "You are so beautiful," he said.

"Thank you," she said, the sandwich almost coming back up.

He went to take a drink of soda, but almost missed his mouth.

"Thanks for the sandwich," she said, then not knowing what else to say, "What are we having for dessert?"

He didn't answer. He seemed to be in a lust-filled trance. "I love you so much," he mumbled at last.

She took a long drink of Coke. Stalling. "You're so kind."

He licked his lips. "I want to make love to you," he said, his voice raspy, full of feral desire.

And there it was. She'd thought she might have a couple of days, at least twenty-four hours, but he wasn't going to wait. "Let's finish dinner first," was all her terrified mind could come up with. If she ate at a snail's pace, that would give her five or ten minutes. Not long.

He grinned and took a big bite of bread and meat, now having a good reason to finish. He was rushing now. Damn. Why couldn't she have said, "Let's wait until the next solar eclipse?"

"We'll be so much in love," he said gulping down his mouthful of turkey and roast beef. "You'll see. You're different than the others."

He shifted his stance and she could see that he was already erect.

Jesus, no… he wasn't going to wait.

She said the one thing that she thought might slow him down. "Tell me about Lauren."

His eyes went wide and at first she thought she'd pushed him too far. Then his head bent forward and he looked at his feet. "Lauren," he mumbled.

"Tell me about her," she said.

He didn't say anything.

"If you want me to be like her, I need to know what she was like." Nothing. "Was she beautiful?"

He nodded. Slow. As if in a trance.

"What did she look like?"

This brought his eyes back up to her. "Like you."

A chill shook her to the core.

"Like the others," he said.

She thought about the six plastic tubs behind the wall. Wondered if Lauren, or pieces of her, lay in one of them. Maybe she'd been his first killing. Or … or maybe she was the *reason* for the others.

"She had the most beautiful hair. Black as the night. It always smelled so nice." His eyes went from Morgan's face down to her hands. "And her fingers. Long. Sensual. The way she held my hand, touched my face, guided me inside her. Let me love her."

His face was becoming flushed, his breathing rapid. He was becoming aroused again.

"She sounds wonderful," she said, needing to steer him away from her physical attributes. "Now tell me what was she like."

He took a deep breath, and for a long moment was silent in thought. When he finally spoke, his answer surprised her. "Giving."

She nodded, letting him continue.

"And she loved me. For who I was."

"Who was that?"

Anger flashed in his eyes. "Not the dumb shit my father thought I was."

She took a guess. "But you married her anyway?"

He gave her a strange look, then shook his head. "I married a good woman. A fine woman. But I haven't found anyone who could love me like she did." His eyes found hers. "Not yet."

Chapter 45

She didn't want to ask the question. Didn't want to know the answer. But she found herself asking anyway. "What … what happened to her?"

"My father. He found out about us. Went crazy. Started beating her. I tried to stop him, but I couldn't. He was too big. Too strong." Tears welled in his eyes. "He beat her. First with his fists, then with a hammer. She kept screaming for me to help her. But I couldn't. I was so scared." The tears flowed down his cheeks. "When she told him she would always love me, love me more than him, I finally gained my courage. I found an old pipe in the garage and while he beat her, I crushed in his head. Killed the son-of-a-bitch."

Jesus. She could hardly breath. "And Lauren?"

He wiped the tears from his face. "She was already dead."

The room went quiet. She watched him, his face twisted in his internal agony. And she almost felt sorry for him. Almost. After a few minutes, his face regained its hardened demeanor.

"That was a long time ago," he said. "And I can't bring her back."

He left unsaid the truth they both knew. *In his own way, he sure was trying.*

She put down her sandwich. She couldn't eat anymore. She already felt bile rising in her stomach.

He, on the other hand, was gulping down his sandwich. Speeding up the process. Becoming excited. "But … you … you're different. You understand. You know what I need."

He bit into his sandwich, tore off a huge mouthful of roast beef and turkey, and she felt another rush of cold air.

Getting her ready.

But for what?

Time.

It was against him. A relentless enemy that could not be stopped. No weapon, no amount of force or discussion would change its course. Time did not negotiate.

And he was losing the fight.

Ransom looked at his watch. Four-fifteen. The morning and most of the afternoon had slipped by without any information on Morgan. He knew they had long ago passed the golden twenty-four hours regarding missing persons. If this was a kidnapping, he would have heard from the kidnappers by now. No contact made Morgan's disappearance an abduction, not a kidnapping. And although he'd known this from the start, he also understood that each hour that went by, the chances of him finding Morgan alive decreased exponentially.

Deep within his heart, he felt Morgan slipping away. He tried to keep a spark of hope alive, but it was doused by overwhelming grief and guilt. Eating him up from the inside out.

After another fruitless day of looking for his daughter, he was back at Laura's dinning room table. Alone. Parker and his officers were all canvassing Sedona and the surrounding countryside. Laura was in the living room. She had left him alone for what he had to do.

He looked down at the cell phone on the table. It hadn't moved in the past ten minutes. Hadn't rung with good news—or, thankfully, bad. Still, he had made no attempt to pick it up to make *the call.*

He knew he should have done it earlier. When he'd discovered that Morgan was gone. But he couldn't. So much anger. So much guilt.

He took a deep breath. What had Laura said? He was here to learn a lesson.

Forgiveness.

It seemed impossible, but he couldn't put it off any longer.

Face your fears.

He picked up the phone and dialed. A number he hadn't used in over a year.

A familiar voice answered, "Hello." Morgan's mother. The woman he blamed for his son's death.

He leaned the pip against the wall and took the last bit of his sandwich. "You'll see, you're going to … going to …" He croaked.

For a long moment, Morgan thought he was unable to contain his lust, then she saw his eyes go saucer wide, hands go to his throat, begin to cough and wheeze.

He was choking! He had been in too much of a hurry to finish his damn sandwich!

She sprang in action, running for the door.

Even in his debilitated state, he stepped in front of her. But she shoved him aside, determination and fear doubling her strength.

She heard the *oomph* as his body slammed into the wall. Didn't even think about it. She was going through that door and nothing could stop her.

Her shoulder struck the door with such force it burst open, and she tumbled onto the concrete landing. Her knee cracked on the hard surface, shooting hot pain through her leg, but she didn't slow down. She began to crawl up the steep steps—

A strong hand grabbed her ankle, pulling her backward.

No!

She clawed at the concrete. But it was slick and she couldn't gain purchase.

She slid back into the room. Kicking, screaming. Then her eyes caught something to her right.

Or, the lack of something.

The pipe.

It should have been leaning against the wall. Right where he had put it.

But it was missing.

Gone.

She spun to her left. Just in time to see it arc down at her. And she knew she hadn't acted quickly enough.

Then her world went dark.

Chapter 46

"Hello?" his ex-wife said for the second time.

"Cathy?"

"Stuart?" she answered, unable to hide the surprise in her voice. "What are—?"

Not knowing how to put it any differently, he said, "I've got some terrible news."

A sharp intake of breath.

"Morgan's missing."

"Missing? Oh, God. How—?"

In short rapid sentences, he explained the situation to her. When he finished, he was met with heavy silence.

"Cathy? You okay?" he said, then regretted it. If she were to ask him the same stupid question two years ago, he would have exploded in rage. Yelling and screaming about how irresponsible she'd been.

Instead, her tone was quiet. "You've got to find her."

He didn't say anything.

"You've got to find her," she told him again.

He knew she wanted some reassurance, for him to tell her, without any doubt, that he would save their daughter. But he couldn't lie and he was stunned by what *did* come out of his mouth. "I'm sorry."

"For what?" she asked.

"For what?" he repeated, amazed that she'd even asked the question. "Morgan was my responsibility, and I … I … failed her. Failed to keep her safe. She's gone because—"

"You aren't to blame, Stuart."

Her words held no accusations. No blame. Only concern.

"I'm sorry," he said unable to stop himself.

"It's not your fault. Neither God, nor I, hold you responsible."

"No," he said. "I'm sorry … for everything." He sucked in a deep breath. "Trevor … I know you didn't mean … that the accident … it was an accident."

"Stuart," she said softly.

"I just wanted to say … to say … that I … I forgive you." He heard hushed crying on the other end of the line. "We *both* did things we shouldn't have. But we didn't intend to harm him. We loved our son and I'm sure each of us would trade our lives for his. I've learned a lot in the past few days. One, if … when … I find Morgan, I'm not going to push her away anymore. I've got to use my time with her to the best of my ability. Two, things happen in life for a reason and I can't spend the rest of my life full of anger and guilt. It's not much of a life."

He ended his soul-cleansing discourse breathing hard. It had been difficult, but he felt as though he was taking his first real breath after being trapped under dark ice for two years.

"Where can I meet you?"

He gave her directions to Laura's house.

"I'll be there in an hour and a half," she said. A moment of silence, then, "Do what you do best, Stuart. Find our daughter."

He clicked off and, hands shaking, placed the phone on the table.

Do what you do best, Stuart. Find our daughter.

She'd said it with a confidence he didn't feel. Hadn't felt for two years. He *had* been a good FBI agent. He used to have a knack for seeing things others had missed. Breaking cases down to their most simple layers. Sifting through all the frivolous crap and focusing on what was important. He'd solved many cases doing that. This was no different.

They were missing something. Something important. He needed to start at the beginning. Back to square one.

But, what did he really know?

He thought for a minute. First, Craig Adams was not a murderer. Weed through all the bullshit and there was no other reasonable conclusion. Then, if that was a fact, the next obvious step was that someone else killed Amanda Pearce. The same person who killed *and* framed Craig Adams. Why? Because Craig either knew who had murdered Amanda or was close to finding out.

And that person was someone he knew. Someone he trusted. Not the guy who had abducted Kristen Tovar.

And now he has Morgan. Took her from Laura's house in the middle of the day. With no sign of forced entry. Morgan was a smart girl, she wouldn't let someone in she didn't trust … or know … or both.

He went through all the people Morgan had met since she'd arrived at Sedona, at least that he knew about and could remember. The first person that came to mind was Hilderman.

Morgan knew and trusted him, that much he was certain. And so did Ransom for that matter. He just couldn't see Hilderman as a brutal killer. But his words to Laura the first time they spoke echoed in his mind, *I've seen fathers sexually abuse their kid, then threaten to kill them if they told anyone. Nothing surprises me anymore.* He tried to remember where Hilderman had been yesterday afternoon. His brother's ranch? Was that what he'd said? Okay, he'd check on that. Next.

Parker. Morgan had met him at city hall the night she arrived. Parker was the police chief, so he also had the built-in trust factor. At least for Morgan. Parker had been unreachable during Morgan's abduction, but appeared to be doing everything he could to find her.

Pearce. He'd been with Parker the first night, so Morgan knew who he was. But was there enough of a recognition factor to let him through Laura's door? Where was he when Morgan disappeared? Unknown. But, could he have killed *and* mutilated his own daughter?

End of list. At least as far as he knew. She could have met someone he didn't know about when she walked to the store yesterday morning. Maybe the store clerk, or someone while she was shopping? She hadn't said anything about meeting someone, but why would she?

Parker already had one of his officers retracing her steps and he hadn't come up with anything yet.

Like it or not, those three—Hilderman, Parker and Pearce—might be the only people she knew in Sedona, and therefore the best suspects.

But could it have been someone else? Maybe a mail carrier or UPS driver? She would trust them if they came to the door. That would make it an opportunistic abduction? Morgan was in the wrong place at the wrong time. He thought about it for a few minutes. It didn't feel right.

Trusting his gut instincts, he went to the final option. Maybe it was someone *he* had met? Someone with a grudge, and who could sweet-talk their way into having her open the door. Who else had he met during his time in Sedona?

Evan. Although Evan had almost pushed him off a cliff, he had just been released from the hospital. He wasn't in any condition to abduct Morgan.

Laura's father. It was obvious that he didn't care for Ransom, but what would he have to gain by abducting Morgan? And he'd left Sedona before Morgan went missing.

Who else? Who would Morgan open the door for?

A police officer. Anyone on Parker's payroll. What about Mosner? She would have opened the door for a cop. No questions asked.

But why—?

His cell phone chirped, startling him. It wasn't the ring of an incoming call, but a missed call. Weird. He hadn't heard it ring before. Then again, maybe someone had called when he was talking to Cathy, and he just hadn't heard the call-waiting click.

He picked it up and snapped it open.

Then his heart stopped. Cold.

He felt the edges of darkness creeping in on him and he could only stare at the name of the missed call.

Morgan.

Chapter 47

Morgan had called him!

"Laura," he called out, relief flooding through him. "Morgan just—"

His voice cut short as he turned toward the living room. Resting on top of the kitchen counter was a red cell phone. Silent and alone.

Morgan's cell phone.

"What is it?" Laura said, rushing into the room.

He didn't answer. Couldn't.

He looked back at his phone. Morgan's name was still displayed on the screen. He pressed the enter key and the call's information popped up. He recognized the number. It *was* Morgan's cell phone. And the time of the call? A little more than four minutes ago.

What was going on?

Laura caught the look in his eyes and said, "What's wrong?"

"I don't know." He handed her his phone. "I don't understand. It says Morgan tried to call me a few minutes ago, but her phone is right there." He pointed at Morgan's phone on the counter. "No one's been in here but me."

Laura studied the phone for a minute, then reached over and picked up Morgan's phone. She started pressing buttons. "Let's see. The last phone call from this phone was at 9:35 yesterday morning, to someone named Cathy."

"Morgan's mother," he said.

"Let's see something." She handed him his phone back, then started pushing more buttons. "Okay … here you are."

A few seconds later, his phone rang. Morgan's name appeared as an incoming call. He pressed the call key.

"Stuart?" Laura's voice came through the phone and from across the room.

He nodded and terminated the call. Then he compared the phone numbers of his last two phone calls.

Identical.

"How is that possible?" he asked no one in particular.

Laura said, "It could have been Morgan."

He stared dumbly at her, not understanding.

"She could be sending you a message."

"How—?" Then he had it. "Morgan's … she … she's dead."

Morgan smiled. She was so happy. Happier than she'd been in a long time.

"Come here, squirt," she said. God, how she'd missed him.

Trevor, his gap-toothed grin about ready to leap off his face, ran to her. She spread her arms wide and he slammed into her, almost knocking her down. Trevor had always liked to roughhouse. They hugged. Fierce and intense. Then came Mollie, wagging her tail so vigorously her entire body swayed side-to-side.

"I missed you," Trevor said.

"Me too."

She could feel the beat of his heart, his breath against her neck.

After a while, he pushed her away with a grin. "Enough of the mushy stuff," he said.

She ruffled his chestnut hair. "It's just so good to see you."

As she gave Mollie a much-anticipated scratch behind her ears, Trevor walked over to an old white refrigerator and popped open the door. "Want a soda?"

She said, "I'm good," then took a moment to check out her surroundings. They were in the kitchen of Grandpa Ransom's house. Bright sunlight filtered through the windows and it smelled like someone had been baking. Her stomach grumbled and she remembered that she was hungry. "I smell cookies."

She walked over and opened the oven door. Inside, a huge baking sheet was filled with cookies. She reached in and pulled out the cookie sheet; the smell of warm chocolate chip cookies, her favorite, drifted upward. Finding the biggest one, she scooped it off the baking tray and took a bite. Her taste buds erupted in pure ecstasy. Nothing ever tasted so good. She quickly finished it and grabbed another. She thought about asking Trevor if he had made the cookies, but decided it wasn't important.

She turned and saw that he was sitting at the kitchen table, sipping the Coke. "Want a cookie?" she said.

"Sure."

She brought him a cookie and sat down next to him. "Where's Papa and Grandma?"

"Papa's fishing. Grandma isn't here yet."

She chewed her cookie. She was so hungry.

Trevor did the same and he winked. "Cookies and Coke. Can't beat it." He gave a piece to Mollie and it disappeared in one gulp.

She shook her head. "Disgusting," she teased, but her own smile was fading. Her head had started to throb. Probably a sugar rush from the cookies. She put the half-eaten cookie down and picked up a glass of milk—though she couldn't remember getting one—and drank the cool liquid..

"Dad's coming," Trevor said without a preamble.

"Dad?"

Another grin. "Yeah, you know, the tall guy who—"

"I know who he is," she said, giving him the raised-eyebrow look.

"You need to go find him," he said, turning serious.

She rubbed her temples. The pain in her head seemed to be getting worse. "I want to stay with you."

Trevor's young, innocent eyes suddenly were filled with ancient wisdom, as though he'd lived millions of years. "You can't. You need to be strong and find Dad."

"Just a little longer?" she asked. "Maybe until Papa gets back from fishing."

He shook his head. "Papa would love to see you," he said, then he was next to her, his small hand on her shoulder. "But there isn't time."

"My head," she said. The throbbing had been replaced with hard pounding. "I need to rest."

He helped her stand. "Later."

He started walking her toward the door. Her vision darkened. Or maybe it was because the sunlight no longer streamed in through the windows. Somehow night had fallen, the sunlight replaced by a dark, bottomless void. The night seemed to draw all of the energy out of the house.

And for the first time since coming here, she was scared. Scared of what lay outside.

Then they were at the door and it was open to the darkness. Thunder rumbled, but she saw no flash of lightning. She turned to face Trevor. "Can't you come too?"

He smiled. Reassuring. "Wish I could, but who would keep Papa company?"

"I don't want to go," she said, her voice small and weak.

Thunder boomed louder, shaking the house.

Trevor said, "Tell Dad I love him."

She could barely hear him above the din.

He gave her another hug. Tender this time. "Love you, sis."

"Love you too, squirt," she said, then she was falling. Falling through the darkness.

Chapter 48

"Morgan … could she be …?"

"It's possible," Laura said. "Electronics are easily manipulated by the recently deceased."

All the air rushed out of him, as though he were a balloon and someone had just thrust a sharp needle into him.

"But it's not the only explanation," Laura said. "Didn't Morgan say something about her TV doing strange things ever since your son's death?"

He nodded.

She said, "Just because the number said it came from Morgan's phone, doesn't mean that *Morgan* originated it."

"Trevor?"

"He could be sending you a message, on Morgan's behalf."

"That she needs my help."

"Right."

He thought for a moment. "And if I had answered the call …"

She shook her head. "He wouldn't have been able to talk to you. It doesn't work like that. But I do think it was *Trevor*, not Morgan."

"And Morgan?"

"She could still be alive."

He drew in a deep breath. "But for how long?"

"Morgan's alive," he said in a low voice, trying to convince himself.

Laura nodded. "Keep telling yourself that. Keep intending she's okay. Picture finding her, alive and well. Having the right intentions goes a long way toward making them come true."

He closed his eyes. Tried to visualize Morgan, safe, smiling and happy. But it was tough. He'd seen so many tragedies during his years with the FBI. And then there was Trevor …

Okay, that wasn't working too well. "I'll leave that to you," he said to Laura. He had better things to do than sitting around, *visualizing* Morgan's rescue.

Start with what you know.

That he could do. He knew that Morgan had met three people during her short time in Sedona: Hilderman, Parker and Pearce.

They were his three best leads. But which one?

Hilderman? Of the three, he was last on the list.

What about Parker? Laura still suspected him because of the whole father/son feeling. He couldn't totally disregard her … instincts … or however he wished to classify her abilities, but he wasn't ready to disregard his own gut feelings—which told him Parker was number two on his list.

That left Pearce. Grieving father.

He used Laura's home phone, wanting to leave his line open just in case Morgan tried to contact him again, and began trying to find Pearce. After more than an hour, he hadn't gotten anywhere. Pearce wasn't answering at home, or work, or on his cell. He tried to get hold of Parker, thinking Pearce could be with him, but Parker was in a meeting. Not to be disturbed. He was about to give up when he decided to call Pearce's work number again.

The receptionist gave him another cool reception at his second call. "No, Agent Ransom. He still isn't here. Hasn't arrived in the past five minutes, I'll give him your message—"

"When's the last time you talked with him?"

"Last night."

"You haven't seen him today?"

"I thought I made that clear already."

"Have you talked with his wife?"

"She's out of town."

"Was he supposed to be at work today?"

"Yes."

"And he never showed up?"

"Do you always ask the same question twice?"

"And you don't know where he is?"

"I'm not his babysitter, Agent Ransom. He seemed quite upset last night. After your visit, who could blame him? Maybe he's taking some time off. Maybe he went to see his wife." A pause. "I've got another call coming in. When he comes in, I'll tell him you called. But I wouldn't expect a quick call back." Then the line went dead.

"No luck finding Pearce?" Laura asked.

He shook his head. "He didn't show up for work today."

"You think—?"

"I don't know. His receptionist and I aren't really on a first-name basis. She could just be covering for him."

Laura thought for a minute. "Why don't you have Hildy call her? He knows everyone in town. He'd have a much better chance with her than you."

Hilderman. "Does his brother own a ranch somewhere out of town?"

"George?"

He nodded.

"I think so."

"Can you give him a call, see if Hilderman was there yesterday?"

Her jaw dropped. "You're not thinking ... Hildy ... he couldn't ..."

He held up his hand. "No. I don't. But I've got to check everything. I can't leave any possibility out, no matter how remote."

"But—"

"Laura. This is my area of expertise. Like you with your angels and everything. This is what I do best. You've got to trust me."

She hesitated, then nodded. "I trust you," she said. She picked up the phone and called George. Her conversation lasted less than a minute. The look in her eyes told him it wasn't good news.

"He does have a ranch. It's about twenty-five miles outside of town. Way out there."

"Did Hilderman go there yesterday?"

"He says he did."

"But?"

"But ... George wasn't there. He was working. He just knows what Hildy told him. No one was there to prove it."

Chapter 49

Blackness. Empty and void of all light. She thought she was falling, but there was no sensation. No feeling of up or down. No sense of time. Nothing at all. Even the sound of thunder had vanished.

She thought of Trevor. She wanted to be with him and wait for Papa to return. Have some more cookies. Stay with them forever. But his words replayed in her mind: *Be strong. Find Dad.*

Why?

He hadn't told her. But Trevor had thought it important, so she'd try. First things first, though. She had to climb out of this black void.

She had no idea how long she'd been in the inky blackness when the light came.

It wasn't like the movies. And it disappointed her. There was no tunnel, no feeling of floating toward a reassuring light ready to welcome her. The light came as a bright flash. Instant. Sudden. Startling.

Her eyes were open, but she couldn't remember opening them. And at first, all she saw was blackness again. But it was different this time. The blackness had a glossy sheen to it. And a smell. She concentrated. Tried to get her brain working. She knew that smell.

After a few seconds, she had it. *Plastic.* The black stuff smelled like plastic! Her eyes took in the scene. Black plastic, like an endless seascape, spread out in front of her. A light—a lantern—glowed a few feet away, making her eyes blink. Where was she—?

Then she remembered everything. She was in his room. His dungeon.

But she wasn't alone.

Though she couldn't see him, she could hear him breathing hard, working on something.

She didn't move.

Play dead, she told herself.

She was lying on her side, on top of the black plastic. It was then she realized that she was breathing through her nose. Something was in her mouth. It tasted like an oily rag. Using her tongue, she forced it out. Took a few quiet breaths through her mouth.

Next, she turned her head. It felt like a hundred-pound pumpkin, but she could move it. Same with her arms, hands, legs and feet. Everything seemed to work and thankfully, she wasn't bound.

Something bumped her foot. She almost jumped out of her skin. Fighting to keep calm, she held her breath, hoping he hadn't noticed. *The dead don't wake.*

When he didn't grab her or shout out in surprise, she exhaled. One slow breath, then another. Tried to make herself relax. He hadn't seen her jump. But what was he up to?

She turned all of her attention to finding out. Although she couldn't see him, she listened hard. He was mumbling to himself. At first she couldn't understand the words, but his tone sounded angry. She concentrated, tuned out the pounding in her head.

His words became less fuzzy.

"Just another fucking bitch," he growled under his breath. "I thought she was going to be different." Something scraped against the plastic and he bumped into her again. "I want to be like Lauren," he mocked in a high-pitched voice. "She tried to fool me ... no different than the others."

Then he repeated the same tirade, more or less, again. Over and over. The black plastic shifted under her. He was working on something.

But what?

"Fucking bitch. Bitch. Bitch. Bitch," he screamed.

His rant was becoming less structured. Building up to a violent eruption. She had to do something. Soon. But she couldn't see a damn thing!

She took a deep breath, then in slow motion, rotated her head.

The first thing she saw was the soles of his shoes. They were next to her and it was his feet bumping into hers. He was on his hands and knees, looking away from her. Working on something on the far wall.

"Just like the others," he shouted to himself.

She rolled her shoulders to get a better view. An assortment of tools and equipment lay next to him. Some could have come from any typical garage: a hammer, chisel, steel vise, extension cord, tree pruning shears, power tools. Others made her skin crawl: a mixture of knives, ranging from small to a large triangular shaped blade; two or three saws; an axe; and that pipe.

"Just another fucking bitch."

He was working on something along the wall. When he turned to the side, she could see the glint of reading glasses set low on his nose as if he was performing detailed work. Hands laboring back and forth. Cutting something? No … no, not cutting, She saw the gray dust filtering through the air.

Oh, God.

He was removing another block. Getting ready to …

It was then she noticed the shoebox sized plastic container angled against the wall. Written in blocky letters on the end was a name.

Her name.

Morgan's stomach erupted into a volcano of acid and she felt as though she was going to throw up. Terror, fiery and hot, swept through her. He was getting ready to chop her up, put her in one of those boxes. Hide her in the wall.

"Just another fucking bitch," he was saying over and over.

She was going to be another trophy he kept inside his wall.

No! She wasn't going to be like the others. She wasn't going to let him cut her up. She wasn't going to end up in her box. Pushing her panic aside, her eyes found the door. She was between him and the exit. A big mistake on his part.

She turned her head back to him. He hadn't noticed her moving. Too caught up in his anger. In making her tomb.

Another mistake.

She took a deep breath. Readied herself. She had one shot at this. Either she would succeed and survive or she'd end up like the others.

Slowly, very slowly, she moved her legs. Brought them up as if she were going to perform a squat press at the gym. When her feet were about a foot away from his rear end, she struck.

Like a coiled spring, her legs shot forward, feet slamming into him. He didn't have a clue what was coming and he tumbled forward. She heard a solid *crack* as his head smashed into the masonry wall.

Then she was on her feet.

For a moment, her world went fuzzy and she almost lost her balance. She willed it away and went for the door.

Her hand touched the wood.

She didn't look behind her. Didn't want to know if he was about ready to grab her.

She pushed.

The door flew open.

The narrow concrete steps again. This time, she didn't fall.

She could hear him behind her. No time to lock him in as she'd fantasized.

So she raced upward.

Into the darkness.

Into the night.

Chapter 50

"That doesn't mean he *wasn't* there," Laura said.

"No. We just want to be careful. Remember, we believe the person who killed your brother was someone who he knew and trusted."

"Hilderman?"

"Anything's possible."

She didn't answer.

"But, we still need him to help us find Pearce."

Although Hilderman answered his cell phone on the first ring, he seemed out of breath.

"You okay?" Ransom asked.

"Decided to get out of the car, talk to some people I know. The restaurant's up a couple flights of stairs."

Restaurant? Probably eating his way through the interview. "Any luck?"

"Nothing."

Ransom was silent for a moment, thinking. "What time did you drive by here again yesterday?"

"I think it was about four-thirty."

"And you didn't see anything out of the ordinary?"

He heard Hilderman gulp, as if trying to swallow his own guilt. "I really wasn't looking for anything … wasn't expecting anything to be wrong. No one was home. I didn't see a car, anyone hanging around. Sorry, boss."

"Something's just not right," Ransom said. "I just don't know what it is. Someone had to take Morgan away. And by force. The blood proves that. But then why didn't someone see something?"

Hilderman said, "Don't know." His voice faint and sympathetic.

"Me either," Ransom said. "But I'm going to find out."

"What do you want me to do, boss?"

"A favor."

"Name it."

"I need you to find Pearce. I'd like to ask him a few questions, but he didn't show up for work this morning and his receptionist isn't helping much. Can you see if you can use that local charm of yours and find him?"

"You got it."

"And Hilderman?"

"Yeah."

"Be careful."

"Don't worry. I always am."

Ransom disconnected, but didn't hang up the phone. Instead, he handed it to Laura. "See if you can get hold of your father. I want to ask him some questions about his visit. Maybe he saw a car, someone walking by."

Laura took the phone and punched in her father's cell number. Her face darkened as each second went by, each ring he didn't answer. She left a brief message on his voice mail and hung up.

"I'm sure he's okay," Ransom said, putting his hand on hers. "Like he said, he just needed to get away. Take a break from all this stuff."

"Think positive? Keep good intensions?" She gave him a sly smile. "You're a fast learner."

"I've got a good teacher." He moved in closer, wanting to—

The sound of a car pulling into the drive made him freeze. Was it Parker arriving with news? Had they found Morgan? Was she alive? Or had she already been cut up in pieces like Amanda Pearce?

Think positive, he told himself.

Laura heard it too and her head swiveled around to face the front entry.

A lone car door slammed shut. A shadow hurried past a window. Three sharp knocks on the front door. A pattern he recognized.

Not Parker.

The three knocks came again, laced with worry and urgency.

His ex-wife.

The air felt cold and the sky was dark except the soft glow of a moon ready to rise above the mountains to the east. But it didn't matter.

Nothing mattered. Only that she was out. Free.

So she ran.

Not in any particular direction. Just away. As fast as she could. Into the desert. Through the scrub brush. Away.

Her bare feet pounded the rocky soil. She wished she'd been wearing shoes when he grabbed her, but she hadn't so all she could do was ignore the stinging pain. She wasn't going to stop. Not because of a little pain. Not because of him. Not for anything.

Neither did she turn to see if he was following her. It would do nothing but slow her down. Or worse, trip her up. She'd seen too many horror movies to know that once you turned to see if they were following you, you tripped. Then, sure enough, they were right there.

No. She was going to run until she knew she had escaped. Knew he couldn't be right behind her. She was at least twenty years younger and should be able outdistance him in no time at all.

So she ran. Threading her way through the brush, she envisioned herself as a jackrabbit. The coyote was on her tail, but she was quicker, more agile.

She would survive.

His emotions, already threadbare, began to do a high-wire flying act inside him. He'd been strong on the phone, but now, face-to-face, he didn't know if he could handle seeing her. It had been over a year since they'd been in the same room.

There had been terrible things said. Mostly by him. Could he just leave all of that anger behind? All of that blame?

"You'll do okay," Laura said as if reading his thoughts. "Remember, you are in control of your feelings … your guilt. It's possible that all the horrible things you think you've done have been forgotten by everyone—except yourself." She gave him a peck on the cheek and headed for the door.

He took a deep, calming breath, but found his feet wouldn't move.

Laura opened the door and invited Cathy inside. His ex-wife's black hair was now cut short. She looked younger than he remembered. As if kicking the alcohol monkey off her back had returned a few lost years. Only her eyes seemed to have aged. But the red puffiness and mascara smears indicated that it was a recent change.

He hadn't known what to expect when he saw her. A week ago, he would have exploded in hate-filled rage, lashing out at her for things he thought could never be forgiven. Now, all that anger was gone. Not hidden away or repressed as his therapist would say. Just plain gone. As if a dark, storm-laden cloud, that had been his constant companion for the past two years, had just up and left. The void left him feeling strangely empty.

Cathy took in the room, eyes searching for her lost daughter, then, not finding her, fell back on him.

"Nothing yet," he said.

With both women next to each other, he realized they could have been sisters. Jesus, was that why he was attracted to Laura?

He took a few steps toward the two women and for a split second his brain hiccupped. After almost twenty years of marriage and out of sheer habit, he had started to angle toward Cathy, but that's not where he wanted to be. After his feet caught up with his brain, he ended up beside Laura.

Both women caught the misstep. Cathy's eyes flicked between them, a look of surprise, then approval.

Fumbling, he made the introductions. Laura and Cathy shook hands. A friendly shake. Laura still hadn't closed the door and when she spoke, he knew why.

"I'm going to find something for dinner," she said. "I've got nothing in the fridge."

Ransom knew her fridge was bursting at the seams, but he also knew what she was doing, and although he would have preferred her to be here, he understood he needed some alone time with Morgan's mother.

"Are you a vegetarian like Morgan?" she asked Cathy.

Cathy shook her head. "Anything would be wonderful, I'm not picky."

"How about chicken? It's easy, and good cold—if it turns out to be a long night."

"Perfect," Cathy said.

Laura gave his hand a reassuring squeeze, then she was gone.

He motioned for Cathy to follow him into the living room. He sat in the chair, while she settled into the sofa. Seemingly out of nowhere, Crackers jumped up on the cushion next to Cathy. She reached out and stroked the cat's back.

Crackers leaned into her touch as if they'd been best friends forever, then worked her way to Cathy's lap and settled in.

"Nice cat."

Ransom rubbed the scratches on his hand. "A real sweetheart."

Crackers glared at him as though he were a malicious vet who'd just taken her temperature—rectally.

Still petting the cat, Cathy looked him in the eye and said, "Tell me everything you know."

"Who could do such a thing?" she said, when he finished.

He didn't know if she was referring to abducting Morgan, or what had happened to Amanda Pearce, but the answer was still the same. "I don't know."

The room fell silent as they both searched for something to say. It was Cathy who spoke first.

"I've stopped drinking," she said.

"Morgan told me. I'm glad."

She took a deep breath. "It was hard. So hard. Especially after losing Trevor … and then you."

"I'm sorry, Cathy."

Fresh tears rolled down her cheeks. "I've been waiting two years to hear those words." She drew in a deep breath. "Every day I have to live with the fact that Trevor died because of me … a mistake I made—"

"We *both* made mistakes."

"It took a long time—and with God's help I was able to forgive myself … at least most days."

"Cathy—"

She shook her head. "I need to say this." Another long breath. "I would give anything to get Trevor back. But I can't. And I've learned to live with it. Asked God for forgiveness." A brief smile. "And for the first year, I wanted you to come back."

He went to open his mouth, but her eyes told him not to.

"I've gotten over that too. No anger or anything like that involved, just a realization that we weren't meant to be together anymore. That you either had to work it out by yourself," she glanced around the house, "or find someone else to help."

"Laura and I—"

"You will and you are. I could see it in both your eyes." Another smile. "And I'm okay with it. Happy in fact. Don't let her get away."

"That's what Morgan said."

Her eyes locked on his. "Morgan's a smart girl."

He nodded.

"You're a good FBI agent. And I'm counting on the two of you working together to get her out of this mess."

"If—"

The sound of Laura's cordless phone ringing sounded through the room. He bolted upward, snatched it up.

"Hello?" he said hoping it was good news.

It wasn't.

Chapter 51

"Ransom?" Parker's rough voice came through the phone.

"Anything on Morgan?"

"No. Nothing. But I've got everyone I can working on it."

Ransom said, "Do you know where Robert Pearce is? I wanted to ask him a few more questions."

A slight hesitation, then, "I haven't seen him since yesterday. Have you checked with his office?"

"They haven't seen him all day."

"His wife's out of town, maybe he went to see her?"

"Maybe," Ransom said, letting his unasked question stand.

Parker sighed. "I'll make some calls after I take Evan home."

"How's he doing?"

"He'll be okay." A long, deep breath. "We had a talk, like you suggested."

"And?"

The phone went silent for almost a minute, then, "He admitted … that … that he and Craig … they were more than friends."

Ransom waited.

"My own son. I can't believe it."

"But at least you still have him," Ransom said. "Don't waste your time together."

"Well, there's that too. We'll have to see how everything works out."

"Just because he's—"

"It's not that," Parker said. "He told me he threw the brick through the window at George's … and started the fire at Craig's house." A long sigh. Admitting this might have been even more difficult for Parker than Evan. "Craig had some pictures of them together," he continued. "When Craig was telling everyone he was going out of town to meet his girlfriend, he and Evan were … getting together in Phoenix or San Diego. He panicked. Craig had hidden the pictures, Evan didn't even know where they were. But he thought someone might find them if they started digging in earnest."

"What about Laura?"

"A huge, stupid mistake. He says he's sorry. And I believe him. I think he went a little crazy after Craig died, but we'll just have to see what the judge says. I'm taking him down to turn himself in tomorrow. We're going to talk with Judge Davenport. I've known him for years. Maybe we can cut a deal."

Ransom said, "Given what you now know about Craig, do you still think he killed Amanda?"

"That's the reason I called," he said, the words coming out with great difficulty. Ransom imagined admitting he was wrong wasn't something Parker was used to. "I am open to other theories. And I just received new information that might shed some light on what happened."

"New information?"

"The computer analysis on one of the smudged fingerprints on Craig's service weapon just came in."

He swallowed hard. "Whose was it?"

"Hilderman's."

She tired much earlier than she expected. Maybe it was the lack of food and water, disorientation from being clubbed in the head, the fiery pain in her feet, or the adrenaline ebbing after being terrified for so long. Whatever it was, she hadn't run very far at all before she needed to rest.

Just for a minute, she told herself. Catch her breath.

"Come on," she gasped, willing herself to keep moving. But she knew she couldn't go much longer. Her legs were weak and felt as though they would fold at any second.

What about him?

She had wanted to be miles away before she stopped. At best, she was half that. Not far enough. Not even close. No matter what she told herself about her youth and ability to outrun him, she still feared he was two steps behind her. That he would be on top of her the instant she hesitated.

Keep moving! A few more feet.

Then her vision began to narrow and she knew she didn't have a choice: Stop now, or fall and break something.

Finding cover behind a small grove of trees, she collapsed to the ground, her burning lungs taking in huge gulps of air. Lifting her head up, she scanned the darkness, half expecting *him* to be there. Ready to pounce.

But he wasn't. Barren desert was all she could see. She listened. Only her pounding heart and raspy breathing.

She was alone.

Thank God.

She took a few moments to congratulate herself. She had done it! Escaped. Her heart soared and she wanted to scream with joy. But she wasn't done yet. She needed to find a safe haven. Get moving again.

First, though, she needed to rest. Think. Make a plan. If she ran in the wrong direction, or in circles, she might not have to worry about him catching her. She would die from exposure before the night was through.

She needed to find help.

To find her father.

Hilderman's prints on the murder weapon.

"Hilderman told me about that," Ransom said. "He said he took the weapon from Craig's father, to keep him from doing something crazy."

"That's what he said. Or he could've just messed up when he tried to clean his prints from it."

"What would be his motive?"

"I don't know. And given there seems to be a lot of stuff going on around here that I don't know about, your guess is as good as mine. I'm going to ask him to volunteer to come in for questioning. Do you know where he is?"

"No," Ransom said. Which was true. He didn't know exactly where Hilderman was. He didn't know why he didn't tell Parker that Hilderman was trying to find Pearce. Maybe because he wanted to talk with Hilderman first. Parker might just arrest him out of pure frustration.

The phone call ended with each promising to let the other know the second they found anything else out.

He turned to see Cathy looking at him from the doorway. He shook his head. "No news on Morgan."

She nodded and went back into the living room, leaving him to do his job.

He didn't move. His brain was working on the new information Parker had given him. Did it really change anything? Hilderman had told him that it was possible his prints would be found on the gun. And why. But could Hilderman be playing them? Could he be a monster hiding in plain sight?

He needed to talk with Laura, and found he was still holding onto the phone. He punched in her number. She answered on the second ring.

"Laura, it's Stuart," he said, "I need to talk with you. How long until you're back from the store?"

"Uh, I haven't been there yet."

"Where are you?"

"We're on our way out to Pearce's house."

"We?"

"Yeah, Hildy and I."

"You're with Hilderman?" Ransom said, feeling the cold dread run down his spine.

"I've already got some chicken in the fridge and I thought you two could use some time to work things out, so I was just driving around, looking for Morgan when I saw Hildy coming back into town. I gave him a call to see if I could help track Pearce down."

"You're with him? In his car?" he said, not hiding his concern very well.

"Yes," she said, the tone of her voice suddenly changing. "What's wrong?"

Ransom dropped his voice to a whisper. "Can he hear you?"

A short pause. "I don't think so."

"Good. Tell him I called to tell you that I need you two to come back here."

"Why?"

"Make something up."

"No, *why?*"

He took a deep breath. "Parker just called. A positive ID was made on one of those smudged prints on your brother's gun. It was Hilderman's."

"He couldn't have—" she stopped herself from saying more.

"You can't take that chance. And I need to talk to him. I think Parker's aiming to arrest him. So, I don't care how you do it, just get back here."

"Okay," she said, her voice small and unsure, then she was gone.

He'd no sooner set the phone down when it rang. "Laura?"

Silence.

He held his breath.

After what seemed hours, a man's voice said, "No, this is her father. Is Laura all right? She left a message but didn't say what she wanted."

He breathed again. "She's fine," Ransom said, hoping that was true.

"Is this Agent Ransom?"

"Yes, Mr. Adams. I asked Laura to call you."

"I really don't want to talk about Craig—"

"This isn't about your son, Mr. Adams. It's about my daughter."

"What about her?"

"She's missing … someone took her."

"Oh, God. I'm so sorry. But I don't understand why you wanted to talk with me."

"I was hoping you might have seen something when you came over here to say goodbye to Laura."

"What? She was taken from my daughter's house?"

"Yes, sir."

"She's okay, right? Laura, I mean."

"Yes. I just talked with her. Did you see anything strange when you were here yesterday?"

The phone was silent for a moment. "No. I can't remember seeing anything out of the ordinary. But I wasn't— I'm still not in great shape. Mentally."

"Maybe even someone you knew," Ransom said, thinking of Hilderman. "Did you see anyone familiar, someone you know, hanging around?"

"No."

"Any strange cars?"

"No … wait. I do remember passing a car parked along the street as I was leaving. I remember it because it was on the wrong side of the road. It was facing … Jesus, it was facing Laura's house."

Ransom's heart raced. "What kind of car?"

"I … I don't know. I wasn't paying much attention."

"Think, Mr. Adams. Was it an American car? Maybe a small car? Or a SUV? Anything would help."

After a brief pause, he said, "American, I think. A big car. Maybe something like a Lincoln or a Cadillac. Dark colored. Burgundy … but, I'm not sure."

"Was there anyone inside?"

"Maybe. I didn't look that close."

"Where exactly was it parked?"

"Across the road. Maybe two houses down."

"It wasn't one of the neighbor's?"

"I don't remember seeing it around before, but it could have been some family or friends."

"Anything else?"

"No, sorry. I wanted out of that Godforsaken town as fast as I could."

"That was about eleven or so?"

"I guess so," he said. "Why?"

"My daughter wasn't abducted until later that afternoon. The car you saw may not mean anything."

"I'm sorry I couldn't be more of a help."

"Where are you now, Mr. Adams?"

Hesitation.

"Laura would feel better if she knew where to find you."

"Tucson."

"I'll tell her."

When he hung up the phone, his hands were shaking. He'd lied to Mr. Adams. The information he'd given to Ransom was useful after all.

He couldn't believe what he'd learned almost by mistake. Ransom had seen a car similar to what Adams had described during his first morning here.

A car that Robert Pearce had driven away in just after he'd told Ransom he wasn't welcome in Sedona.

Chapter 52

Ransom began making phone calls. But he didn't call Parker—not yet. Parker was too close to Pearce, so he called one his colleagues at the FBI.

In less than five minutes, he had the answer. Robert Pearce owned a 2009 dark burgundy Cadillac DTS. It was very possible this was the car Adams had seen parked by Laura's house. Then again, maybe Adams had been mistaken. Just a coincidence.

Possible. That was, if Ransom believed in coincidences.

He didn't.

Morgan had been abducted a few hours after Adams had seen a car that matched Pearce's lurking near Laura's house. And now, Pearce had disappeared.

No, it wasn't coincidence. He was convinced of that. But he needed proof.

And that meant finding Pearce.

After he hung up, he looked at his watch. It had been ten minutes since he'd talked with Laura. And he felt like he'd been holding his breath the entire time. He was halfway through dialing her number when the door opened and she walked in. He was more relieved than he'd thought possible.

She must have seen the concern in his eyes. She walked up to him and touched his shoulder, telling him she was okay.

Gaining his breath again, he asked, "Where's Hilderman?"

"I don't know. He just dropped me off."

"What happened?"

"Right after you called, I was thinking of a good excuse for him to take me back here, when he received a phone call. It didn't last more than thirty seconds, but when he hung up, he had changed somehow. Then he told me that he had to take me home. I didn't argue. I asked him who had called, but he clamed up. Didn't talk to me at all on the way back."

"You told him I wanted to talk with him?"

"He said he didn't have time."

"Did he say where he was going after he dropped you off?"

She shook her head. "Do you think Parker is going to arrest him?"

"That'd be my guess," he said.

"Maybe he got a call from a friend warning him?"

"Maybe."

He crossed his arms over his chest and asked her a question that had been bothering him since they'd first met. "What's up with you and Hilderman anyway?"

She didn't answer him. Not right away. She licked her lips, as if what she had to say was difficult. "Hilderman has a thing for me," she said.

Now who was being the master of understatement?

An uncomfortable cough. "But I guess you already knew that."

"My FBI training didn't all go to waste," he quipped, trying to lessen her uneasiness.

It didn't work. She looked down at the floor, and her face developed a soft red glow. "I went out with Hildy's brother in high school—"

"George?"

She nodded. "When I returned to Sedona, I visited him and his wife. That's when I met Hildy. He was so nice and ... and I was all messed up from the divorce. I needed a shoulder to cry on." She took a deep breath. "I wanted a friend. Needed a friend. Hildy's family had moved here from California when he was young, so we had that in common. And ... Hildy ... well, he took it for more than it was. One night he tried to kiss me ... said he loved me ... that he would leave his wife for me. Would do anything for me. If you didn't guess it already, he's the one who got copies of the police report I sent you."

Ransom had, and wasn't surprised by her confirmation. "Then what?"

She looked up at him. "I told him he was sweet, but I gave him the old cliché ... said I just wanted to be friends."

"How did he take it?"

She walked over to a cupboard, grabbed a glass and filled it with water from the sink. Took a small drink. "Badly … at first. Especially when his wife asked him for a divorce."

Ransom raised his eyebrows.

She shook her head. "Nothing happened between us. He tried to kiss me. One time, that's all."

"Did his wife know about it?"

She nodded. "Yeah, the big lug told her. They were already having problems, that was just the nail in the coffin."

Stating the evident, he said, "He still loves you."

She let out a long sigh. "I know. He's like a stray puppy you invite into your home. He never wants to leave." Another sip of water. "But I love him too … as a friend. Or … a brother now that Craig is gone. He might be the only *family* here I've got left."

She didn't mention her father by name or the fact that she was concerned he'd kill himself, but the implication was clear.

Which reminded him of the last phone call. "I spoke to your father."

"Where is he?" she said.

He told her about her father being in Tucson.

"He always liked it there," she said.

Then he told her about the car.

"And you think it was Pearce's car out there?" she asked.

"Matches the make and color."

"So do about twenty others in Sedona."

"That's why I'm going to talk to your neighbors again. I'd imagine most people here know what Pearce looks like, maybe they saw him and just forgot about it."

"Want some company?"

"That's okay." He angled his thumb toward the living room. "Can you keep Cathy busy? And I want someone to stay here … answer the phone, just in case …"

"Done. I'll have her help me with dinner. It'll help keep her mind off Morgan."

Night had already settled by the time he walked out the door. He tried to imagine Morgan was with him, that they were taking a father-daughter walk. *Tomorrow,* he said to himself. *I hope that's what I'm doing … not looking at pictures of her horrified face.*

No more negative thoughts—only positive thoughts, he reminded himself. He lost what little optimism he'd conjured up after two of

Laura's neighbors didn't have anything to add to Howard Adams' story.

Then he talked to the young mother.

He spent a half an hour with her. Asking questions. Confirming what she'd seen … and what she hadn't. He even tracked down the preschool director. Called him to confirm pickup times. Finally satisfied that she could offer no further information, he thanked her and almost ran outside. He needed to get out. Get some fresh air.

Once outside, he sucked in a few deep breaths, focused on the cool desert air going in and out of his lungs. The information the neighbor had given him had led him down a path he didn't think possible.

It just couldn't be.

But as much as he tried to squash the thoughts, they seemed the only logical conclusion.

He had to be sure. He'd been wrong so many times during this case. So wrong. And this time he couldn't afford to be.

The computer search he had done in his hotel room two mornings ago had held the key to all of this. He just hadn't known it at the time. He dialed his colleague at the FBI again. The guy was a workaholic, just as Ransom had been a few years ago, and was still at the office. Ransom told him exactly where to look, gave him his number to call back when he had the information.

Ransom clicked the phone shut, but didn't move from his spot on the street. He didn't want to return to Laura's. Not yet.

He'd told Laura he was here to find out the truth. And now, finally, he might have uncovered it. He shivered. Sometimes, knowing the truth wasn't all it was cracked up to be.

He took a deep breath and started for Laura's house.

Apparently, there were lots of secrets in Sedona.

Secrets worth killing for.

Chapter 53

Laura was waiting for him on the front porch and motioned for him to sit next to her on a curved oak bench. He shook his head. He couldn't just sit down. Not now.

Laura stood and came to his side. He said nothing. After a few long moments, she said. "Beautiful, isn't it?"

His eyes found what she was looking at. The full moon, swollen and impossibly large, had just climbed over the mountains to the east. Its pale light reflected off a thin line of clouds, painting the red rocks below a deep crimson. For an instant it looked as though the moon was bleeding, spilling its life force on Sedona itself.

In a whisper, Laura said, "Beautiful … and unfortunate."

He turned to face her.

Her focus remained on the moon. "The Anasazi called it the Devil's Moon."

"The Devil's Moon?"

"That's the rough English translation. The Anasazi, or 'Ancient Ones,' didn't believe in the Christian Devil as you and I know it. But they did believe in the essence of evil." She put an arm around his waist. Not to comfort him, but her. "The Devil's Moon only happens every ten years or so. Modern meteorologists say it has something to do with a specific combination of water vapor, clouds and temperature. When everything's just right, the moon looks like—"

"It's bleeding," he finished.

"You saw it too?"

He nodded, but when he looked back, the illusion had vanished and it was just a moon rising over the mountains.

"Anasazi legends speak of the moon as the daughter of the mother earth and father sun. When the daughter bled, the Anasazi took it as a warning."

"A warning?"

She held him tighter. "That evil is within the valley. Malicious spirits inhabiting living flesh, performing acts of treachery and violence. Death among family and friends always followed."

"And you believe this?"

"If I believe in angels and goodness, I have to believe in their opposite."

"Satan and the Devil?"

"It doesn't matter what you call it, there is evil out there. You should know that by now."

He nodded, remembering the atrocities he'd seen during his time with the FBI. Yes, there was evil in the world. It had been in Craig Adams' basement. But, he wasn't convinced it was nothing more than simple human malevolence.

"Besides," she continued, "many legends are based, at least in part, on some truth."

"Wait," he said as a long-forgotten piece of information surfaced, "I didn't think the Anasazi left any recorded history. How do you—?"

Her look gave him the answer. One he wasn't ready to accept yet.

His phone chirped, startling both of them. Laura released her grip on him and he snatched it from his belt. "Ransom."

He listened for a few minutes. Numb. His suspicions had been correct. He hadn't wanted them to be. But he couldn't refute the facts.

"Are you sure?" he said.

The man said he was.

Ransom's stomach felt leaden. Cinched into a tight, heavy ball. He ended the call and clipped the phone back to his belt.

Laura caught the look in his eyes. "What is it?" she asked.

He didn't answer. Couldn't. Just stared down at his feet, wishing his phone had remained silent. Wishing he hadn't come here. Wishing Morgan had stayed home.

Laura put a hand on his shoulder. "What's wrong?"

Without looking up, he said, "Do you know a James Martin?"

"I don't think so."

"Ever hear the name before?"

"No. Why—?"

"He's got some property outside of Sedona. Ever been to 19648 North Red Canyon Road?"

She thought about it. "I know where Red Canyon Road is. It's up north, near Lost Mountain. I've been on a couple of hiking trails near there, but the address doesn't sound familiar. What's there?"

When he looked up, he said, "Morgan. If she's still alive."

The crash of breaking glass.

Ransom twisted toward the sound.

Cathy. Standing in the open door. A broken glass at her feet. "Morgan?" She whispered. "Is she okay? What's she doing there?"

Ransom met her eyes. "I don't know."

Laura said, "And who's James Martin?"

He took his keys form his pocket. "He's the man who killed Amanda Pearce … and your brother."

"Oh, God … Morgan," Cathy said, in such a low voice it seemed she was miles away. She ignored the broken glass and went to her knees, started praying.

Laura didn't flinch. "But *who* is he? And why did he take Morgan?"

"That's what I'm going to find out," he said. Which wasn't entirely true. Ransom knew who James Martin was, but he had no idea why he'd killed Amanda, Craig … and now maybe Morgan.

"You think he's got Morgan up there?"

He shrugged. He didn't know for sure, but given the information his FBI colleague had told him, it was the best lead he had.

"I want to go with you," Laura said.

He shook his head. "Not this time."

"But—"

"No!"

She looked at him, her green eyes questioning.

He closed his eyes, inhaled deeply, then opened them again. "Please, Laura. You can't go with me. You … it's … it's … not safe."

"Then call Parker," Laura said. "You can't do it alone."

Another shake of his head. The FBI manual would want him to wait for a SWAT team to drive up from Phoenix. But he couldn't wait. And if he told Parker, they would try to handle it themselves. Go in, guns blazing. Not a good option. "If I can … resolve this … without any bloodshed. Especially Morgan's—"

"What about yours?" Laura asked.

"Morgan's all that's important."

"Not to me. You matter, too."

He said nothing. What could he say? Just yesterday he'd thought he *wanted* to plummet a hundred feet to his death. Join Trevor forever.

"Listen," she said, "I know you have your reasons. I don't need to understand them, that can wait. And I want you to know I trust you. Trust you to do the right thing. Whatever that may be … but, I'm not giving you carte blanche to throw your life away."

"Laura—"

She held up her hands. "You've got twenty minutes. Then I'm calling Parker."

He didn't hesitate. It was more than he thought she'd give him. "Deal. Now, tell me how to get there."

Chapter 54

Fifteen minutes later, he was turning right onto Red Canyon Road, tires spitting gravel. He wasn't concerned about other cars. The pavement had ended a few miles ago and he hadn't passed a single car since then.

Laura had given him directions to Red Canyon Road, but didn't have any idea where North 19648 was. It would have been nice if there were mailboxes to help him, but there weren't many houses out here to receive any mail.

This was open ranch land with just a few widely scattered homes. No lights that he could see. Just empty desert. Lost Mountain loomed in the distance.

After a mile, a dirt drive branched off to the right. He slowed, flicked on the high beams. A large wooden sign, supported by two tall rough-hewn posts, hung above the road. It read, *Bar Q Ranch*. No address.

He didn't think it was what he was looking for.

Another wooden sign a half mile farther, on the left. This one stated the property belonged to *The Thompsons*. And it had an address: 19206 North Red Canyon.

Close.

He continued driving, maybe another three miles, until he reached a white mailbox on the right. No name, just the address: 21197.

Too far.

He pulled into the drive and turned around. Damn, he hadn't seen anything since *The Thompsons*. Maybe he'd been going too fast. He slowed down, eyes searching the pinyon and acacia trees along the shoulder. After a mile, he thought that he'd missed it again when he saw an almost invisible trail weaving its way into the darkness with no sign or mailbox. But what did he expect? A glowing neon poster stating, *Bad Guy Here*, and an arrow pointing down the lane?

He pulled up to the drive.

Somehow he knew this was it. No close neighbors, and no prying eyes. No one to hear the screams.

A perfect spot for murder.

Morgan stayed hidden in the trees for a long time. Gaining strength. Making sure he wasn't out there. She didn't want to leave her hiding spot. It felt safe.

But she was getting cold. She needed to leave the protection of the trees and find someplace warm. She rubbed her arms and searched the darkness for the hundredth time, this time not for him, but for a direction to continue.

Dark mountains loomed in front of her.

Maybe she could hide up there until morning. She looked down. Her feet were torn up pretty badly. She wondered if she could make it all the way to the mountains plodding her way through the desert at night.

She swiveled her head. Behind her, a few lights twinkled in the distance. Miles away. Again, she wondered if she could make it through the desert at night all that way. But that wasn't the only problem.

If she headed for the lights, she would be walking back toward him. And she wanted to be as far as possible from him. But she was so cold. She wouldn't last the night out here. Blowing warm air into her hands, she knew she had to make a decision.

That's when she saw the lights. Moving lights. And the sound of an engine.

A car!

A road must be nearby.

If she could get to road, wave down a car …

She hurried back the way she'd come, never thinking that he could be using a car to try to find her.

He turned off the headlights, rolled down the window and looked toward the east. The full moon had risen above the mountains possessing none of the malevolence he'd seen earlier. The Devil's Moon was gone. But would its influence still be felt?

He shook himself. It was just an old legend. Tonight, instead of being something to fear, it was a blessing. He could use the moon's light to guide him to Morgan.

He angled the car off the road and crept down the drive. As his eyes grew accustomed to the moon's glow, he found the path wasn't difficult to follow. After almost a quarter mile, the drive opened into a wide clearing, a dark shape near its center.

A tiny, box-like house outlined in sharp angles and a high-peaked roof hinted that it had been built decades ago. Its windows were dark and it appeared abandoned, except for the car parked in front.

A car he'd seen before. He couldn't tell the exact shade in the moonlight, but it was a dark color. It didn't matter. That shape told him whose it was.

Robert Pearce's Cadillac.

Chapter 55

Morgan didn't even come close to catching the car, but she did find the dirt road. Walking on its gravel surface wasn't easy in bare feet already bloody and full of cuts, but she wasn't complaining. It was far better than the rough desert. And the road meant people. The car had proven that. She would follow the direction the car had gone. She didn't care if it led to someone's house, or Sedona. The one thing that did matter was finding someone to help her. Find her father. Before she succumbed to the cold desert air.

She gritted her teeth and continued taking small steps, the stones bruising her already battered feet.

Ten minutes later, as she was rounding a sharp corner in the road, she didn't see the headlights or hear the racing engine until the car was almost on top of her.

Staring at Pearce's car, his mind went through everything he'd learned so far, and it didn't take long to make the connections.

He listened for any sign that someone had heard him approach. There was no sound except for the quiet popping of his car's engine cooling. He took his worry stone out of his pocket and began rubbing it furiously.

Jesus, why—?

Snap! The stone broke in half.

He shook his head. Morgan had bought it for him. Would Laura think that was a bad sign? *Enough!* He slid the broken stone back into his pocket. He wasn't going to get spooked.

He reached up and turned the dome light to the off position. No use advertising his presence when he opened his door. Next, he pulled a small flashlight from the glove box.

Using only the moon's ambient light, he crept up to Pearce's car. Touched the hood. Cold. No surprise. A quick peek through the windows revealed the car was empty.

He edged up to the house's front door. Stopped. Listened.

Nothing.

He put an ear to the door.

Quiet.

The door was old, paint cracked and peeling. He touched the handle and turned. The latch clicked open.

He took a deep breath, gritted his teeth and gave the door a nudge. The air inside seemed to rush out and invade his nostrils. The stench was unmistakable. Blood. Lots of it.

Morgan's?

The thought that he might be too late was too horrifying to contemplate. He pushed all negative thoughts from his mind. *Morgan's still okay. This isn't her blood. I'm not too late.*

His gun entered first. The house was dark, with only a tiny sliver of moonlight shining in from the windows. But it was enough for him to see into a small living room. Three dark shapes—a couch and two chairs—rose up from a wood floor. Off to the left was a dark entryway into what looked to be the kitchen. A closed door, probably to the lone bedroom, was on his right.

He waited.

Nothing moved.

The house felt empty. But had to make sure.

He stepped inside. Closed the door, counting his blessings that no one was there to greet him.

Kitchen or bedroom? Which one to check first?

Kitchen. Someone could pop up from behind the counter and he'd never know it. Anyone leaving the bedroom would have to open the door. Hopefully, he would hear the door pop open.

Hopefully.

He worked his way along the wood floor. Each small creak and groan sounding as if he were beating a drum to announce his presence. The kitchen was almost full-on dark. The small window was on the opposite side of the room, and none of the light from the living room penetrated beyond the entryway.

He bent low when he reached the counter. He willed his own breathing to slow, then angled his head around the edge of the counter. His eyes stared into the blackness. He waited for them to adjust. They didn't.

Shit.

He angled the flashlight to where he thought the most likely place someone would hide, aimed his Glock at the same point in space.

Click.

Bright light flashed, illuminating the area in front of him.

Click.

Then it was dark again.

The entire sequence had lasted less than a second, but it was enough for him to know he was alone. No one was hiding in the shadows. The kitchen was small and Spartan. A wooden countertop containing a small sink sat underneath dilapidated cupboards along the far wall. Everything looked old, but recently used. He also saw what looked like bags of groceries on top of the counter.

Now, the bedroom.

He retraced his steps to the closed door on the opposite side of living room.

The doorknob rotated without much effort and he eased the door open.

A loud squeak.

Damn. Now, *he* was the one announcing his arrival.

Too late to go back, he shoved the door the rest of the way open, then hit the flashlight's on button. It was a lame tactic, but if he could blind anyone in the room, just for a second …

He was looking at a tiny bedroom, a single mattress its lone furnishing. No dresser. No nightstand. No closet.

And no human beings.

At least not living.

A body lay on the floor next to the bed.

No …

A closer look revealed it wasn't that of a teenage girl's.

Thank God.

It was a man's body.

He moved closer. The flashlight's beam roamed over the fallen man. His face and head were caked with dried blood the color of dark chocolate. Someone had crushed in the side of his head.

Even with the damage, he could tell who it was: Robert Pearce.

A large pool of blood stained the wood underneath his body. Pearce had been killed here. Lured to this house by the killer, James Martin.

Ransom shook his head. After talking with Laura's neighbor, he'd known Pearce hadn't taken Morgan. Or killed his daughter. No, both he and his daughter were just unlucky victims.

With the house empty and Pearce dead on the floor, his big question now was, where was Morgan? Had Martin already—?

His thought was interrupted by the unmistakable sound of a door opening.

The front door.

Ransom spun around, his flashlight casting a wide arc of light. By the time he'd turned 180 degrees, a familiar shape was silhouetted in the moonlight.

Laura.

No!

Ransom's heart nearly exploded. "Laura! What are you—?"

"Morgan—" Laura started.

Then another figure entered behind her. One that almost filled the entire doorway. One holding a gun.

"Hi'ya boss," Hilderman said with a lopsided grin.

"Stuart!" Laura said rushing up to him, wrapping her arms around his waist.

What had she done?

Hilderman's smile widened. "I've got a surprise for you." He took a step forward, then the air filled with gunfire.

Two sharp blasts. Two flashes of light.

Hilderman pitched forward and crumpled to the floor.

"Hildy!" Laura shouted.

Ransom, still entangled in Laura's grasp, was unable to meet the threat until it was too late. Another form had taken Hilderman's place in the doorway.

This one also held a gun. One pointed at Ransom's chest.

"Don't," the man said.

Laura gasped as the figure stepped into the light. "Dad?"

"Drop the gun," Howard Adams said. With his free hand, he swiped at the blood seeping from a cut on his forehead.

Ransom considered his options. No way he could raise his weapon before he or Laura were shot.

"Now!"

"Okay, okay," Ransom said. "Take it easy." He let the Glock fall to the floor.

Adams said, "Kick it away."

Ransom did as he was told and sent the Glock into a dark corner of the living room.

Laura unwrapped herself from Ransom. "Dad … Hildy … why … what are you doing …?"

"He should have kept his nose out of my business."

"Business?" Laura said.

She stared at her father, waiting for an answer. But he didn't seem to be in a hurry to provide one.

Ransom stepped in. "It's him, Laura. He killed Amanda Pearce."

"No," she said.

Adams said nothing, just continued to stare at Ransom.

"Dad?" Laura said, her voice wanting him to refute Ransom's accusations.

But he didn't.

"Dad," she whispered again, more to herself than her father.

Still no answer.

Laura held onto Ransom for support as the realization that her father was a killer hit her. "Oh, God … why?"

After a long moment, Adams said, "I wanted her to love me … like I loved her."

Laura stared at her father. "You *loved* her? You didn't even know her."

"She was so pretty. So much like your mother."

"And Lauren," Ransom added.

Adams' eyes almost jumped out of their sockets in surprise. "How … how do you know—?"

"Who's Lauren?" Laura asked.

"His stepmother."

Chapter 56

"Stepmother?" Laura began. "I never—"

Ransom held up his hand. "Your father was born as James Thomas Martin, the only son of John and Sally Martin. Sally left when James was thirteen, tired of John's drunken abuse. John quickly remarried, to a barmaid named Lauren Adams." He nodded at Adams. "Am I getting this right?"

Adams didn't answer.

"Anyway, John worked as a mechanic aboard freighters and was gone long periods of time. I guess Lauren became lonely, because when your father turned fourteen, she seduced him and they became lovers—"

"Your stepmother?" Laura asked.

"Leave her out of this," Adams said.

"John found out about the affair and beat her to death, but that wasn't the end of it. The juvenile records my friend at the FBI was able to pull up showed that *fearing for his life, sixteen-year-old James Martin beat his father to death with a pipe.* When James turned eighteen, he legally changed his name to Howard Adams, taking his stepmother's last name. He tried to escape his past, but I'm guessing he couldn't forget her. Went searching for someone like her."

"My mother," Laura said.

"She was enough like his stepmother to fill some inner need—"

"I loved her … almost as much as I loved … Lauren," Adams said.

"When she died …" Laura started.

"He needed to find a replacement," Ransom said. "And I don't think Amanda was his first one."

"No," Laura said. "God, no. And what about Craig? Did you kill Craig too?"

Adams' face hardened. "He suspected I'd taken Amanda."

Ransom risked a peek at Hilderman. He lay facedown, unmoving. Fresh blood oozed from his wounds. Nothing he could do for him now. Two bullets from such a short range? He was most likely already dead. "How did he know?" Ransom asked.

"He called me to his house. Started asking me all sorts of questions about Amanda. Asked me if I knew anything about her disappearance. Things like that."

Ransom risked another look at Hilderman. His pistol lay a few feet from the man's hands. About ten feet away from Ransom. Ransom edged his left foot forward a few inches. *Just keep him talking.* "What did you say?"

"I told him I didn't know what he was talking about, but he didn't believe me." He took a deep breath. "Then he showed me the necklace. Said he found it in my car. In the trunk when he borrowed it last week."

"The one with the golden angel?" Ransom remembered it had been left with Amanda's head in Craig's basement. Craig had also been asking Robert Pearce about the necklace, confirming Amanda had owned one.

Adams nodded.

Ransom edged a few inches closer, pulling Laura with him. "What did you tell him?"

"That I would never do anything to hurt Amanda. But he didn't believe me. He kept asking me where Amanda was." He shook his head. "I told him it was none of his business."

"So you killed him? Made it look like a murder-suicide?"

"I didn't want to. I loved Craig … he was my son … his middle name given in respect to who I once was. But he wasn't going to leave it alone. He called me a monster. Said he was going to see Parker." He waved the pistol at Ransom. "He didn't know I'd bought this a few years ago. And was still in shock when I led him into his cellar. Didn't think I'd be able to go through with it. I almost didn't." The man's shoulders slumped as a horrible sadness seemed to come over him. "I guess I am a monster."

Ransom shuffled his feet, moving a little closer to Hilderman's pistol. "What about Robert Pearce?"

Adams' eyes shifted to the bedroom. "He kept calling me. Wanted me to find some way to make you leave Sedona. Both of you. That you were causing trouble. I ignored him. I was supposed to be out of town. But he saw me driving away from Laura's house yesterday. Followed me here."

"And Morgan?"

Adams twitched at the mention of her name. "I had planned to leave town when I stopped by the house. I wasn't going to come back. Ever." The way he said it made it clear that when he'd told Laura goodbye, it was meant to be his last. "But then I saw her. Sitting on my daughter's sofa."

Shit. When Ransom had thought about the people Morgan met in Sedona, he'd forgotten she'd been in Laura's house when Adams stopped by. *They hadn't even introduced her—*

"She was so beautiful," Adams continued. "So beautiful. She looked just like Lauren. I had to have her."

Ransom felt a chill sweep through him. He'd thought he had prepared himself for this. *But having Adams confirm it....* Through clenched teeth he said, "Where is she?"

Adams ignored him. "She said she was different. I thought she was. I thought I had finally found someone … then she …" He rubbed his head. "She lied to me. Tried to get away."

"Where is she?" Ransom repeated.

"The fucking bitch was just like the others," he said, anger flaring in his voice.

Ransom clenched his fists. "Just tell me where Morgan is."

"She never loved me either. Just like the others."

"Where—?"

"She tried to trick me. I told her what would happen …"

The man's hand was shaking so badly that Ransom thought he might be able to make a grab for Hilderman's pistol and take a shot before—

"In the cellar," Adams said, regaining his composure. His hand had stopped shaking and Ransom threw out any idea of a quick escape.

"The cellar," Adams repeated.

Ransom didn't know if he was answering the question of where Morgan was or telling them where to go. "Cellar?" he said. He hadn't seen any doors leading to a cellar in the house.

"Outside," Adams said, motioning toward the door with his free hand.

Ransom didn't move.

Adams rotated the gun away from Ransom. It now pointed at his Laura's head. "Don't make this any harder than it already is."

"Dad? You … can't …"

Ransom knew he could. He'd killed Amanda Pearce and his own son. He pulled on Laura's hand. Now wasn't the time to make a stand.

Ransom held no illusions about what going down in the cellar ultimately meant. Regardless of whether Morgan was down there— dead or alive—Adams planned to kill them in the cellar.

But if he made a move now, Laura would be dead before he got to Hilderman's pistol. He might be able to take Adams down before being shot himself, but in the end, Laura would be just as dead. And that wasn't acceptable.

He didn't want to go to the cellar. Didn't want to see what was down there. Was terrified to the core of what he might see. But he would go. Better to live a few more minutes, wait for a better opening.

Adams led them outside and around the building. His car was parked behind the house, hidden from view along the front. A pair of dilapidated wooden doors stood open against an angled concrete entryway leading into the ground beneath the house.

An exterior root cellar. Ransom had played in his grandmother's when he'd been growing up, but he doubted if this one was filled with canned fruits and vegetables. He looked down the narrow stairs. Light filtered around an open door at the bottom of the landing. He couldn't see what was inside the cellar. There was no movement in the light.

It smelled of death.

And he knew this was where he had killed Amanda Pearce. And the others.

Possibly Morgan too.

Chapter 57

Ransom hesitated at the bottom of the stairs. The smell had deepened. Rotten flesh. The stench of death, but it was old death.

His nose didn't detect the metallic smell of fresh blood. It wasn't like it had been upstairs with Robert Pearce. He allowed his heart a small beat of hope. Maybe he hadn't killed Morgan yet. He had waited a few weeks to kill Amanda Pearce.

"Open the door," Adams said, "then go to the far wall. Stay where I can see you."

It was then that Ransom realized he'd made a huge mistake. He'd led the way to the cellar, wanting to shelter Laura from the horrors it might reveal, which meant Laura was between him and her father. If Ransom had made her go first, he would have a good chance in taking Adams' gun away in the confines of the landing or when they entered the cellar. With Laura between them, there was no way to do that effectively. At least without Laura being shot.

He cursed himself for the blunder. One that might cost both their lives.

"Move."

Ransom gritted his teeth, pulled the stout wooden door open.

The first thing he saw was the black plastic. And he knew what it meant. Easy cleanup. A lantern sat near one wall, its bright light conflicting with the cellar's inherent gloom.

Then he saw the knives. The power tools. The axe. He knew what that meant too.

What he didn't see was Morgan. Neither dead nor alive. He hadn't wanted to admit it, but he'd half expected to see her body, all in pieces on the floor.

No body. No blood. Did that mean she was still alive?

"The far wall," Adams said.

Ransom moved, his feet squeaking on the slick black plastic as he crossed the small room. His eyes caught the half-excavated block, the plastic bin.

His heart stopped. Morgan's name was scrawled on the end. Maybe he had …

His feet still moved, but he wasn't consciously directing them. Then he was against the block wall.

"Turn around and sit down," Adams directed.

They did as they were told. Laura sat heavily into the corner, Ransom settled in next to her. He wondered about Laura. She hadn't said anything since leaving the house and her eyes were distant. Still in shock. He couldn't blame her. It was taking superhuman strength not to shut down himself.

"Listen," Ransom said, "we can get you some help. Show me where Morgan is. We can make a deal," he lied.

Adams didn't respond. He seemed preoccupied.

"Parker knows the truth. He's on his way here. You won't be able to claim Hilderman's and our deaths were suicides. It's over. No one else needs to die."

"I just wanted someone to love me."

"I loved you … love you," Laura said, her voice hoarse.

"No," he said. "It's not the same. You … you're my daughter."

"But these girls … Amanda … how could she love you?"

He said nothing.

"She was so young and she didn't even know you. You can't expect her to love you." She gulped in some air, the next words even harder to swallow. "Then what do you do? Kill them if they don't love you? Chop them to pieces?"

"No … I … loved them."

"You need help, Dad. Killing us isn't going to solve anything."

Adams said, "You sound just like Craig."

"He was right," Laura said.

"He said I was a monster!" he roared, anger flaring as quick as a match catching flame.

"No … just sick—"

"A monster!" he repeated, started pacing in front of the door. Black plastic crinkled under his feet. His face was flushed red and Ransom could see veins popping out in his neck. "I won't go to jail!"

"Maybe—"

Ransom grabbed Laura's hand. She was trying to argue with an illogical, insane mind. She wasn't going to win. And if he lost all control …

"A monster!" he said again, then, "all the same. They were all the same." His anger rose as he talked to himself. "Fucking bitches." He kicked the tools, smashed the plastic bin with his foot. "She was just like the others. A lying whore."

Ransom shifted his weight. Ready to spring. It was obvious that Howard Adams was beyond the point of no return. He was working himself up into a boiling rage. It wouldn't be long before he turned it on them.

"Goddamn bitch. Where the fuck is it?" Another hard kick sent the knives scattering.

Then he turned to look at the door.

The opening Ransom had been looking for.

Ransom leaped.

But he'd forgotten to take into account the plastic covering the floor. It shifted like wet ice under his feet and he felt himself falling forward.

"No!" Laura screamed.

Adams spun around, eyes blazing.

Ransom was still five feet away when the gun fired.

He felt the bullet rip into his flesh and it was as though he'd been slugged with a fifty-pound hammer. But he kept moving forward in awkward crawl-like leaps. Desperate to reach Adams before he could pull the trigger again. Before he could turn it on Laura.

It wasn't to be. He was still three feet away when he saw the revolver's hammer cock back.

Shit.

He thought of Morgan. Laura. Trevor. All in that instant. Wishing he could have lived the last few years of his life differently.

A shadow flashed and the gun fired again.

But this time, he didn't feel the bullet.

Instead, Adams pitched forward and Ransom barreled into his gut. Why Adams had lost his balance, he didn't care. He was entirely focused on getting the gun away. He spun, letting Adams' body roll under him.

The gun had tumbled from the man's hand when he fell and Ransom snatched it up before Adams gained his senses. Then he was on his feet, pointing the revolver at Adams, who was lying on the floor, on his back, eyes wide in fear.

But he wasn't looking at Ransom.

He was looking behind Ransom.

A shadow emerged behind him from the dark landing.

"Morgan?" Adams said in a horse whisper.

Ransom couldn't help it. He whirled around.

"Looking for this?" Morgan said, bringing a heavy pipe up like a baseball bat. "Doesn't feel so good, does it, asshole?"

Ransom's heart seemed to burst with unbridled joy at that instant, but it didn't last long. He heard a snarl behind him.

Adams.

He turned to see the man crouched like a rabid tiger, ready to pounce.

Laura screamed, "Don't!"

But he did.

And Ransom pulled the trigger.

Chapter 58

Ransom slowly lifted his eyelids. They were heavy with sleep and medicinal narcotics. He would have liked to doze a little longer, but he sensed someone in the room.

"Oh, good, you're awake," came a soft voice.

"I am now," he croaked out in a pitiful attempt at anger.

Morgan's face came into view, and he felt his lips curve into a huge smile. As it had done for the hundredth time since he'd found her—rather, she found him. He couldn't help it. Even now, two days later, he still couldn't believe he'd gotten her back, untouched and in one piece.

"How'ya doing Dad?" she said.

"Ready to go home," he said, wincing as he used one hand to push himself up into a half-sitting position.

She pressed a button on the hospital bed's remote control, and the back began to rise. "Not for another day or two."

"It was just a scratch," he said, but both of them knew it was a lie. The bullet from Adams' revolver had entered just above his scapula, breaking it before turning south and puncturing a lung. The ER doctors had done a good job stitching him up, but it still hurt like hell, and he did have at least another day of observation before he could go home.

"Hilderman?" he asked, as he'd done for the past two mornings.

This time, her face lit up. "He's awake, and they're saying he's got a good chance at pulling through."

Ransom let out a deep sigh, which caused him to wince again. Hilderman had it worse than him. Two bullets in the back. One had hit a rib, shattered it, and didn't go any farther. The other entered his lower back, creating all sorts of damage in his abdomen. Lots of blood loss. Organs needing to be sewn back together. Very touch-and-go.

But now Ransom allowed relief to flood through him, and his smile widened even more: something he didn't think possible.

"He wanted me to ask you if you had any openings in the FBI when he gets back on his feet. He says you owe him one."

He chuckled, but cut it short when a new wave of pain erupted in his shoulder. *The master of understatement strikes again.* Ransom did owe him. Big.

Laura had called Hilderman after Ransom left. She had an overpowering feeling she needed to be with Ransom, so she'd convinced Hilderman to drive her to Red Canyon. About a half mile away, they found Morgan walking along the dirt road. She was Hilderman's big surprise, the one he'd wanted to tell Ransom when he came through the door.

When they arrived, Hilderman had told Morgan to stay in the car. Which she did, until she heard the gunshots. Then she went back into the cellar—extremely brave after what she'd been through—but found it empty. Except for Howard Adams' pipe.

She'd taken the pipe and climbed back up the stairs to *find Dad*. That's what her dream with Trevor had told her to do. She'd also remembered what Laura had said to her before Adams kidnapped her: *Be strong. Find Dad.* And that's exactly what she had done.

As she was coming around the house, she heard voices. Saw Adams leading Ransom and Laura into the cellar. She hid, then snuck back down the stairs, arriving a little too late, but in time to see Adams fire the first shot. Then she used Adams' own pipe on the back of his head.

"You tell Hilderman that I might be the one looking for a job," Ransom replied. Roger Phillips had come to see him the day after his surgery. Although Ransom was officially cleared of killing Howard Adams, his actions leading up to the shooting were still under review by the FBI. The case had drawn national attention, and even though Ransom had gotten the bad guy, he didn't know if he could salvage his career. He would be on administrative leave for a minimum of thirty days while things got sorted out.

Truth be told, he didn't care if he went back to work for the FBI or not. Maybe he would learn the plumbing business. Or go up to visit his sister in Oregon for Christmas after all.

The one person who didn't have a job was Chief Parker. His attempts at covering up for his friend Robert Pearce, and the misguided investigation of his daughter's murder, had been brought to light, and Parker had been forced to resign.

Howard Adams hadn't been so lucky. The bullet fired from his own gun had killed him instantly when it penetrated his skull.

But the man *was* a monster.

It had begun to unravel when Ransom talked with Laura's neighbor and realized she'd seen Adams' car at Laura's house after 12:00. *After* he had told Laura he was leaving.

Ransom's phone call to his FBI colleague that night had changed everything. That's when he'd found out that Howard Adams wasn't Howard Adams at all. And James Martin had been a bad boy.

The partial remains of six murdered girls were found in his cellar. They'd also found six graves in a corner of the property, and were busy identifying bodies, contacting families, finding out what had caused Adams to lose control.

Ransom thought it had been the death of Craig and Laura's mother, Sandra. She looked a great deal like his stepmother, as did all the murdered girls they'd identified so far—including Morgan. Ransom guessed Sandra kept Adams in check, either by sheer will—Laura had said her mother was a strong woman—or just by the fact that she so closely resembled his stepmother.

When Sandra died of cancer almost ten years ago, Adams seemed to slowly sink into the depths of insanity. The first murder occurred a year to date after Sandra's death. A five-year gap, then they came with more frequency, until he just couldn't stop.

Of course, none of this had ever been seen by Laura or Craig. Laura had thought of her father as a decent man. That her father's parents had died in an automobile accident. He'd put up the perfect front, at least until his sickness overcame him.

Now she knew the truth.

The truth.

It was hard, but she seemed to be accepting it—with the help of the people of Sedona. Some living. Some not.

Ransom still didn't know if he believed in all that stuff, but he couldn't deny what he'd seen and heard. And when Morgan told him about her "dream", they had cried together. But it was a good cry. Morgan said although Trevor missed them, he seemed happy where he was.

"Dad?" Morgan's voice brought him back. "Earth to Dad."

"Sorry, sweetie," he said. The smile returning to his face.

She took hold of his hand. The scratches, bruises and bumps were healing twice as fast as his. She didn't even walk with a limp anymore. The benefits of youth.

"Mom and I are heading back to Phoenix today," she said.

"Right." His smile faded, but not too much. He'd be seeing her soon. "Tell her we'll all get together when I'm back on my feet."

She bent over, kissed his forehead. "Sounds great. I'll tell her." Then she rose to leave.

"Do you have to go so soon?"

She grinned. "Don't worry, you won't be lonely. If I'm not mistaken, you've got another visitor coming down the hall as we speak."

They both turned toward the open door. Then, he too, heard the footsteps. Two seconds later, Laura's sculpted frame filled the door.

She broke into a wide smile when she saw both of them staring at her. She was carrying a bouquet of flowers and the morning newspaper. "What?" she said.

Ransom shrugged, then pointed to the flowers. "For me?"

Laura gave him a playful slap on his good shoulder. "And ruin your rough-and-tough G-man image?" She handed the flowers to Morgan. "Have a safe trip back to Phoenix, and come back and see me soon."

Morgan promised she would, then added, "Take good care of him."

"Don't worry. I will. The way I see it, he's all mine for at least thirty days." She tossed the paper on the table, right next to a smooth black stone Morgan had bought him the morning after the shooting. It was almost identical to his old one, except he hadn't felt the need to use it anymore.

Morgan kissed him goodbye and strode out the door, leaving him alone with Laura. She pulled up a chair and took his hand.

He looked into her bottomless green eyes and thought he couldn't be in better hands. *Maybe more than thirty days.*

And they talked. Not about what had happened. They were done with that. They talked about the future. What *might* happen. What they wanted to happen.

It felt good. He hadn't felt this good for years.

And, later, he was glad he hadn't read the paper's headlines that day. There would have been nothing he could do. Nothing but worry for the girl who had been abducted the night before in Albuquerque by the same man who'd taken Kristen Tovar in Flagstaff.

No. He would have ample time to worry about that in a few months. When the Devil's Moon would shine its crimson light on him once more.

About the Author

Matt has always enjoyed writing, which probably comes from his love of reading. Not surprisingly, his favorite books are mysteries and thrillers. Give him a good mystery and you won't see him for a couple of days.

In 2004, he began freelancing for *Arizona Highways* magazine as a contributing writer, followed by a humor column in *Irish Dance Magazine*. No, he can't dance a lick; remember, it was a humor column.

Then he got a brilliant idea: he was going to write his own novel. One full of all the action, mystery and suspense he craved. It was going to be easy. All he had to do was scribble some words together and bam, his book would be born. Yeah, right. Although it took a few years and he lost a great deal of hair in the process, Devil's Moon lives!

But that's not the end of the story. Matt's hard at work on his next novel. His continuing goal is to combine his love of Arizona and writing into the perfect mystery/suspense novel.

Originally from Michigan, he considers Arizona—the backdrop of Devil's Moon—his home. He lives there with his wife, children, four cats, two horses, a couple of dogs and one cat-dog. When Matt's not writing fiction about the evil in rural Arizona, he enjoys exploring the state by bike, boot and Jeep—something he's done for almost thirty years. Putting his knowledge to use, he authors a popular outdoor adventure website called Experience Arizona (www.experience-az.com). You can also find info on Matt at www.mattmarine.com.